WINDOWLIGHT

Also by Ann Nietzke

Solo Spinout
Natalie on the Street

WINDOWLIGHT

ANN NIETZKE

The following lyrics are used by kind permission:
From "If You Could Read My Mind" © 1969 by Gordon Lightfoot.
Published by Early Morning Music; From "Imaginary Lover," by
Robert Nix, Buddy Buie and Dean Daughtry, published by Lo-Sal
Music, Inc., Copyright 1978.

Published by
Soho Press, Inc.
853 Broadway
New York, NY 10003

"Danny" and "Pissing" appeared in *Bachy 18: New Poetry, Fiction, Translation Annual*, published by Papa Bach Editions, Los Angeles, Spring 1981.

Library of Congress Cataloging-in-Publication Data

Nietzke, Ann, 1945–
    Windowlight / Ann Nietzke.
        p.   cm.
    ISBN 1-56947-060-X (alk. paper)
    1. City and town life—California—Los Angeles—Fiction.
    2. Women—California—Los Angeles—Fiction. 3. Venice (Los Angeles,
    Calif.)—Fiction. I. Title.
    PS3564.I36W5   1996
    813'.54—dc20   95-50724
                                                                          CIP

CONTENTS

for Doug

*With special thanks to Jean Samuel, Judith Brown,
Holly Prado.*

PREFACE

WINDOWLIGHT is a work of autobiographical fiction. While many of the experiences and incidents depicted in this narrative did actually occur, few occurred as written. The characters are products of the narrator's imagination, and the narrator, of course, is a product of mine (her I, my eye). Various names of people, streets, and places (with the obvious exception of Venice, California, itself) have been changed, not to protect any person or place from the "truth" of this work so much as to reflect more accurately the extent of its fiction.

Ann Nietzke
Venice, California
Fall, 1981

Chapter One

Danny

I already know who he is—know his name, even—from seeing him on the boardwalk so often. He is one of the hard-core winos who hangs out at the pagoda at Westward and Ocean Front Walk. Maybe he is the hardest-core of them all, because I have seen him out there going strong with a bottle of Night Train Express at midnight and back again when I head out for my jog at 6:00 A.M. Bleary-eyed, sometimes filthy, sometimes clean with a bright red handkerchief tied around his head, but always energized and never stuporous. His name is Danny. He is a short, brown man who always stands tall and proud, often with his arms folded across his chest, even as he talks to people, even as he approaches passers-by for spare change.

I hope it is change he wants as he approaches me for the first time in front of my building. I have vowed not to donate to any of the daily down-and-outers who habitually ask for money. I have vowed to establish myself in their eyes as a resident of Venice and of the boardwalk and not a "tourist," not an easy mark. I will refuse to be nickeled-and-dimed to death; I will refuse to contribute so blatantly to anyone's self-destructive needs. I steel myself and am always prepared to say no.

"How you doin' this evenin', pretty thang?" he says with sweet insinuation as I start up the steps to my front door. My stomach tightens—it isn't money he is after. I keep my voice neutral as I say "Fine" and find my key.

"You gonna invite me up for a cup of coffee?"

"No."

"Watch TV?"

"No."

"What's yo' room number?"

Silence, fear.

"How come you so unfriendly?"

I look him in the (bloodshot) eyes. "I guess I don't like to talk to strangers," I say as I get the door open. He takes hold of the knob as I go in.

"Well, if you don't talk to strangers, how you ever gonna make any new friends? That's what I wanna know."

"You've got a point there," I say. I have to smile. I start pulling the door to, but he is holding it open, not coming in, but showing me he can hold the door open. I pull harder, and he slowly begins to let it shut but keeps pulling slightly, just enough. There is something sexual about the way he does this—a nice tease, nothing scary. But my response to it scares me and lets me know how hungry I am. It feels dangerous to have let myself get so hungry that something in me is enjoying attention from a man like Danny.

"What you wanna go up there and be by yo'self for?" he says through the crack in the door just before I jerk it shut. "*Shit*, girl."

I feel unnerved.

The next time he approaches me is a bright Saturday afternoon as I come out of the Ocean Front Market and head around the corner toward my car. I do not break stride as he appears beside me, positioning himself just an inch or two too close, marginally invading my personal territory. I edge away, walk faster.

"You one beautiful woman, did you know that?"

Such sweet insinuation. I feel angry. I may be a beautiful woman, but not in any way that he could possibly know about. He has his hands stuffed in the pockets of his jeans, is wearing a bright red dashiki and looking well groomed, but his red eyes and putrid breath give him away. I wonder how old he is. Hard telling, but surely not over thirty-five. A contemporary. Handsome, if you are more partial to character in a face than fine features.

"Look," I say earnestly. "I get tired of being hassled all the time. I really don't like your following me."

"*I* know it," he says, taking his hands out of his pockets and folding his arms across his chest. "That's why I'm walkin' *beside* you instead of *behind* you." He grins triumphantly. I feel exasperated. We keep walking.

"Where you from, anyway? Peoria, Illinois?"

This astonishes me. How did he know? What was I saying or doing or wearing that gave me away? It is probably an insult, but its accuracy takes me so by surprise that its hostility barely registers.

"Thirty miles west," I almost say spontaneously, stopping myself only by a self-protective instinct that tells me how foolish it would be to get into such a conversation with Danny. Of course he doesn't know or care where I am from. Peoria is just a hip, catch-all word for Hicksville, for nowhere at all.

By the time we get to the car I am uneasy and beginning to resent the intrusion—the threat of pleasure with the threat of violence just underneath it.

"Don't you wanna take me with you now?" He says this with innocence, as if he really thinks I might say yes. "You take me for a ride, I take you for a ride . . . a nice long ride . . . huh?"

I blush with the familiar image, feel my privacy violated, hate him for it. I am behind the wheel and he has his hand on the top of the door, forcing me to pull against him again in order to close it. I jerk hard and it slams. I lock it fast.

Danny doesn't back away from the car; in fact, he steps closer and plants himself, arms folded across his chest, just three or four inches away from me. I start the motor, but he stays planted. When I give him a glance just before pulling away, he shakes his fist in my face. It is a mock gesture, but for a second I am afraid he might break the window. I leave him standing there and drive away in a sweat.

I begin using the back door to my building more, preferring to climb to the fourth floor up the fire escape over the chance of getting hassled on the boardwalk. I worry sometimes that Danny might know more about me than I want him to. After all, I know quite a bit about him just from looking out my window. Has he seen me watching? Does he know which room is mine? Will he get crazy enough or drunk enough or doped up enough to try to get to me? Somehow I don't really think so but feel cautious, always double-lock my door, am more diligent about my shades at night.

Meanwhile he enters my fantasy life peripherally, almost against my will, and I resent it. "Take you for a nice long ride, baby?" The rawest part of me says, "Yes, yes." I keep hearing "Imaginary

Lovers" on the radio:

> Imaginary lovers never disagree.
> They always care; they're always there
> When you need.
> Satisfaction guaranteed.

I am feeling vulnerable all the time, lonely, homesick for something I don't even want anymore. It used to be easy to handle passes.

"How about a date tonight, sweetheart?"

"I don't think my husband would appreciate that," I used to say, and I had the ring to back it up. If you already belong to somebody, they figure you're not going to become theirs. If you don't belong to another man, you're free game. Belonging to yourself doesn't seem to count.

One Sunday afternoon I sit on the grass among a large crowd across from a nearby sidewalk cafe, watching the L.A. Connection, an improvisational comedy group. Having watched their routines several times, I know that they are much less improvisational, much more highly structured than they would have the audience believe. When Danny suddenly appears right in the middle of their stage area and stands there with his head thrown back, draining his brown-bagged bottle of wine, I can see that the performers are barely concealing their uneasiness and resentment: upstaged by a wino, and who knows *what* he will do next? The situation calls for true improvisational talent.

"We need the name of a character," the group leader says to the audience, doing his best to ignore Danny, who stands right in the center of things with his arms folded across his chest, empty bottle at his feet. "Give us the name of a character for our story."

"TINKERBELL NIGGER!" Danny shouts, and gets the biggest laugh of the afternoon and a round of applause. The actors are then stuck with using that name in their story, and every time one of them says it, Danny starts to prance around yelling, "I'm Tinkerbell Nigger! Right here and right now! Tinkerbell Nigger!"

The audience laughs and Danny laughs hardest of all. It is his show—he is both starring in it and directing it—and the L.A. Connection people are only bit players. He takes several professional bows at the end of the skit and drinks in the applause.

"I *hate* him, I *hate* him," one of the actors says to the audience, and everyone laughs, knowing that it is true.

Maybe somebody in the crowd gives Danny a good, long drink to celebrate his triumph. Maybe several somebodies do. When I see him on the boardwalk an hour or so later, he is staggering and muttering to himself and gesturing wildly. A young girl who apparently knows him stops to speak, and he slips his arm around her waist and speaks into her ear. She looks startled and begins to pull away. Danny grabs her breast roughly, and she pushes him hard, so that he almost falls. It is ugly, and I turn away, suddenly afraid that he will see me. I do not want to be the one who will have to kick him in the groin.

But bizarre as it seems, I feel a slight twinge of jealousy. Something childish and irrational in me wants to be Danny's exclusive object of (unwanted) attention, while all the rest of me genuinely hopes I will never be subjected to another encounter with him. I suppose if you honor someone with a place among your sexual fantasies, he also wins the privilege of arousing illogical possessiveness. At any rate, I begin going to greater lengths to avoid him on the boardwalk, while my observations of him from my window intensify.

I wonder where he sleeps and if he ever eats. He seems to be on the boardwalk most days from early morning until late night, and I have never seen him eat anything. He is thin but not emaciated, and he appears to have tremendous stamina and energy. I wonder if the energy comes from drugs of some kind. I wonder how he pays his rent, if he pays rent, and where he gets his clothes. It is difficult to imagine him going into a store, even a Goodwill Store, and it is difficult to imagine him cooking anything for himself or even sitting down and containing himself long enough to eat in a restaurant. It is, in fact, hard for me to imagine Danny going anywhere or doing anything except surviving somehow on the boardwalk with his brown bag and his pals and his sense of humor and his menacing charm. I wonder if he has ever loved anyone and if he has ever been loved back. And where did he come from? Wherever it was he has brought some dark, internal ghetto with him, and it seems not to matter at all that in Venice the air is clear and the sun shines bright and the ocean rolls in fresh moment-by-moment.

People come here on weekends for a good time, and they give

Danny and his pals money and cigarettes—out of guilt or fear or kindness—and pretend that everything is cool, while anger and contempt fester just beneath the surface all around. "I'm Tinkerbell Nigger," Danny shouted, and the white-faced crowd laughed hard with relief that he, not they, had said it.

My heart always goes out most to Danny when I see him sitting all alone on a bench at the pagoda, huddled up in his green army jacket against the damp night air, the cold fluorescent streetlight pouring down around him and his bottle. When his cronies are with him, they all buoy each other up, with lots of laughing and signifying and soul-brother handshakes. But to see any one of them sitting there alone is to feel, undisguised, the sordid sadness of a life gone to waste.

One evening the boardwalk seems especially deserted and quiet. There is a bit of a chill in the air, and fog has begun to accumulate. It is a good night to stay in and snuggle under a quilt, but Danny is out on his bench alone, smoking and hugging himself for warmth. Sometimes he will get up and pace with the intensity of a caged animal, and twice I see him stop suddenly and point to himself and address no one that I can see: "Hey—this Daniel is one mean mothafucka. You better believe *that*. A *mean* mothafucka."

He walks over to an overflowing trash barrel and circles it, then in a flash gives it a kung fu kick that sends it into a crashing and rolling disgorgement of cans and bottles and garbage. There is the tinkle of breaking glass, and then Danny stands rather proudly surveying the mess, arms folded across his chest in his typical fashion. His exaggerated stance is that of an Indian chief in a B-grade western, waiting for the white man to approach his teepee.

My heart sinks when I see him kneel down then and begin to sort through the debris, searching for a drink. Carefully, he shakes each beer can and brown-bagged bottle, sometimes holding them up to his ear, tossing the empty ones disdainfully away, raising the others full-tilt to his lips. I cannot bear to watch him sit there doing that. My stomach recoils, and I move away from the window. Something in me wants to fetch him a cold, clean beer from my refrigerator or pour him some decent wine into an elegant glass. Something in me even wants to go down there and drink with him beneath the streetlight—I could spread a red tablecloth on his bench, and we could have a good talk, and I might somehow manage to save him from himself.

Danny

I pace in my tiny room—as Danny did in front of his bench—until good sense gets the better of me. I pull my shade without checking on him and pour myself a generous shot of Jack Daniels. It is definitely a good night to snuggle under a quilt. I undress and get into bed and let the whiskey ease me down to sleep without looking out the window.

Within an hour I am jarred awake by a loud commotion on the boardwalk. In my grogginess it seems as if Danny must have attacked another trash barrel, but as I come to consciousness I hear the passionately angry voice of a black woman projected with the kind of power that an actress uses to touch people in the back rows of a large theater. Every word is clear, and her lines have a spellbinding cadence and rhythm. I sit up and look out at her, unable to believe what I am hearing:

"I don't suck *no* white man's dick no mo'. I *hate* white men. White men is *shit*. If they think I be suckin' *they* dicks anymo' *they* in for some *news* tonight, honey. I *hate* white people. I get so *sick* and so *tired* sometime I just wanna give it *up*. All they want is somebody to suck they *dicks* and they treat they *dogs* better than a black-ass woman like *me*. I *hate* white people because they ain't nothin' but *shit*."

She stands center-stage at Danny's pagoda, repeating the lines again and again with slight variations as Danny paces slowly back and forth in front of her, giving out an occasional "Right on" or "You say it right, sister." When some white people pass by, she takes a step or two toward them and raises her voice defiantly, and the nightwalkers quicken their pace. She is a large woman, solidly built, and she wears a ragged print dress with no sleeves. Unkempt she is, and distraught, and full of rage. She cannot seem to stop saying the lines over and over.

It is after midnight, and gradually almost all the lights come on in the building directly across from mine as the white tenants, like me, appear at their windows and crane their necks to find where that powerful litany is coming from. As her words sink in, they one-by-one withdraw and close their windows and turn their lights back off. Her delivery is mesmerizing, but the message hurts too much. It is somehow the blues twisted inside out—mournfulness turned to fury, sentiment rubbed raw, sadness wrung into madness. I feel it all the way down in my gut and want her to stop. But I cannot close my window against her. Sometimes, attention must be paid.

She is getting louder rather than letting up, and Danny gradually stops encouraging her and then stops his pacing to look at her. She seems oblivious to his presence. When he eases up beside her and puts his hand on her shoulder, I am struck by his size. She dwarfs him and makes him look frail, and I feel that she could knock him down with little effort.

There is a gentleness in his stance as he speaks calmly to her, and whatever it is he says makes her hush for a bit. He leads her over to his bench and sits close beside her and pats her knee tenderly, but she does not look at him. She sits with her legs apart, her back stiffly containing her fury. I wonder if they know each other and somehow sense that they don't. He approaches and touches her with the tentative manner of a compassionate stranger, the kind of reaching out we all do when we come face-to-face with someone whose suffering is greater than our own—or just the same.

On the rim of the pagoda behind them, someone has scrawled in unsteady white letters, "JESUS LOVE JUSTICE MY DOG LIVE." I see Danny turn and look at the message as he speaks quietly to the woman. With sudden violence she flings his hand away.

"You leave *me* alone. Don't you *come* around here with that *Jesus* shit. Jesus is *shit.*"

Danny gets up quickly and backs away from her but points to the scrawl with determination, and she turns to read it.

" 'Jesus love *justice* my *dog* live'—SHIT. *Jesus* love *justice* my black *ass* an' he don't give no *shit* about yo' mothafuckin' *dog*. You a *fool* if you *believe* it. I *hate* that *Jesus* shit an' I *hate* some stupid *nigger* tryin' to shove it down my *throat*. I don't suck *no* dicks no mo' an' I don't suck no *Jesus* dick *either*. You get *away* from me with *that* shit."

She has gotten up and moved toward Danny, and with the final words she lunges at him and sends him reeling backwards. He comes to a halt and regains his balance and then stands his ground to show her he is not afraid. He folds his arms across his chest and walks with a slow swagger to the overturned trash barrel and gives it a fierce kick. Then he jams his hands deep into the pockets of his jacket and walks away down the boardwalk, abandoning the woman to her streetlit stage.

"I don't suck no *black* dick, either," she spits after him and then falls silent. Something she does with her hands then—the way she pulls at her tattered dress—makes her look like a tiny lost child. She stands staring after Danny, and her left hand seems almost involuntarily to tug her dress hard in his direction. Hesitantly, she lets the hand and the tugs draw her down the path he has taken, and she disappears from view.

My gut by now is in more of a knot than I can stay in bed with. I feel such a helpless, hopeless agitation. I hope the police will pick her up because this feels to me like the stuff that suicides and murders are made of. But no, I don't want the police to pick her up—the thought sickens me. I want someone to help her, but what therapy could ease her anguish or soften her truths? My black sister. I know something about that rage and something about that tugging hand.

I pace around chain-smoking and sipping whiskey until I feel numb enough to get back into bed. I toss and turn and finally doze, but I know it is no dream when I hear long, deep sobs. They tear at my heart before I am even fully awake and able to focus my eyes out the window.

Danny and the woman are inching through the fog back to the pagoda. His army jacket is draped around her shoulders—or rather around one of her shoulders and one of his own, for she is leaning on him heavily as he guides her with one arm around her waist. He looks as if he might give under the weight, they are so clumsy and off-balance together, and she is sobbing more loudly and deeply and mournfully than anyone I have ever heard in my life. When she takes a breath between sobs, she cries out, "I hate *white* people and I hate *black* people, and I hate *myself*. I don't want *nothin'* but to *die, nothin'* but to *die*."

As before, she cannot seem to stop repeating the words, and as before, the repetition intensifies rather than scatters the impact of her pain. I find myself crying, too. Danny eases her awkwardly onto his bench and stays right with her, both of them huddled under his meager jacket. It is 2:30 in the morning and cold, and there she sits with no sleeves in her dress and—I see now—no shoes. Where did she come from, and where does she have to go back to?

As if by magic, Danny pulls what appears to be a new bottle of wine out of his shirt and makes her drink. Maybe it was his kindness that started her crying, because after she takes some, she sobs even harder. "I just want to die," she says over and over. "I want to die."

Danny takes a long drink and nestles up against her, and if she were not the noisy one, it would look as if she were comforting and protecting him—she the big mamma and he the little boy, head almost at her breast. But he sucks only from his dark green bottle while she weeps on, and I have to close my window and draw my shade and pull the covers over my head, because I am starting to feel as if I am drowning in the endlessness of her tears and the uselessness of my own.

When my radio comes on at 6:00, I feel as if I have drunk a quart of Night Train Express myself. I peek around the shade out into the gray morning and see that the bench is deserted. It is a relief not to find them there. I wonder if they have gone to Danny's place, if he has a place, and if so, how was it with them, together there? Did they sleep, and will the new day make any difference at all? I never see the woman on the boardwalk again, and I never think about her without wondering if she is still alive.

But the next afternoon Danny returns in full force. He struts back and forth in front of his bench, which is loaded down with the pagoda regulars, some sitting on the seat and some on the back of it, almost as if posed for a family snapshot. Danny is shirtless and carries a battered looking burgundy colored guitar. At intervals he breaks into what appears to be a drunken, out-of-tune B.B. King imitation. "Ain't nobody home," he sings. "You mothafuckas come knockin' at my do' an' ain't *nobody* home."

During one of his quiet spells, the men on the bench begin a spontaneous, off-key rendition of "I Shot the Sheriff—But I Did Not Shoot the Deputy." This is the only line they know, but they sing it over and over until it makes a whole song, while Danny plays a mock accompaniment on the guitar. He is strumming all the strings at once with a random beat, the way I used to play my badminton racquet as a child to keep from getting bored while playmates fetched the birdie out of the hedge.

The louder Danny bangs away, the louder the winos sing in order to drown him out. As he gets more and more frenzied in his movements, it is hard to tell whether he is just throwing himself into the act or whether he has lost control of himself. Suddenly he takes the guitar and smashes it against the boardwalk. It breaks off at the neck with the first blow, and then he uses the neck as a club to shatter the rest of it. I suppose it is a rock concert parody, but it is frightening instead of funny. The men stop singing and watch with glazed expressions as Danny destroys the instrument, shouting, "Take *that* you mothafucka. Take *that* and *that* and *that!*" He throws down his club then and walks away, and the men begin to sing their one-line song again, as if nothing at all has happened. They pass a brown bag around as they sing, each one carefully replacing the bottlecap before passing it on. Danny is out of sight, but I hear him yell back at them, "Next time shoot the mothafuckin' *deputy*, too, you stupid niggers."

For the next several weeks, Danny appears to be in a constant rage, itching for a fight or whatever sort of trouble he can stir up, making a general nuisance of himself. He does his best to insult one or another of his cronies—it's motherfucker-this and motherfucker-that until he coaxes them into a bleary-looking, slow-motion fistfight that seems more like a dance. All the brothers are taller and more solidly built than Danny, and all are unwilling to give him the punch in the face that he asks for by taunting them. The tight-fisted dances always end with a laugh and a soul handshake and a genuine, unself-conscious hug—and of course the passing of the bottle.

I wonder if the black woman's rage has kindled or rekindled Danny's. He begins to carry a waist-high piece of twisted driftwood with him all the time, using it as a cane as he walks. It gives his gait such an odd rhythm that he sometimes looks as if he might indeed have a hurt leg rather than a need for such embellishment of his style, such an eloquent character prop for his boardwalk persona. He stands in front of his bench with both hands on the cane planted between his feet, then leans forward on it heavily and precariously, and from that vantage point he harrasses the passers-by.

"Hey, Mister Man, come here. I got to ax you somethin'. How come is it that some folks has all the money while us poor niggers is out on the street hungry? You wouldn' happen to have a dollar for a poor little nigger boy like me now, would you?"

Nervous whites back away, cross to the other side of the boardwalk and hurry off.

"I'm gon' fuck you in yo' ass, white boy!" Danny calls, waving his stick wildly, sometimes throwing it after them like a spear. There is something ominous about the way he constantly handles the driftwood, as if it contains his fury which he might let loose any second, as if it is much less cane than spear and club.

I suppose he finally throws it or shakes it at the wrong man, since after awhile Danny appears without the stick, exhibiting a grossly swollen eye that looks cut and bruised and in need of attention that I am sure it will not receive. He stands outside the windows of the Napoleon Cafe one morning as I sit at the counter trying to convince myself that for a dollar I am getting a bargain with the breakfast special of two pale-yolked, underfried eggs, grease-laden hashbrowns, and margarine-soaked toast. Suddenly he starts banging the plateglass with his fist to get the attention of people sitting in booths all along the windowed south wall of the place. His red T-shirt is torn from the neck nearly to the waist, and his puffy eye gives his face the grotesque and distorted look of some tortured Francis Bacon painting. My appetite vanishes at the sight of him.

He shakes his fist at the customers and mutters incoherently, then raises his voice and bangs on the glass some more.

"Feed yo' white pigfaces, mothafuckas!" His cry is shrill with rage and anguish, but the people in the booths ignore him as best they can, which infuriates him even more. "Look at me, goddammit! Look at me right now!"

The manager of the restaurant calmly leaves his griddle to go out and shoo Danny away. Danny shakes his fist at the man and protests, then backs off slowly and resentfully, no doubt under threat of having the police called if he doesn't. The manager comes back, wiping his hands on his grease-spattered white apron, and resumes his cooking. My breakfast congeals on the plate before me while I drink weak coffee and watch him fry a total of sixteen eggs. I need to make sure Danny is good and gone before I set foot back on the boardwalk.

The small-town coincidences that can happen in Los Angeles amaze me. The very next day Danny's name comes up as I make conversation with a social psychologist whose office at the university is near the one where I work. I make conversation with him because I dislike him and therefore refuse to talk to him about anything meaningful. Preston is good-looking and wears all the right clothes, is deliberately charming, unflaggingly personable, stylishly liberal. He is climbing

Danny

the academic ladder, doing research on alcoholism by mailing out questionnaires to "problem drinkers." He is just divorced, eligible, a "prize catch." He flirts with all the women, and all the women flirt back, and I know he wonders why I am so tight-lipped. Sometimes I wonder myself. He persists in trying to get me to talk about my writing, but I always change the subject, and then he begins to talk about Venice, intrigued by the fact that I actually live here. He comes down from posh Brentwood to hang out on weekends and watch the carnival of freaks and fags and street singers and winos.

"That's quite a crew who hang out there around the Napoleon Cafe," he says conversationally.

"Yes," I say, neutral-toned.

"Have you ever seen that one—I think his name is Danny—who always wears a red bandana on his head?"

"He doesn't always wear it," I think to myself, not answering. I feel as if my privacy is being invaded.

"He's really bad news," Preston says. "He's crazy. It's a wonder he hasn't been locked up."

I feel oddly threatened and resentful at hearing an outsider's view of Danny, particularly from Preston. I turn back to my typewriter so that he will leave. "Something in me likes something in Danny better than something in me likes anything in you," I think as the door shuts behind him.

A few mornings later I am awakened by the unmistakable sound of Danny's voice so close in my ear that for a groggy second I think he is in my room.

"Get down, Mojo! Get down here right now!"

I look out my window down to the flat, one-story roof of the market next door, where Mojo, the most bizarre of the black winos, is prancing around in his immaculate white panama suit, mumbling to himself and tipping his white straw hat to invisible passers-by. At random, his mumbling escalates into a burst of surprisingly authentic sounding operatic song which displays the depth and resonance of a trained voice—and the intensity of a man possessed.

At the far side of the roof, Danny stands between the prongs of a ladder, apparently left overnight by the artist who is painting the mural on the side of the market. His eye looks a little better, though still ugly. It is unnerving to have him right outside my window, and

I take special care that he does not see me watching from behind my shade. His tone with Mojo becomes that of a strict parent.

"You get over here and climb down right now, Mojo. I mean *right now!*" He bangs his fist on the top ladder rung for emphasis, and his good eye begins to twitch as he sees that Mojo is not going to mind him.

In fact, Mojo sings his way to the very front edge of the roof and steps up onto the curb-like rim that borders it.

"Ladies and gentlemen," he shouts like a barker on the midway, "the show is about to begin!"

He situates his Panama upon his head as if it were a top hat and proceeds to walk the edge of the building like a tightrope. His movements are all pantomime and have a certain staggering grace about them, and it is very much a pretend-show, except for the fact that a slight misstep could easily plunge Mojo to the concrete twelve or fifteen feet below. The lone regular who lies stretched out on Danny's bench applauds uproariously, while two little Mexican girls halt their sorting through a trash barrel for aluminum cans long enough to give Mojo a thorough, solemn stare, neither surprised nor delighted as circus children are supposed to be. They move on to the next barrel, dragging their black plastic garbage bag noisily behind them without looking back.

Danny is outraged. "Get away from there, fool!" he orders as he climbs the final ladder rungs onto the roof and marches directly up to the weaving aerialist, interrupting his song. "Come on with me back down the ladder, Mojo," he insists, quickly grabbing Mojo's elbow and yanking him off the raised curb, then pushing and pulling him gently across the gravelly, tarred surface to the paint-spattered ladder. Mojo responds to the tugging and nudging as docilely as a wandering senile patient being coaxed back to bed by the night nurse. As he obediently climbs down the ladder, Danny stands guard on the roof, carefully monitoring the descent to assure himself that the rescue mission is complete.

Then instead of following Mojo down, he turns to explore the rooftop and the view of familiar territory below. He picks up a bright yellow Frisbee and sails it expertly beyond the pagoda and out to the sand, then retrieves a child's red felt cowboy hat which the wind has deposited in a far rear corner of the roof. By mashing his natural down with it he almost forces it to fit, and he secures it by sliding the wooden ball along its cord tight under his chin. He hooks his thumbs into the front belt loops of his jeans then and gives his walk a sort of bowlegged, ultra-masculine accent as he reaches the front of the roof and looks down on Mojo, who is sitting on one end of Danny's bench, so straight-backed in his coat and tie and hat that, except for the reclining wino beside him, it might be a church pew.

"Look here, Mojo, I got me a new hat," Danny calls down. Mojo acknowledges this bit of information with one brief operatic outburst and gives no sign of remembering that he has recently been up on the roof himself. Danny retains the hat but drops the cowboy pose and then picks up a barren, rusty umbrella frame, which he tries unsuccessfully to open. I have often wondered how the umbrella came to be on the roof, though I feel no sense of mystery at all about the next object Danny approaches—a dilapidated, rusted-out, heavy, old Underwood typewriter whose carriage has been almost entirely torn off, undoubtedly when the machine made its crash landing from an upper window in my own building. I am sure that some frustrated, agonized, would-be writer at last gave up and thus attempted to murder all literary aspirations with a final stroke of drama. I spent part of one rainy afternoon gazing down at the word machine and wishing for the camera and talent to record such a stark if melodramatic image of destructive waste that characterizes so much of life visible in Venice.

Now Danny pokes at the rusty keys with the tip of his umbrella, then kneels down to press his fingertips against them.

"Look here, Mojo," he calls, though he is too far back to be seen from the boardwalk. "I'm gon' write me a book now, man. *The Book of Daniel. The Story of Daniel P. Mothafucka.*" He pretends to type for a bit, then abandons the typewriter and walks to the front of the building carrying the umbrella on his shoulder like a rifle or a fishing pole. He steps up onto the concrete rim where Mojo did his tightrope act, but Danny walks it casually and with no theatrics.He walks it, in fact, exactly like what it is—a curb—and suddenly I feel twelve years old, sitting in a tall cane-bottomed rocker on my Aunt Opal's huge, shady porch in Overton, Tennessee.

"Look yonder, Robert," Aunt Opal is saying to my father, pointing up the street where two shirtless young black boys are walking the curb, carrying bamboo fishing poles on their shoulders. "Looks like them little niggers has caught 'em a mess of fish, don't it?"

It is a sleepy, humid summer afternoon, and the three of us rock without speaking as we watch the fishermen move delicately toward us. The creaking of rockers on gray wood is punctuated by the ping of peas Aunt Opal is shelling into the pan in her lap. As the boys get nearer and see that we are watching them, they step off the curb and into the middle of the street, each one holding a string of small fish just high enough to clear the ground as they amble on. They do not look up at the porch but catch us in the corners of their eyes.

"Looks like ya'll caught you a big dinner," Aunt Opal calls out, and the boys look at her long enough to say "Yessum."

"Have ya'll been up at Miz Luvie Overton's pond?"

"Yessum."

"Was ya'll usin' worms?"

"Yessum, sho was."

"Well, it looks like you done all right."

"Yessum." They keep moving, heading toward the rows of shacks at the far end of the street where the pavement becomes a gravel road. I wonder how they can walk on the gravel barefoot, since up north I seldom even take my shoes off outside the house.

"Bobby Mac'll be fit to be tied when he hears them nappy-haired pickaninnies has caught fish right where he's failed for the last two days," Aunt Opal laughs. Bobby Mac is one of her twenty-seven grandchildren, a second cousin my age. "They're cute li'l ol' boys, though."

"They won't be that way long," my father declares. "Before you know it they'll be two more big black bucks."

Twenty years later, I sit again with Aunt Opal on her porch, having come south for a last visit before moving to California. She does not approve of my decision and is not shy about letting me know it. She is way up in her eighties now, fat as ever and slow-moving, short of breath, hard of hearing. She has a dip of Garrett's snuff tucked into her lower lip and, as we talk, she occasionally spits deep into a three-pound Folger's coffee can, then wipes her mouth with a brown-stained hanky. It feels good to rock with her, oddly comforting to hear the ping of spit in the can. We are surrounded by pink peony bushes all abloom, and the smell of honeysuckle hangs heavy in the air.

"I cain't for all the world think why you want to go way off out there by yourself. It's too far away. What'd you do if you was to get sick out there? Right here you got kinfolks that cares about you. You could move upstairs here as private as could be and set yourself down and write about Overton. There's stories galore right here—you needn't to worry about that. But *Los Angless,* of all the places in the whole country to pick. I b'lieve there's more crime and dope and meanness and I-don't-know-what-all in Los Angless than there is just about anywhere. But then you never *did* have good sense, anyway." She spits with emphasis.

This last statement shocks me, for I feel that I have lived a quint-essentially sensible life—or at least it's impossible Aunt Opal should know about my real acts of foolishness. I can't imagine what prompted her remark, but she begins to talk about a time when I was in high school, living with my parents in Mississippi during the heyday of the Civil Rights Movement.

"And that time I come down there to see y'all, I'll never forget," she says. "You jumped on that bicycle of yours and rode it clear across niggertown just to see a li'l ol' colt. *Clear across niggertown by yourself* to see a li'l ol' colt one of your girlfriends had. And I set there worried sick the whole time you was gone. So I know you never had real good sense." She spits again, then looks through me through her rimless spectacles.

The sound of breaking glass makes me pull back my shade once more to peek down on Danny. He is methodically picking up wine and beer and soda bottles on the roof, ten or twelve in all, and tossing them one-by-one onto the boardwalk or into the street or into the alley at the back of the building. He does this without apparent malice, rather as if it is his civic duty to clear the roof of litter, just as he took it upon himself to rescue Mojo. Maybe he does it simply to hear the liberating, almost musical sound of glass crashing to pieces on concrete. He checks around to see that there are none left, then straightens his cowboy hat, retrieves the umbrella skeleton and manages at last to jerk it open, hooks it over his shoulder like a parasol, and disappears down the ladder.

I lie back in bed. Maybe Aunt Opal is right that I don't have good sense. Here I am 2000 miles from anyone who cares about my past, spying on a half-crazed black man in a community notorious now for its crime and dope and I-don't-know-what-all. I suppose I am a little mad myself. It's the I-don't-know-what-all that drew me here.

Spring arrives gradually, and the evenings lengthen. Every sunset on the water is a post card without gloss. I feel the need to drink my way through the poignancy of twilight and go often to have wine at the nearby sidewalk cafe where there is noise and music, sea breeze, and a view of the horizon. I go armed with a book, not so much because I wish to read but because a book somehow makes me less a lone woman, less approachable as prey. Sometimes there is a crowd, and it is necessary to share a table, which I dislike. I hate to eat or drink with strangers so close, can bear neither awkward silence nor small talk. "But if you don't talk to strangers," Danny asked, "how you ever gonna make new friends?"

One evening the hostess seats me at a small table with a heavy-set woman in her fifties. She is drinking rosé and reading Erica Jong's *How to Save Your Own Life* and barely acknowledges my arrival. I am relieved—perhaps we can enjoy some solitude together. I prop Volume VI of Anaïs Nin's *Diaries* in front of me as I wait for my wine, but I do not read, partly because the sun commands my attention and partly because I am nearly finished and do not want the diaries to end so soon. Over the past several weeks I have devoured all six books, buying each one separately as a gift to myself, and now there are no more to buy. My employer has been out of the country, and I have spent several workdays earning $5.22 an hour for reading Anaïs Nin. I savor the grand, grand larceny of it and am bitterly aware of the irony that no one paid her a cent to do the writing. I am intrigued with how she kept her diary peculiarly devoid of sexuality while supporting the likes of Henry Miller and sometimes writing pornography for a dollar a page.

It is good to be sitting at a sidewalk cafe in Venice, California, with a glass of red wine and a remarkable piece of literature on the table. Never having been to Paris, this is as close as I have come to the cafes that Nin describes so lovingly. In fact, she had a fondness for the Venice of the '50s, too, because of its European flavor and sense of artistic community. At one table behind me, a man reads a poem aloud, while at another a guitarist is singing how he hates to see the evening sun go down. People of all sorts stroll by quietly on the boardwalk, and the fading light lends everything an orange afterglow, makes it all look soft and special.

Suddenly I spot Danny alone on the far side of the boardwalk, leaning against a telephone pole with arms folded, one foot crossed over the other. I have to stare to make sure it's really him, because this man is wearing a new outfit—pure-white, natural cotton drawstring pants with a matching V-neck shirt, belted by a long, silky, elegant-looking, orange patterned scarf. There is a looseness about the clothing, and the way it hangs on him as he leans against the pole is very sensual. There is something suggestive about his posture, too, which lacks the sense of defeat I have so often observed in him alone at the pagoda. He looks taller to me. The sunglow is warming up the whiteness around him and intensifying the colors in the scarf. His skin is a rich brown, his face unmarred. But yes, this is Danny. Can it be that he is sober?

As he stands there watching the sun descend, I realize that this is the first time I have ever seen him look west. At the pagoda he always sits or stands with his back to the ocean. It is curiously touching to see him face that way now with an aura of peacefulness. He has the look of a man who is thinking things over. He has the look of an ordinary, attractive black man who has come to the beach at the end of his day.

His reverie is abruptly broken by a skinny little snow-white puppy that first sniffs at Danny's sandaled feet and then begins to jump up and down against his shins. Danny bends to pick it up, and the dog is ecstatic, unable to contain its joy. It licks Danny's face with the abandon that only puppies are privy to, and Danny does not pull away. He submits smilingly to the squirming pup's affection until at last it brings forth from him a genuine, feel-good kind of laugh, the kind I remember emitting as a child with my own dogs before someone convinced me of germs. I sit grinning with my wine, and then Danny does something that pierces my heart with its tenderness: he squats down and places the dog carefully on all-fours in the grass, then holds it still with one hand while he ever so gently cleans the corners of its eyes with the forefinger of his other hand, wiping the residue unself-consciously on his new shirtsleeve. My eyes fill up at the sight of such a rare, unsolicited, even unnecessary act of caring, at once so exquisite and humble. The puppy trots away wagging its tail. Danny lights a cigarette, and so do I.

"I *met* her when I was a girl in New York," the woman at my table says suddenly, pointing to the book in front of me. "What's-her-name Nin. She used to read all the time in a bookstore in my neighborhood. My parents knew the people who owned it."

I am excited. This woman has seen in the flesh someone I revere in print. I want to know what she read, how she read, what she looked like, who was there, what year it was. But the subject seems to bore her.

"Oh, I don't know. She was a little bit of a thing and had big eyes. Everyone made such a fuss over her, which I couldn't understand at all. I guess she read from her novels—I don't really remember. Of course I was in my teens and didn't know she would get to be so famous. That was before I met my first husband. I tried to read one of the diaries once but couldn't get into it *at all.*"

She pauses. I can think of nothing whatsoever to say.

"There are some real characters down here on the boardwalk, aren't there?"

I nod, glancing back at Danny automatically, feeling uncomfortable now at the table.

"I saw *that* one expose himself right here in front of the cafe one night."

"Which one?" I say, knowing who she means.

"That one in white by the telephone pole."

"Are you sure?" I search her face for any signs of doubt.

"I saw him *do* it—pulled it right out and paraded around."

"I know, but I mean, are you sure that man over there is the one?" I say this with a certain delicacy, not wanting her to think that I think she thinks they all look alike. One Sunday afternoon I found myself walking behind a small black man in a trench coat that had "Exhibitionist" pencilled across the shoulders. At the time I took it for a joke, but maybe it wasn't. Maybe she has him and Danny mixed up.

"I think he's the one," she says, lifting her glasses to squint at him. "Though it does look like somebody cleaned him up a little."

I drain my wine and say nothing, motioning for my check.

"Have you read this?" the woman asks, holding up her book.

"Yes," I say. "I didn't care for it."

"You're *kidding,*" she says. "Why *not?* I just *love* it."

"I don't know. I guess because it didn't tell me how to save my own life."

"Well, I don't think you should take the title so *literally*," she says irritably as I move toward the cashier and wave goodnight.

I am feeling irritable myself and forget to avoid Danny.

"Hey, Peoria," he says softly as I pass him in the semi-darkness. "How you doin' this evenin', darlin'?"

I nod, then quicken my step, though he makes no move toward me. I think it over and decide not to believe the woman's story about him. I do not trust her memory or her perception or even her eyesight. She strikes me as a woman on whom too many things are lost.

Some evenings when solitude crowds me out of my room, I take bread and salami and beer down to the edge of the water. I climb the splintery ramp to the lifeguard's shack and sit shielded from the wind, not wanting sand in my food. Even so, I sometimes hear the grit of it between my teeth, and as I breathe in the salty air and feel the ocean spray against my face, I am enveloped by the unrelenting power of the sea. The waves never fail to mesmerize me with their inability to cease, never fail to stir me with their perpetual coming, never fail to make me glad that I am female.

One evening early in May I roll my pants up to the knee and follow the curving shoreline with bared feet. I flirt with the water, make a guessing-game out of where it will crest, perform a running dance in order just to miss wetting any cloth. At times I taste salt on my teeth and know that I have been smiling. As the tide rises, staying dry requires more concentration than I am willing to invest, and as I stop for a swallow of beer, a wave catches me with all its force, nearly flipping my feet from under me. The soft cotton trousers are soaked now up to the very top of my thighs, and suddenly I am glad to be wet. I walk a slow, straight line and let the water overtake me as it will.

Darkness sets in and I worry about broken glass. My pants become waterlogged and refuse to stay rolled, and, oddly, it is the wet fabric descending my calves that inspires a penetrating chill, the likes of which I have not known since my last icebound midwestern winter (our shivering bodies on frigid sheets warmed each other where blankets failed). I hurry toward my jacket, shuddering fiercely. The beach is deserted now, and all at once I am terrified of dark water, crashing waves, isolation. Trembling makes me afraid in the way that crying sometimes makes me sad, and the jacket does not faze the chill, much less the fear. I select my building from the distant row along the boardwalk and take comfort from the warm, welcoming look of its large, lighted front windows. More than anything I want a hot bath in the safety of my room. No, more than anything I want someone to hold me until the shaking stops.

The air feels warmer with every step away from the sea, and I will myself into a studied calmness. The goosebumps disappear, which seems to allow me awareness that my thighs are itching from the saltwater. Damp sand covers the tops of my feet and will not brush off. I twist open the last of the beers to distract myself along the way, but coming back always takes longer than going out.

I reach grass at last and am glad to see people still out on the boardwalk. Skaters whizz by on the bike path, and I hear music from several radios at once. Not until I am nearly home do I focus on Danny leaning against the yellow brick front of my building, shirt-less in his white pants, calling out repeatedly in the sing-song voice of a street vendor:

"Whiiite women! Whiiite women! I *love* whiiite women."

He has already seen me, and there is no way to dodge him.

"I *do* love white women," he declares earnestly as I start up the steps. When he tugs at my elbow to turn me around, I feel the warmth of his hand right through my sleeve. Heat and fear and resentment all surge through me.

"I love nigger women, too," he says with a grin, "if they be righteous." He keeps his hand on my arm, watching in silence as I dig into the damp depths of my pocket for keys. I become keenly aware of the crease at the tops of my thighs where the dark, wet cloth ends and dry cloth begins. I feel exposed.

"M-*mm*. You got some healthy legs on you, girl."

This feels like a real compliment, and I am flattered in spite of myself. Danny is not sober, but neither does he seem as frenzied as usual. He is wearing the red bandana as a tie. He stares at my crotch, then looks into my face with twinkling eyes.

"Looks like you done went and got yo'self *wet*. M-*mm*."

I pull away, but not before he catches the hint of smile on my face.

He wants me to look at him to show I know what *wet* means, but I head for the door.

"Come back here, girl!" He jerks my arm and whirls me against the wall beside the door—not hard, but I feel just on the verge of panic at his unpredictability. He stands slow-dance close but folds his arms across his bare brown chest. One of his hands is wrapped in a blood-soaked strip of cotton cloth.

"Now you and I have spoken before." His voice is calmer than I've ever heard it and has a mellow sweetness. "Now, I thought we was gonna be friends. What you so afraid of? I ain't gonna be hurtin' you. Peoria must be one cold town, the way you act." He puts on a boyish expression that conveys mischief and mock hurt at once.

"Well . . . I have to go now," I say, hoping to end the scene as casually as a phone conversation. "Here—why don't you take this?" I hand him the sack with beer in it, and he pulls out the half-full container.

"Let's us have us a little drink together before you go in then," he says, offering me the long-necked brown bottle. He watches me lift it to my mouth, and I watch him watch me, and in the look we both know before it gets there that it's cock. I sense him quickening against my thigh, and I yearn to play it out for him—want to caress my lips with the brown tip before I drink, insert my tongue just inside before I pull it away. Instead I take a quick sip, avoid his eyes, offer him his turn.

"You keep that, girl," he says gently, neither moving back nor pressing against me. "I rather be watchin' you drink it than be drinkin' it myself." I feel as if he saw me doing what I didn't do and begin to blush. I move sideways and set the bottle down on the porch.

"Take care of your hand," I say. "It doesn't look good."

"Oh, that don't matter," he says softly, putting it in his pocket. He is quiet for a moment, then comes on again in his old style. "Why you want to go in there and suffer and leave me out here sufferin'? Let me come in one time. I guarantee you not to regret it. There be so much margarine nowdays you women don't even know what to do with real butter. You know that?"

I am halfway in the door and turn to say goodnight.

"All right, then," Danny shouts for all the passers-by to hear.

"That's *it*. Now it's gonna cost you a hundred dollars. I *was* gonna do it for you free, but *now* it'll cost you a hundred dollars. You just let me know when you got the money an' the itch at the same time an' I be waitin' on you right here, girl." I pull the door to and head for the stairs, suddenly too cold again to stand waiting for the ancient elevator.

I can't fill the tub fast enough. I pour myself a shot of whiskey, light all the candles around the edge of my old-fashioned tub, and climb in while the scalding water still runs. To get properly immersed I have to be nearly flat with only my head erect, calves crossed yoga-style. I ruminate on why this bathtub is so short. Were people really that much smaller sixty or seventy years ago? I decide I am stuck somewhere on the ladder of evolution of the American bathtub, for if you grew up as my parents and aunts did, using a wooden tub in the middle of the kitchen floor on Saturday nights, sitting with your knees right under your chin in stove-heated water that several brothers or sisters had already washed in, then a bathtub like mine would be a luxurious sign of progress. I begin to appreciate it. Once when I asked Aunt Lucinda if she hadn't gotten awfully dirty and smelly between Saturday nights, she shook with laughter.

"Well, I reckon we did, sugar. But we never thought nothin' about it. I reckon we must've smelled like the dickens after working hard as we did all the week, but we never paid no 'tention to it. I reckon one of us smelled 'bout as bad as the next 'un, so it didn't matter. Course we never heard of any such thing as deodorant back then. But that ol' lye soap we used to make—you wouldn't want to use *it* too often, anyway, for it'd eat your skin right off."

I am warm now and safe. I sniff my oval bar of lavender soap. The luxuries I allow myself these days are good Tennessee whiskey, half-and-half for my coffee, fine stationery, haircuts by an authentic Frenchman, and lavender soap. Through the wall I catch one faint line of a familiar country song: "If I have to live alone, I'd rather do it by myself." Yes. My husband used to love me in the scent of lavender. I want to cry and can't.

Danny smelled of almond oil—perhaps it was in his hair. I might have been wearing a dress, naked underneath, wearing a silky, knee-length, lavender dress, inviting a hand to slip along the inner thigh. Brown hand along the inner thighs, against the wall among the shadows on the porch, finding me. The sweetness of being found. Untie his drawstring slowly, slip white cloth below dark hardness. He lifts me slightly against blonde brick, my thighs on his, hands on the back of his neck. He nuzzles my breasts with the rich brown fragrance of almonds. He is in me, in me, up me, up me, both releasing too fast for awkwardness. It is all right, all yes, all over and done and roughly beautiful. It is all I want.

I sip whiskey and look at myself through candlelit water. It is ironic how in the long months of hunger I seem physically to have ripened and entered my prime. I have become the cautious but earthy "older woman" who stares obsessively at young men in tight pants. In a way I feel like some sort of macho male's dream woman—bruised and sickened by love's complications, too lusty to need courtship or subtleties, preliminaries or patience.

I muse upon the idea of a reputable bordello for women. Good, clean, hard man-fucks for a price. No questions asked, no strings attached, no fear, no danger, no bullshit. The whiskey is taking hold, and the honesty of this fantasy appeals to me immensely: get into my cunt and stay out of my life. But I laugh aloud at one hitch—men can't fake erections the way female whores do orgasms.

Now Danny pretends that he will charge me a hundred-dollar stud fee. But he does not fit the requirements of the fantasy. Such a complicated, sad, funny, awful, wonderful, tender, frightening man. My tiny room could never contain his energy or his demons. He is too unpredictable, too full of anger, always too close to violence. He is often not clean. He might be diseased. He would probably expect an encore. He might brag to every wino on the boardwalk.

My poor Daniel. I have already seen too much of your noisy desperation. You neglect and abuse yourself and obscure your own existence. There may be no last name in your obituary, but you are not anonymous enough to be my stud, because I already give a damn.

I begin to sweat and my hair is frizzing from the steam. I examine my water-shrivelled fingertips, and the instant thought of old age pierces me. Perhaps it is time to stop using soap on my face. Perhaps it is time to start creaming away the early signs of mortality. I get out of the tub and gaze into the mirror but cannot tell how old I am.

I looked this way when I was twelve, only less so. Something about my mouth was never young.

Suddenly my chill is back in full force. Its absurdity in the warmth of the bathroom angers me—it is coming from the inside out, like Danny's ghetto. I climb into bed without looking out the window and unfold the flannel quilt Aunt Opal made me such a long, long time ago. I draw up like a fetus but cannot stop shaking and have to delve deep into the closet for my mother's rough, heavy woolen patchwork quilt, which gradually warms me. I straighten my legs out and concentrate on how the weight of the covers bends my icy toes backwards until at last my feet collapse sideways. It is a girlhood game.

My mother shivering and shaking violently on her deathbed. Her feet have not been warm for days. I keep ringing the nurse for blankets, finally take all the bedding off my army cot and spread it over her gently, but the weight of it makes her scream with pain, and I jerk it off. She sits up wild-eyed, out of her mind with pain and morphine together.

"Your mother is dead!" she shrieks. "Your mother is dead!"

It is terrifying to see her drop her stoic front at last and cry out the truth of her agony. I am numb and brave now myself. I speak in calm, reasoned, sixteen-year-old tones.

"No Mother, lie back down. You're not dead."

"Yes I am! Yes I am! Your mother is dead!"

"Who's talking to me, then? You're talking to me, so you *can't* be dead, can you? Hold onto my hand." But she is right. The woman I know is already dead, and the excruciated, odorous pile of flesh on that bed is very soon to follow her. My mother is dead. I have been my own mother for a long time, and I watch out for myself.

I get up again and drink half a shot of whiskey neat and soon am able to drift into sleep. Sometime in the night I'm aware of tears on my face but do not quite wake up, do not quite remember the dream, and do not struggle to.

At sunrise I nudge myself awake before the radio clicks on. Danny appears naked beside my narrow bed with a magnificent morning erection and a proud, vulnerable smile. I throw back both quilts, give in to him at last, and please myself.

In the days that follow, I realize that surrendering has somehow freed me. I no longer search Danny out from my window, and I no longer design my comings and goings on the boardwalk to avoid him. I trust that his pride will not allow him to approach me again, for he has set it up himself so that I have to make the next move, and I am safe now in the knowledge that I will not make it. The boisterous, unkempt man I see at the pagoda no longer bears real resemblance to the sober, immaculate, hard, whole Daniel who visits my bed upon command and leaves me always silently renewed.

One humid morning as I return panting and sweating from my run, a bleary-eyed Danny is sitting on the steps of my building. I tense up at the sight of him but am not afraid. He is wearing the white outfit, though it is dingy now with one sleeve badly torn. He stands up with a slow smile as I approach.

"How far you go everyday?" he asks.

"A mile and a half," I say, becoming conscious of my thighs.

"How come you not to go by the water? You runnin' on that cement be hard on yo' legs, girl."

"Yes, I know," I say. "I know you're right about that." I do not tell him that the morning ocean overwhelms me, that the last time I jogged along its edge I ended up lying in the sand staring at the waves for half the morning.

"An' I tell you somethin' else, too," Danny says earnestly. "You ought to be stoppin' yo'self back up there a little ways and walkin' yo'self on home—so yo' blood have a chance to settle down some. That be better on yo' heart." I am touched that he is concerned about my heart, surprised that he has observed so closely.

"I should have you for my manager," I say, smiling.

"M-*mmm*," Danny grins. "I like to be yo' *manager* all right. M-*mmm*." I have to grin back as I open the door. "I still be waitin' on you, girl," he says softly, standing very still, and for a long moment before I let the door come to we look at each other with special regard, as if we share an important secret.

Inside, I wonder if he has had any breakfast and must suppress a fleeting impulse to re-open the door and invite him to the Napoleon Cafe. Yet I discern the paradox in the look we just exchanged, for it carried both our first real hello and some kind of goodbye. The way things can suddenly redefine themselves astonishes me. Already I feel the loss of the Danny I never had, and his inability to be the

Daniel of my fantasies makes it feel as if the rejection is as much his as mine. Somehow I do not think that he will visit my room again.

As summer deepens, every day at the beach begins to feel like Saturday, jammed with sunbathers, surfers, skaters, musicians, children, street vendors, cars, bicycles, and a thousand dogs. One late afternoon I find the sidewalk cafe so crowded and noisy that I leave before my name is even called for seating. I walk a few blocks south to the weightlifting pen and sit to watch several grossly over-developed men work out with iron, unable to decide whether I find what they are doing to themselves attractive or merely repulsively fascinating. I gaze unabashedly at their bikini trunks, musing upon the possibility (or impossibility) that their penises could be proportionate to the rest of their bodies.

All at once a little white pup that has been lying in front of the bench I'm on jumps straight up into my lap and starts licking my face before I can defend myself. I submit until my kidneys can't bear another poke, but only after I've set him down do I recognize him as the dog that made Danny laugh so beautifully. Suddenly I realize that I have not seen Danny anywhere for weeks and weeks. I stroll back home keeping an eye out for him, wondering where he has disappeared to. Jail is the first place that springs to mind.

I find myself leaning out my window sometimes when there is a crowd around Danny's bench, checking to see if maybe he's back. One afternoon I hear his name called out amidst a commotion of greetings. He is getting out of a battered old silver Cadillac with a young black woman at the wheel. He is clean-shaven with what looks like a fresh haircut, is wearing a new turquoise dashiki and walking lively. It seems to me he has put on some weight. I am glad to see him and wonder instantly who the woman is. She waits patiently in the car while he clowns with the regulars.

"We done thought they thrown away the key on you, nigger!" one of them finally says with a loud laugh. "We better have us a little celebration here."

As he starts to pull a bottle out of his shirt, the woman throws open the car door and stands beside it, hands on her hips, watching Danny. She is lean and pretty in sequined jeans, and the way she stands there with such obvious pride makes me wonder if she is his sister. Their skin tones are the same rich brown.

Danny

When Danny takes the bottle and begins to unscrew the cap, she marches straight up to him, grabs it, and smashes it on the concrete. As if by reflex Danny slaps her face. It is a very quick blow and not terribly forceful, but I feel stunned by the sudden violence of it. The woman runs back to the car crying, one hand on her cheek, and Danny follows slowly, pleading forgiveness.

"Wait a minute," he says. "Wait a minute. I didn't mean it. Wait a minute."

She slams the car door and starts the engine with a vengeance, jerks it into reverse, and takes off with squealing tires. Danny has to run to catch up as she slows to turn around. She reaches over to lock his door, but he pulls it open too quickly and jumps in beside her. The car remains poised for a moment, then zooms away up the narrow street. The winos pass around a fresh bottle and give no outward sign that anything unusual has happened, but the impact of that slap lingers in my mind for days. I no longer think the woman is his sister.

One late August morning I hear a loud quarrel and lift my shade to see the silver Cadillac below.

"Quit that be-a-man shit, bitch," Danny is shouting. "I *am* a man. I *am* a man. That's why I don't stand for no bitch tellin' me what to do. Get the fuck away from me! Get the fuck out of here!" He pushes her backwards and walks toward the pagoda.

The woman is still and silent, but I can feel the fury in her posture. She gets into the car and starts it up and then, incredibly, she floors it after Danny, who just barely jumps clear before she crashes into the concrete side of his bench. She backs up and aims toward him again, but this time he is ready and not in danger. Her crunched-up left front fender grazes a parked bicycle and then topples a trash barrel before she speeds off down the crowded boardwalk, where only police cars are legal.

Danny picks up a bottle and hurls it after her, then sits down on the damaged bench and folds his arms across his shirtless chest. The wide-eyed black man who sat there throughout the crash offers him a brown bag and Danny empties the bottle in a long series of gulps, then throws it, too, in the direction of her departure.

"That woman loves you, Danny," I say to myself. "She loves you enough to want to kill you."

The weeks that follow take Danny farther and farther down. He drinks constantly and stays filthy, shouts obscenities at everyone and mutters incoherently to himself. He wears an ugly, oversized flannel shirt that I know he got from one of the pagoda regulars, and he begins to carry a ragged looking pink cotton blanket with him everywhere. Gradually it dawns on me that he really has nowhere to stay now, that he must be sleeping somewhere along the boardwalk. Early one morning I run by him sitting huddled under the blanket on his bench. He does not acknowledge my wave, and I am chilled by the vacancy of his stare.

Soon, along with the blanket, which he often wears draped over his head and shoulders, he begins to carry a thin stick that is actually longer than he is tall and has a slight curve at the end, suggesting a shepherd's crook. He has a beard now, and his walk has become the stooped shuffle of an old man. The transformation is bizarre and disturbing. Dogs bark at him and threaten to attack, and people, even the other winos, tend to stay as far away from him as possible. I see men get up and move when Danny approaches where they sit. The young man who owns a plant shop in the neighborhood tells me how he came in one day and started knocking pots off the shelves with his stick. Eric bodily threw him out into the street and regrets not calling the police. I watch Danny almost coldly while something deep within me mourns.

One Sunday afternoon I walk the length of my corridor to the tiny front balcony that overlooks the boardwalk four floors down. Danny is standing stiff and glassy-eyed directly across from my building, arms folded to keep his blanket and crook in place. A couple of young black men are tossing a football back and forth, and when one of them misthrows, the other runs smack into Danny in order to make the catch. The collision knocks him hard onto the concrete, but Danny lands on his side with his arms still locked in the same position and hardly blinks an eye. He makes no move to get up, but neither does he give any sign that he is hurt.

"He didn't mean it, Danny," the one who threw the ball says nervously. "You all right. He didn't mean nothin' by it."

"I didn't mean nothin', Danny," the other says. "You know I didn't."

No one goes to help him up. The boys move off to resume their game and do not hear when Danny softly says "I know it" and uses the crook to pull himself to his feet. Suddenly he lashes out into the air with it and speaks to himself as if someone were confronting him.

"This is the last time, nigger. I got to kill ya now. I am one Daniel Mothafucka, and this is the *last time*." He keeps hitting at the invisible enemy with his stick until I have to turn away.

Late that night a flashing red light draws my attention to the pagoda, and I see a policeman at Danny's bench poking him awake with a nightstick.

"Move on out," he says gruffly, "and don't let us find you sleeping here again." Danny gets up slowly and arranges the blanket over his head, then shuffles off into the damp night, leaning on his staff.

Months pass, and I do not see Danny again. I suppose he is locked up somewhere. Maybe the woman is taking care of him, though I doubt it. Twice I have violent dreams that tell me he is dead.

One evening my old phantom Daniel suddenly reappears in my bed, but he makes me too sad to take any pleasure. I get dressed and need to get out of the room, so I take some wine and stand on the front balcony, listening to the moonlit waves and watching the passers-by. Two of Danny's pals are sitting on his bench, and for a moment I think I will go down and inquire about him, but fear of learning the worst holds me in check.

A man and woman stroll by arm-in-arm, and he looks up, then points me out to her. They view a solitary woman outlined against the dim hallway light, leaning over the balcony with her glass of wine. I toast them with a smile, and they wave back. They take me as a part of the Venice scene.

Chapter Two

Roaches

Sometimes I can't tell if the roaches are getting better or worse. Some days I don't see any at all, and then again I'll see one here, there, and everywhere I look. I don't know if it's my diligence in looking that runs in cycles or if the insects' visibility varies with their daily patterns. Sometimes I feel as if our habits are in concert, though. I would never have got into the habit of checking around the baseboards for carcasses, for example, if the roaches had not fallen prey to the occasional habit of eating the poison sprayed or sprinkled there. And I would never have got to be so quick and deadly with a Kleenex if the roaches were not capable of vanishing instantly at the first slight sign of hunt or battle. (Never look away when stalking a roach, I've learned, or you'll lose the game as surely as tennis when you don't watch the ball.)

I see that our relationship is not without its symbiotic overtones. When I am feeling centered, I can mash a roach with lightning speed and efficiency, never giving it a second thought. But if I'm a little scattered and anxious, I may miss entirely and then be unable to fall asleep for imagining that some roach is about to crawl under cover up my leg. And so it goes. I fight a good fight and win many battles, but I know the roaches will take the war through sheer power of numbers and the psychological edge they have. After all, they are the ones who are ceaselessly and unself-consciously on the offensive, and, as far as I know, they suffer neither the vulnerability of possessing active imaginations nor the handicap of awareness of their own mortality. I may kill a thousand roaches but know that roachdom will persist undaunted. This most ancient of insects has been around for 345 million years, and ultimately I must yield as gracefully as possible to its documented talent for endurance.

I have a recurring dream in which my steering wheel locks on the freeway. I wake up as soon as I hear the click, but panic shoots through me at the sound of it. For days then I question every little noise my car makes, check the steering constantly, test the brakes in advance of every stoplight, triple check for cars before I change lanes. In my efforts to be careful, I suppose I get to be a very bad driver.

After this last time, out the corner of my eye I think I see a roach in the car, moving along the passenger side of the dashboard. I have to pull over and try to determine where it disappeared to, if it was there, and how it got there, if it was there, and why I saw it, if it wasn't there. Could I have brought it into the car on my clothes? I shudder. Surely not. But I've never seen one outdoors before. I decide it must have been a shadow of some kind and drive on. When I park and move to get out of the car, my thigh twists the steering wheel and the lock clicks into place. That awful click. I flash back to childhood and feel a giant roach squish under my bare foot on the kitchen linoleum. That click, that snap—that oozing of guts onto bare flesh. I yank my leg up, get a paper towel, and don't go barefoot in the house at night anymore. I have forgotten until now about those huge, black roaches in the house where I grew up, perhaps because my mother was always so ashamed of them.

"You needn't to go around telling everybody in the neighborhood we've got roaches," she informed me after hearing me tell a friend about stepping on one. "They'll think we're not clean, when it's just that the basement is damp. This house is clean. I know that, because I'm the one who cleans it." This was true. I don't know why the roaches were there—or why rats the size of small squirrels infested our garbage cans in the alley out back. But both were sources of fear and humiliation. No wonder I am outraged when I move into this apartment and discover it is already occupied.

The place seems reasonably clean, though it has the smell of ancient plaster and stale hallways. I hang sachets about and burn honeysuckle incense to sweeten the air. One room is newly carpeted and both are recently painted, but the roaches undercut for me the landlord's attempts to improve his property. I am in love with the charm of the place—its ocean view, its access to sunlight, its tall ceilings, its old-fashioned, compact design. But every roach I confront suggests that this new home cannot be as pleasant as it looks. I scrub everything in sight with the naïve and moral hope that roaches are repulsed by simple hygiene. I don't let food or dirty dishes accumulate, don't keep garbage around, don't entice or encourage the pests through any sort of negligence, yet within a few weeks they seem to have increased rather than diminished. I resist buying poison but begin to suspect its inevitable necessity.

Gradually it dawns on me that the infestation probably has nothing to do with me or the young couple down the hall who lived here before me. If there are roaches on the fourth floor, it seems likely that the whole building has been invaded. When I go by the realty office to pick up a new mailbox key, I shove down all embarrassment and let my outrage surface.

"I'd like to leave a message for the landlord," I say with icy calm. "The apartment I'm renting is full of roaches." Does this pot-bellied, puffy-faced man actually stifle a yawn, or am I imagining it?

"How do you like living at the beach?" he asks, as if I had just commented on the weather.

"I love it," I say. "But the place is full of roaches. Aren't you going to write that down somewhere—you know, make a note of it or something?"

"Oh sure," he says. "I'll just make a note of it here somewhere and pass your message along." His hands are locked together on his belly, and he makes no move toward pen or paper. I head straight for the store to get a can of poison powder.

After I get it sprinkled all around the sink and tub and woodwork and water pipes, I wish I had bought the spray instead, even though I detest its odor, for the trails of greenish-gray powder make the place seem instantly unclean, in spite of all my careful scrubbing. And picking up the few powder-covered corpses that accumulate along these trails is almost more repugnant than killing them myself. Besides, it appears that most of the roaches find the stuff no more appealing than I do—they quickly become adept at avoiding it, no matter where I sprinkle. Late one night I watch what looks like a grandfather roach crawling half an inch from the poison path—and precisely parallel to it—all the way around the bathroom floor and then out into the kitchen. I smash him hard in exasperation but not without due respect for his intelligence. In the morning I vacuum up much of the visible powder.

The next time I pass Mr. Andrews sitting in the first-floor parlor, I decide to inquire about the roach population in the building. Mr. Andrews is the manager, though since he is in his nineties now, I figure the title is more honorary than practical. I start to say, "I've got roaches," but can't quite get those words out.

"I suppose all the apartments here have roaches," I say in a friendly, conversational tone.

"Oh, sure," Mr. Andrews says pleasantly, nodding his head of thick white hair. "Yip. Sure do." There is a long pause. "'Cept mine." His smooth-skinned face breaks into a smile that is a wonderful combination of boyishness and manly serenity.

"All except yours?" I say. "You mean you don't have any?"

"Nope." He beams with pride and waits for the next question.

"Well, what's your secret?" I ask, really wanting to know.

"Bug Death," he says matter-of-factly and falls silent again.

"Bug Death?" I laugh, thinking I've misunderstood him.

"Yip. Bug Death. Comes in a spray can. I get the large size m'self."

"Bug Death, huh?" I say. "And it really does work?"

"Course it does," Mr. Andrews replies, sounding a little offended that I could doubt it. "Just spray it all over good once a week. It'll take care of 'em all right. I get the large size m'self."

I go to three different supermarkets in search of Bug Death. "Do you carry Bug Death?" I inquire of stockboys in the first two stores.

"Bug Death?" they both ask. "I don't think so." We exchange embarrassed smiles. On the third try I settle for Professional Strength Raid ("Stops Crawling Bugs in their Tracks!"). I get the large size.

The black-and-red-and-yellow can is a foot tall, and one whole side of it is covered with fine white print which yields detailed directions and cautions for use. "Kills even resistant roaches," the label promises. "Kills with residual action." I read everything twice, open all my windows, and begin to spray. When bugs are driven out, the instructions say, spray them directly. I feel myself tense up, expecting a herd of roaches to come scurrying out of every crevice and corner. I spray and wait, spray and wait, keeping the can poised for action, but not one solitary roach appears. The only detectable effect the stuff seems to be having is on my own eyes and sinuses. I open my door and let it stand that way, despite the sense of vulnerability and uneasiness it gives me. The place is so tiny that having the door open to whoever might pass by in the corridor feels like a serious invasion of privacy.

I am uneasy about the young man who lives across the hall, anyway. He seems to stay in his room alone day in, day out, night in, night out, radio or stereo blaring rock music constantly. The few times I've seen him he has answered my cordial hello with silence and a frighteningly vacant stare. Once I caught a glimpse inside his apartment, which appears to be totally devoid of furniture. I keep wondering if he sits in there all the time cross-legged on the floor, tripping out on some kind of drug—or whether his brain has already been burned enough that he no longer needs to take anything. I try not to connect him with all the news interviews I've ever heard with neighbors of murderers. ("He was a quiet fellow," they always say. "Didn't go out much. Kind of a loner, you know.") I wonder in passing where he gets his rent money. His dark hair is shoulder-length, matted and greasy looking, and I have nicknamed him the Hamburger Hermit because nearly every evening he fills the corridor with the heavy odor of frying meat. Tonight it seems to be worse than usual—an almost rancid smell of grease wafts its way through my door to compete with the insecticide.

I lean out the window to get a few fresh breaths of salty night air. It was foolish to wait until so late to do the spraying. I should have done it some morning before leaving for work. Now I have to sleep in the poisoned atmosphere, and, for all I know, the "residual action" of Professional Strength Raid may work all night, driving hundreds of roaches out from hiding and into my living space. I close the door against the rankness from the hallway, but this stops the crosscurrent from the windows and my eyes begin to water again, so I resign myself to leaving it open.

I wash my hands carefully and start to light a cigarette but remember the warnings against it on the can. Sometime in my late teens I resolved not to die an absurd death if I could possibly help it, and I am not about to die by fire or explosion in a war against cockroaches at the hands of my own nicotine habit. I sit on the bed feeling helpless until suddenly the whole thing strikes me as hilarious. I half roll over, laughing and laughing, then stop myself, feeling foolish and hoping none of my neighbors happened by to catch sight of me. I once read a newspaper account of a man who laughed himself to death. Someone told him a joke, and he began to laugh uncontrollably until he had a fatal heart attack. I've always sort of wondered what the joke was, even while appreciating its irrelevance, but at any rate, I keep that man in mind as good evidence for my belief that it *is* possible to die a sensible death. I gather my cigarettes and keys and money together and stand laughing in the doorway.

"All right, you guys," I say half aloud, "it's all yours. You win. Enjoy yourselves." I head for the sidewalk cafe.

The atmosphere is different at night—fewer people, certainly fewer "tourists." The overhead electric heaters are burning on the patio, and I am lucky enough to get a table to myself right under one of them. I recognize several faces of people who spend a lot of time on the boardwalk—roller skating, bicycling, performing, or like me, just walking or running or checking out the scene. I order cafe au lait and sit smoking, determined to relax a bit and forget what might be going on in my apartment.

At the next table, a thick-spectacled, heavily bearded man sits totally engrossed in Ram Dass' *The Only Dance There Is*. It is an unusually quiet night on the boardwalk, and I am beginning to wish I had brought a magazine to keep me company when suddenly Mojo's operatic tenor pierces the silence, though the man himself is nowhere in sight. Several patrons interrupt their conversations to shift in their seats, anticipating his arrival, and sure enough, within moments he staggers around the corner into view. The white suit and hat make his face appear even blacker than usual under the fluorescent streetlight.

He is carrying a Christmas gift-boxed bottle of whiskey, which he grasps in one hand and gestures with as he sings. The top flaps of the box have been torn off, and the bottle is capless, making the booze very accessible both to Mojo and to whomever he offers a drink at random. He moves to center stage on the boardwalk directly in front of the outermost tables of the cafe and begins his circus barker act with perfect enunciation.

"Ladies and gentlemen, I am here to tell the story of Mary Bethune. I will begin it very soon. But first the story of a bloody battle. Before your very eyes I'll tattle. The bloody battle of Kotex, fought each month by the fairer sex." Here he pauses to do a little operatic riff and take a swallow of whiskey, while his audience variously applauds or turns away. The tall young man with the beard has not looked up from his book.

As Mojo's voice rises on the scale and in volume, I have a quick flash of him dropping his bottle onto the concrete and kneeling down to save what he can of it. Just then a skater comes whizzing down the boardwalk, and Mojo extends the bottle toward him a little too quickly—the boy's arm flies out in a defensive gesture and knocks the box straight up into the air. The bottle is propelled out of its container and crashes right near the wrought-iron gate at the entrance to the cafe. From where I am sitting, I can tell that there is nothing to salvage—only the neck of the bottle is intact. It is curiously upsetting to have foreseen this, though it hardly takes a psychic to predict that a drunken man will drop his drink. Some people begin to clap as if it all were part of Mojo's show, and he responds to their cue.

"Do not worry, do not fret," he says, weaving his way over to the puddle. "Mojo will have him a drink yet." He lets out a long, demented-sounding laugh and falls to his knees dangerously close to the jagged bottleneck. Then supporting himself on his palms, he lowers himself to the whiskey and begins to lick it up, guiding his tongue carefully among the shards of glass. The group of seedy-looking young men in motorcycle jackets who have been encouraging him all along begin to howl and applaud and call out "Chugalug," and Mojo keeps at it until the liquid has disappeared into the porous asphalt. Miraculously, he has not cut himself. He rises and brushes off the knees of his pants, launches upon yet another operatic scale, and moves off down the boardwalk with what looks like the world's most dignified stagger.

The gang turns back to their pitcher of beer, and the very young man behind me says to his girlfriend over his Coke, "God. Don't you just about get grossed out every time you come down here?"

"Really," she replies, taking a long sip through two straws.

The guy at the next table gives the impression that he still has not looked up from his book. I sit despising them all, wanting to go home but not quite ready yet to cope with insecticide and rancid meat. The thought brings back the image of roaches scurrying in herds out of corners, and for a moment I wish I were "safe"—back in my big old house in my big old marriage bed.

It is 9:00 here, which would make it 11:00 there, so he is asleep—he and whoever. I'm sure he's found someone to be with by now. I wonder if he lets her use my desk. But of course he does. It wouldn't do, really, to say, "Oh, and by the way, don't use the desk in the upstairs study—it was *hers*, you know." Maybe he has sold it. I hope he sold it. I wonder if she cleans the house, lugs that aged vacuum cleaner up and down that long staircase, cleaning as she goes. My two closest friends made fun of how clean I used to keep those seven rooms.

"You're the least likely housewife of anyone I know," Janet would tell me, "yet your house is the most immaculate." This always made me feel a mixture of defensiveness and pride, inferiority and superiority. Actually, I hated housecleaning so much that I would set aside one morning each week and make myself do it, no matter what. I lived with the secret fear that if Wednesday morning came and went and the job did not get done, it would never, ever get done, at least not by me. And so, by virtue of phenomenal negative energy, I had the most sanitary kitchen floor in the neighborhood.

That apartment I moved into the first time we split. On Walnut Street, lined with giant oaks and maples. Built to survive in 1856. Four large rooms with fourteen-foot ceilings and perfectly waxed hardwood floors and a white marble fireplace for $185 a month. I never had to pick a day for cleaning it. Sometime every few weeks I would clean the bathroom and run the dust mop and dust the tiny bit of furniture I had brought there with me. I kept it clean partly by not doing much living in it. I ate out or carried food in, spent the quiet, silent evenings watching TV or brooding in front of the hickory fire, recuperating from eight solid hours of medical transcribing. Spent the weeks waiting for the weekends when he would come to get stoned and sleep with me and we would do our very best to have us a good old time, succeeding just often enough to keep us going despite the pain. Licking up the sweetness among the shards of glass. Not wanting to let him go on Sunday night, not wanting to let him stay, not wanting to go with him.

The anxiety attacks begin there in that narrow bed, though I don't know what to call them yet. I wake up in a sweat at 3:00 or 4:00 or 5:00 in the morning in total panic for no apparent reason. The feeling is that something unspeakably horrible is just about to happen, though I don't know what it is, and because I don't know what it is, it feels as if it must be my own death. My heart is going wild, and I can't get enough air. The crown of my head tingles as if I have some sort of leak, and I have to get up and turn on all the lights, sit bundled up in a stuffed chair and force my self to breathe evenly until the nausea subsides.

One deep winter morning I manage to sleep all the way through until 6:30 when Janis Joplin rasps into my ear that "Freedom's just another word for nothin' left to lose." It is 15° below zero with a wind chill factor of 30° below. The ground is covered with ice-packed snow, but I will run my mile-and-a-half, because it's the only thing I do these days that feels worthwhile and serves to reassure me that death is not immediately imminent. It takes ten shivering minutes to get dressed in double and triple layers from head to toe. No one else, nothing else, is stirring in the house.

The gray wood snaps with cold as I step out onto the porch. It is a stunningly clear morning—already the sun begins to sparkle in the icy tree branches in the park across the street. Four times around the square and I'll have it made. I will not slip, I will not collapse, I will not fall, I will not freeze. I will complete the run and know what a strong woman I am. I may be crazy, but I am not weak. I may be crazy, but I am not sick. I may die sometime, but it won't be soon. Freedom's just another word for everything to gain.

The cold and the challenge and the crunch underfoot make the run even more exhilarating than usual, and I work up a good sweat. There is a burst of warmth as I open the door and remove my snow-covered shoes and breath-moistened ski mask. Suddenly there is a flash of black across the living room, followed by a solid thud against the frosted window.

"Jesus Christ!" I am startled by the sudden movement and unsettled by the presence of the large blackbird that is waddling stunned beneath the windowsill. "Jesus Christ." I see ashes scattered out from the fireplace—he must have followed warmth right down the chimney. I re-open the huge door and move slowly and gently around the edge of the long room, hoping to get behind the bird and encourage him out, but as soon as he regains enough sense to feel my presence, he hurls himself past the exit, through the dining room, and once more against the glass.

"Jesus Christ," I keep saying. It is unreasonably frightening and eery to have that powerful flutter of wings in the house. I get a broom and open the back door, intending somehow to guide the bird gently into the proper flight pattern, but once again as I approach, he flings himself upward, this time straight into the dining room wall. I stoop to pick him up, thinking I might catch him while he is stunned, but when I touch him, he goes into such a fluttering panic that I am too scared to hold onto him. He shoots back into the living room, and I see a little brown puddle of diarrhea on the floor beside my foot.

The apartment is freezing, and the old furnace is going full blast, so I shut the doors and try to think of a rational plan, deciding to leave him alone awhile so we can both collect ourselves. I'm afraid he will kill himself or at least injure himself badly if he keeps flying into things. As I stand there, he swooshes past me again and clips the edge of the refrigerator before plopping onto the linoleum and leaving another brown splash. I know just enough medical terminology to feel sure I will contract histoplasmosis from his droppings.

"Calm down," I say softly to the blackbird and to myself. "Just calm down. I'll get you out of here all right."

I do not hear him at all while I am in the tub, and when I get out and dress for work, he is nowhere in sight. The silent disappearance is as creepy as his appearance was. I look behind the refrigerator and stove, try to see up the chimney, search everywhere, at last find him under my bed, huddled in the corner. I slip the broom under the bed, stand it on its edge to trap him there, then crawl across the mattress and reach down to get him. He is trembling and does not fight me. I am so moved by the feel of his life in my hand that I talk to him like a baby all the way to the porch. When I open my fingers, he struggles to his feet and pushes right off my palm without a moment's hesitation. It thrills me to see him soar. I talk about him all day at work and watch him fly between my lines of type.

A year and a half later, I am all packed for California. An old friend and I drive through the humid spring night to the park on Walnut for a farewell walk together. As we head up the block across from my old apartment, a very large blackbird drops to the ground from a leafy branch just above us. It is startling, but even more startling is that after one final flutter of wing, he is perfectly still. We stand staring in disbelief for several moments, then let out deep sighs and move on. Strange to feel no grief, no disturbance, no panic at the sudden brush with death. I wonder if it could be the same bird that was so frightened of entrapment when I was so afraid of freedom. At dawn a few days later, Aunt Lucinda stuffs me with waffles and sorghum and packs me biscuits and country sausage for the first day of the drive.

"You're awful brave to be headin' off like this, child," she says. "I reckon you ain't afraid of the devil hisself."

"Yes, I am, too," I say, beginning to cry in her warm, fat arms. "Yes I am."

All of a sudden a frantic young woman comes bursting through the exit of the indoor section of the cafe. She rams into the back of my chair so that my knee bumps the table and sends what's left of my coffee into my lap. A very blonde and drunken young man follows right on her heels, catches her elbow just past me and whirls her around.

"You bitch!" he shouts. "You bitch! I'll smash your face in!"

I jump up fast and move clear of them, find myself recoiled against the brick wall beside a bin of dirty dishes.

"Don't, Bobby, don't," the woman begs, putting her hands up in front of her face. She is drunk, too, and the way she holds her hands is more a gesture of helplessness than a tactic of self-defense. Bobby's eyes are glazed, and his mouth has a mean twist. I can see that he really is going to hit her and brace myself for it as I do for a violent movie scene. He lunges at her stiff-armed and pushes her backwards into an empty table, then does it again hard enough that she reels back and takes the table with her as she goes down. The customers close by get up and move to other tables where they resituate themselves to watch the fight. There is an electric charge in the air, something I can almost taste and smell. The woman landed slowly and loosely and does not appear hurt as she starts to her feet. Bobby towers over her, waiting—waiting for her to get up so he can knock her down again. I wish I were a big man and wonder just what I'd do if I were. I see that the reader of Ram Dass is leaving. The burly manager comes striding out onto the patio flanked by two effeminate-looking waiters.

"All right, all right, that's enough," he says, seizing Bobby firmly by both shoulders from behind and guiding him toward the boardwalk. "Take your little spat home and stay the hell out of here." Bobby moves at his own pace with fists clenched but does not protest, and the young woman follows him out crying into her hand as one of the waiters holds the gate open for her. The other sets the table upright and replaces the broken ashtray, and I walk a little shakily back to my coffee-covered chair. Before I can sit, the Mexican busboy appears with a new cup for me, smiles and shrugs as if to say, "What can you do?" and soaks up the spill in his dingy yellow rag.

Bobby and the woman are arguing as they weave their way out to the grassy area across from the cafe. Two men and a woman pass behind me.

"He's been drinking all day and itching to pick a fight," the woman is saying angrily. "He can't seem to control that temper, and she just eggs him on." The three of them head toward the couple, but before they arrive, Bobby gives the woman a smack on the cheek with his open hand. When she starts to pound his chest with her fists, he pushes her down and kicks at her thigh once, then sits on top of her, holding her wrists against the ground.

"Look at that shit," a tall black man standing at one of the far tables says loudly to the cafe at large. "They'd rather fight than fuck." There is a burst of laughter from the crowd, loudest from the motorcyclists.

"*Fuck* 'er, man," one of them yells in Bobby's direction. "*Fuck* 'er."

I stop one of the waiters on his way by. "Has anyone called the police?" I ask.

"The police?" he says, looking surprised. "What for? They'll just be at it again next week." I am both angry and relieved at his casualness. This whole thing must not be as serious and disturbing as it seems. Maybe it is all more tame and controlled than it looks, and maybe she does't get hurt. Maybe it's for show. Maybe it enables them to make some kind of awful love.

The two men pull Bobby off the woman and hold him in check while the other woman helps her up. Suddenly Bobby whirls free and begins to shout threateningly.

It's between me and her," he says. "You all stay the fuck out of it." The three friends try to persuade the young woman to go with them, but she refuses, and they edge away slowly, unwilling to tangle further with Bobby, still reluctant to desert her entirely. They linger at the edge of the grass, talking quietly and keeping an eye on the couple, who lean against a tree glaring at one another for a bit and then embrace. The motorcyclists cheer and applaud as Bobby and his woman head off down the boardwalk with arms entwined.

"You ain't a man," a wrinkled, old black man says quietly, pointing his brown bag at Bobby's back. "You ain't as much man as a roach."

As I leave, the police are cruising slowly by on their regular run. "Good evening," the officer driving says pleasantly to me.

"Good evening," I reply, not breaking stride, just wanting to get home.

The smell of Raid is definite but not overwhelming. When I take off my stained jeans and put them to soak, I see that my skin is slightly red from the hot coffee. I wonder about the smell of violence, what it was at the cafe that I could almost taste—something that the people were giving off, maybe, some kind of animal response in the attacker, the attacked, the watching herd. I smell my own fear when I strip to put on a robe, see the woman's hands crossed in front of her face as he lunges, wish I had done something—called the police, brushed a bit of ashtray glass off the back of her sweater. Something, anything. I wonder if it cut into her when he got her down on the grass. Will they discover the wound in bed?

My parents talking too loud in the kitchen, him drunk and waving that big butcher knife around until I lift my knees and hang on his arm crying so long he has to switch hands and put it down. Nothing so serious as it felt to me. Things went on.

Three dead roaches stop me from filling the tub. I scoop them up, flush them away, and get into bed unbathed, not wanting to chance seeing more. I do not check the baseboards and won't let myself pull off all the covers to inspect the bed, but I put my underpants back on to sleep in.

I am jogging down a gravel road. It seems to be somewhere in Michigan where we stayed in a cabin once. I pass the couple with us, sitting on a porch without a house. Some of the rocks are a little too big, and I feel them through the soles. I am pouring sweat, can hardly breathe in the humidity. A swarm of flies begins to follow me, must be after the sweat. They keep landing on my hair and face and neck if I don't keep beating them off with the long blue scarf or even if I do. It doesn't matter how fast or slow I go, but if I stop they bite. The reddish earth is high on either side of the road with thick tree roots exposed. If I can latch onto the roots and climb up, the flies will fall away. I feel the roots of my teeth and must get to the river to soothe my mouth. Jump in afraid of the water but the flies are gone. A catfish snaps a scab off a sore on the back of my hand which starts to bleed in the water. Wake up or you will faint or drown if the fish doesn't come back.

I am not afraid, just wide awake. That kind of humidity is so oppressive. I can smell myself in the bed, try to examine the back of my hand in the dim light that filters through the shades from the building across the street. Such an odd sensation when the fish struck, more a quick peck than a bite, and yet it tore off the scab. For a moment I think I see a roach on the ceiling, but it is really much too dark for such perceptions. The ceiling could be covered with them for all I know—a black, overcrowded ceiling with no open space left for them to crawl in, so that the ones who can't get a footing on the plaster drop down onto my bed and scurry. All those noiseless falls. Into my hair, maybe, or what if I fall asleep with my mouth open? Worms. What really happens after they bury you, really. That mummy I stared at so long, the caverns of the face exposed. The worms crawl in, the worms crawl out, the roaches play pinochle in your snout. I finally get back to sleep on my stomach.

In the morning I am dense and off-key, unable to concentrate on material for the article I'm writing and unable to find anything I want to read, in spite of having a stack of eleven brand new, if slightly yellowed, books which I got from a closeout sale at the Frigate Bookshop for 20¢ apiece—everything from Kafka's *Metamorphosis* and Theodore Reik's *Of Love and Lust* to a Tolstoy trilogy and an annotated *Death of a Salesman*. Today I wish I were a reader of mysteries, science fiction or Harlequin romances. Today I regret not owning a TV, am yearning to see some old rerun of *Gunsmoke* or *Father Knows Best* or tune into some talk show conversation where nothing real intrudes. I find California Street on my map and drive to the Venice library to read magazines.

Roaches

I am better as soon as I get inside. The place has the feel and smell of all the small libraries I've ever been in. The one in Columbus was in an old, two-story white frame house, complete with porch and pillars, while the one in Overton occupied a grocery store building for awhile, and the one in Alton is now in a bank. But their essences are all the same. This large room with the high wooden ceiling is admirably designed with many windows and a good-sized alcove to the back that one enters through tall, wide-arched doorways. The fireplace on the west wall is closed, but over it, carved rather charmingly into concrete, are three sailing ships, a few waves, and a verse from Emily Dickinson:

> There is no frigate like a book
> To take us lands away,
> Nor any coursers like a page
> Of prancing poetry.

The bookshop must have been named from this, not merely because of its proximity to the ocean.

The long, rectangular wooden tables remind me of junior high school. If I concentrated hard, I'm sure I could hear Miss Schwartz emphatically stamping due dates on *Sue Barton, Staff Nurse* or a biography of George Washington Carver, freshening the ink after each entry so there could be no excuse for an overdue book. I take some *New Yorkers* to the children's side, where the tables and chairs are lower versions of those on the adult side. There is nothing quite like the sound of one of those straight-backed wooden chairs being scooted in on a linoleum-covered concrete floor. I feel safe with my knees right up under the table, even though it appears that everyone is speaking only Spanish. I try to read some book reviews but really just want to look at cartoons and finally give in to them, lulled by foreign whisperings in the background.

When my eye catches a dark movement along the left edge of the table, I know instantly that it is a roach and am quite surprised to look up and see a centipede. My father used to call them thousand-leggers, and I have not seen once since I was a little girl and got a bad bite that swelled up and stung for days. It's as if my sitting in the diminutive furniture has called this creature forth, but he disappears before I can consider whether, or how, to kill him. I used to think they really had a thousand legs. And those grasshoppers I used to catch so I could watch them spit what my father told me was tobacco juice—how shocked I was to learn in biology class that they were the locusts I had heard about in Sunday School. The plague on my house could be worse: at least I do not have centipedes.

I move to a full-sized table at the other end of the room, right near the encyclopedias. Every once in awhile a salesman would come to our door and do his best to convince my mother that I would probably fail in school if she didn't buy a set. When I was in the eighth grade, one almost succeeded by telling her they were a must if I was going to go to college. No one in our entire family had ever gone to college, but the counselor that year had said I should, and so Mother began to think it over, measuring how badly I needed them against spending money she could not spare.

"I don't want them," I said, and meant it. "I can always use the ones at the library." I did not want the burden of having all those facts at my immediate disposal, fearing, I guess, that if I owned a set of encyclopedias someone would hold me responsible for all that knowledge, while I preferred to be reading *Jane Eyre* or *Babbit* or *Of Human Bondage* or Nancy Drew if a new one appeared. The salesman gave me a dirty look and commented on his way out that young people don't always know what is best for themselves, and perhaps he was right.

I reach for volume "R," but the entry is under "C" for cockroaches. There is a color photo of a big old roach perched on a greasy red-and-yellow ham wrapper, and I wonder whether it was a candid shot. From the diagrams, I see that the giant ones we had when I was a kid were the American variety, while the ones I live with now are the smaller Germans. I can see that this insect has impressive credentials: it is not only the oldest bug but is one of the fastest runners and was the first animal ever to fly. There is a word for *cockroach* in nearly every language, because they inhabit the Arctic, the Antarctic, and almost everywhere in between. Apparently the reason they can live almost anywhere is that they can eat almost anything, even books or—I feel the little hairs on the back of my neck stand up—the nails and eyelashes of sleeping children. This latter I simply choose not to believe, just as I know that none of the several roaches I've seen in my medicine cabinet has ever crawled over my toothbrush. Besides, it says that although roaches have often been accused of spreading disease by walking over filth and then onto food, *this has never actually been proven*. Suddenly I've an urge to adhere to the strictest scientific criteria for truth. I bet they're not half as bad as everyone makes them out to be nowadays. Sometime, somewhere, it says, somebody used to mash them with sugar and apply them to sores for healing and fry them in oil and garlic as an aid to digestion. I replace the volume and exit, feeling a rather pronounced desire for fresh air.

As I open my door, I sniff carefully but detect only the Raid and potpourri from the sachets. It said they emit a foul odor when they congregate in large groups, so maybe I don't have so many after all. I wonder if it's that each one smells on its own or if there's something about being in a crowd that causes the stink. Only one carcass, on the kitchen counter, a female—I can see the egg case protruding from the rear of the abdomen, just like in the diagram. Each case holds fifteen to forty eggs, and a female can deposit fifty or more cases in her lifetime. So fifty times, say, twenty-five eggs is 1,250 new roaches for every old female. Do they copulate, or what? That information must have been censored. "To find hiding places," the encyclopedia said in its practical tone, "enter a dark room quietly, turn on the lights, and notice where the cockroaches run." Big news.

One evening a few weeks later, I catch the tail end of a radio commercial that sounds like a joke—something about motels for roaches. "They check in, but they don't check out," the announcer says. I sit and listen for the ad to repeat. Having discovered that my Raid tolerance is lower than ever, I get excited about the possibility of trapping instead of spraying, although the smashing with Kleenex has by now become such an automatic response that I no longer even shudder. In fact, I killed a moth in the elevator in the same spirit, though with immediate regret—I should have caught him and put him outside instead of stomping him in the corner of the ratty old carpet. That evening as I sat with a candle at my window, three of his relatives kept fluttering in and out to haunt me. Such vulnerable creatures in their sweet and silent, erratic journeyings. I shooed them all out and shut the window, knowing I would feel responsible if one should fly into the flame that attracts them so irresistibly. The pale, dry wings of their cousin lay in the elevator for weeks until, I suppose, Mr. Andrews finally got around to vacuuming.

Newlyweds with me so young, coming out from Sunday morning breakfast to find our yard blessed with hundreds and hundreds of Monarch butterflies. They cover the trees, the hedge, the passionflower vine, the telephone wires, the roof of the garage, resting brilliant, weary wings that may have carried them from as far away as Texas. It is awesome to think of these frail, quiet splashes of orange and black making such a trip, uncanny and moving that they have chosen our yard to land in. We sit right down on the still-wet grass and do not move until the last of them has taken to the sky again, heeding some mysterious, silent signal. Then we carry pink wine back to bed and bask in the fragrance of cherry blossoms blowing through the big, screenless window, beginning to joke afterward about whether the visit was real and half scolding ourselves for not thinking to document it with a photograph. I am glad now that we didn't, would not have wanted to decide which of us should keep it.

There is a disturbance at the pagoda, and I look down to see a bicycle skidding across the concrete on its side. The dark, red-turbaned man who is yelling at the woman with the baby must have kicked it over to show her the force of his anger. She cringes with the infant, while several of the regulars observe from the bench behind her. I cannot understand what he is shouting, but in a moment, she begins to answer him with loud, tearful emphasis: "I didn't fuck him, Leroy, I swear. I *didn't*. I *didn't*."

"Don't lie to me, white bitch," Leroy says. He raises his hand to slap her, but she protects herself with the baby, who is wrapped only in a small, light blanket against the damp night chill. Leroy grabs the child away from her and plops it into the lap of a startled wino, jumps back and finishes the blow he started. The woman rubs her cheek and backs away from him, saying, "I didn't, Leroy, I swear." She retrieves the lightskinned, fuzzy-headed infant and then begins to shout her side of the story at Leroy, bitterly listing women's names, all the "whores and bitches" that he has betrayed her with. It appears that she is even drunker or more drugged than Leroy as she staggers about with the child. I have seen them around before, her with long, straight blonde hair, unkempt and wearing too much eye makeup; him icy cool in his turban and tight black pants; the baby usually quiet, looking to be about seven or eight months old. Now they push each other back and forth, taking turns at verbal abuse. First he takes the baby away from her, saying her mind is too fucked-up to take care of his son, and then she grabs him back, saying she loves the boy more than he does. One of the winos steps up to intervene, taking the baby with him to the bench, but soon the mother comes back for him, and it starts all over again.

I am getting very nervous and concerned about the child, who is crying fairly constantly and begins to shriek as his parents trade slaps. When Leroy pushes the woman so hard that she almost drops him to the concrete, I can no longer sit still. I pick up the phone and realize that I have never in my whole life called the police about anything. I feel myself freeze and stop dialing mid-number, terrified of getting involved. I wonder just what it will mean—whether I will have to sign a complaint or go to the police station and confront the couple in some way. I go back to the window. Maybe this fight is winding down. They've been at it for fifteen or twenty minutes. How much longer can it last, anyway? But I see that it continues at the same meaningless pitch and with the same disregard for the infant's safety. I take a deep breath and make the call, telling myself that intervention by the police may jar the man and woman into not abusing their child in the future. I sound like the perfect concerned citizen as I describe the situation to the female operator, who repeats in monotone my complaint and the location and takes my name and phone number, which I give reluctantly but quickly.

"Can you ask them to hurry?" I say. "It looks like the baby could get hurt any second."

"Right," she says, just before the click.

In these few moments the scene apparently climaxed. One of the winos has the now-silent baby perched awkwardly on his knee, and it looks as if Leroy must have hit the woman hard this time—she sits on the far edge of the bench with her head on her knees.

"You better git on home now," a bent old black man says to the woman, bringing the bicycle up close to her. "Take yo' young 'un an' get on home. It looks to me like Leroy about to get sho 'nuf mad now." He helps her to her feet and holds the bike steady while she rather shakily mounts it, then he gently places the baby in the large metal basket attached to the handlebars. There is no pillow, nothing to protect his head from bumps.

After a couple of false starts, the woman manages to balance herself and weave her way slowly out of my view as Leroy stands sullenly watching. Not until fifteen minutes later, when I've nearly given up, do the police come cruising by on what surely is just their usual run. They slow down at the pagoda but see nothing that warrants a stop. They don't even bother to question the regulars, and Leroy is long gone.

"Roaches check in, but they don't check out," the deep radio voice says again enthusiastically. "No poison, no unpleasant odor, no mess with the Roach Motel. No need to clear out cabinets, no need to pick up dead roaches throughout the house. Just throw away the Roach Motel when full! Stops roaches twenty-four hours a day!"

It is nearly ten o'clock, but I drive straight to the grocery store in search of a miracle, and sure enough, Lucky's has a fresh stock of black-and-pink-and-yellow-and-orange colored boxes, each of which contains two white cardboard "motels"—5 x 3 x 2-inch traps that have one-inch strips of glue-bait running all around the inside. When I unwrap them in the kitchen, a sickening sweetness rises to make me distrust the ad claims—if this is their idea of "no unpleasant odor," what is their idea of efficiency? Still, I am very pleased to have something new to try. I have never before responded to a commercial so positively and quickly and consciously and gratefully.

I place four of the traps in strategic locations, checking them often the first few days as roaches do indeed begin to accumulate on the pale pink strips of glue. It is only upon careful examination the third or fourth day that I perceive the roaches I've been seeing in there are still alive, antennae still moving, the leg or two not completely stuck stretching feebly and uselessly toward some apparent dream of escape. "No poison," the ad boasted. It appears that they just get stuck in the glue and starve to death, which seems to take several days. Christ, I'd rather mash them than listen to their silent screams. And yet I stare into the trap with as much fascination as compassion, with a certain sense of triumph, and with a certain renewed respect for American ingenuity, for it looks as if the Roach Motel will indeed live up to its own potential and its marketers' promises.

My sense of relief overcomes my distaste for cruelty. I check the motel on the kitchen counter everyday for the arrival of new tenants and the final stilling of old ones, and I feel safety in their growing numbers. I can see them. I can see them, and they can't crawl on me or hide from me or multiply. One afternoon, I see that one of the newer females has managed to push her egg sac out from its pocket at the rear of her body, and spilling from the case right into the waiting glue are twenty or thirty tiny, still black dots with legs. The mother's antennae are jerking about feverishly, but her babies apparently experienced birth and death almost simultaneously. I feel sorry and go for days without looking into the trap. I feel sorry, and yet am glad.

"That's just too bad," I tell myself. "That's just too bad. It's the way things are. It's the way things have to be."

Early on a dull, gray Sunday morning I wake up to the awful sound of someone crying out for her mother. "Mommy," she says over and over, sounding angry and sad and scared and impatient all at once. "Momeeeeeeeee!" I peek out my window but can see no one except a small group of people waiting for the Napoleon to open. They give no sign that they hear what I hear, and I wonder if it could be someone in my building—maybe one of the young women on the third floor reduced to a little girl by Saturday night's bad trip. "Momeeeeeeee!" The word pierces, seems to cut through to the very center of me. It could make me cry if I let it. Mercifully, as I start to shut the window, the woman falls silent.

Lying in that stiff hospital bed, waiting for the night to pass so that I can get my womb scraped clean. I have put up with the bleeding for months dreading this violation, fearing what it might reveal. I am sure I do not have my mother's disease, and yet I bleed wrong, too much at the wrong time, too little at the right time, until I no longer know which is which. How is it that I cannot regulate myself?

Everyone else on this ward is swollen with child. "How many do you have?" my roommate asks, and when I say none, she says she is sorry. I do not want her to be sorry. I do not want children, and yet when she says she is sorry, I feel sorry, too, and turn on Walter Cronkite overhead. Husbands come in and fidget until we send them home as guilt-free as possible, and then someone begins to cry for her mother. "Motherrrr," she wails like a child. "Motherrrr!"

"God, I hope *that* doesn't go on all night," the roommate says and turns up the TV, but it doesn't help. I figure she must be in labor, wanting her mother, wanting her mother. I wonder if her mother is far away or dead. I want mine, too.

I haven't asked Janet to come, but now I call her, and of course, she says, of course she will be here by 6:45, or earlier if they will let her in. "It's routine," she says. "Don't be afraid."

"I know," I say. "I know. I've typed a hundred D&C reports. It's no big deal."

The lights go out, but sleep won't come. "Motherrrr," the woman starts again. "MOTHERRRR!" I don't want them to knock me out and stick whatever it is up inside me, farther up, deeper into me than anything has ever been, where I don't even know what I look like, and it's not fair for anyone else to know. It is rumored in town that my doctor is a homosexual. I hope he is not the sort who hates women and takes accidental revenge. But no, he has a kind face. I hope he is sober tonight. "Motherrrr, Motherrrr." Why don't they give her a sedative? But the real question is, why doesn't her mother come? I wait numbly for daylight.

Janet sits right up on the side of the bed to hold my hand after they give me the shot. I start to fade a bit, panic, don't want to lose sight of her. She walks alongside the stretcher holding my hand as they wheel me down the hall.

"It's just like 'Marcus Welby, M.D.'," I say feebly.

"Oh, I love that show," one of the nurses responds cheerfully. "He don't ever bore me somehow." He don't, he don't, I think. I don't want her in the room when I am unconscious and bleeding. I think she will enjoy it, and how could she have got through school without ever noticing that it's *he doesn't*, not *he don't*? What else did she fail to notice? What kind of person wants to be a surgical nurse, anyway? No wonder they wear masks. Janet trails off, and I am in a room with too much metal. They situate me on a very cold, hard table with stirrups.

"He's here," one of them calls out, and the Marcus Welby fan takes my arm.

"Would you mind if I just gave you a little poke with this?" she grins behind green cloth, showing me the needle.

"Yes, I think I would mind," I say as she does it. I'm gone before she even puts my arm down.

"You're fine now. You're awake," someone is calling into my ear. "Doctor says everything is fine, just fine. The lab report looks fine so far, just fine."

"Did that woman's mother come yet?" I hear myself ask, or at least I think I hear myself. "Did that woman have her baby?"

"What is it, honey? Do you want water already?"

"That woman who kept crying for her mother, did she come?"

"Oh, is your mother waiting for you, dear? I'll let her know everything is fine." This jars me into total consciousness.

"My mother is dead," I say, enunciating each word slowly. "I want to know about that woman who was screaming all night."

"Oh, *her*. No, honey, she's two floors up from you on the burn ward. Just about burned to a crisp, and seems like 'Mother' is all she can say for the past two days—and her mother right there in the room, too. She's just real mental, but it sure can get on your nerves, can't it? Here, honey, let's hold this extra pad down here 'til we get you back to your room."

As I descend the fire escape for my run, the woman begins to cry out again, this time more insistently. "Momeee," she calls between what seem like measured pauses, "Momeeee!" When I get onto the boardwalk, I hear her more clearly—it is "Bobby" she is saying. "Bobeee!" It is the woman from the fight at the cafe sitting alone on a bench some distance ahead of me. She is filthy looking, wild-haired and wild-eyed, her face puffy from crying. "Bobbeee!" she shouts, and the fury of it seems to come from the bottom of her spine all the way up and out through her tortured mouth. I gravitate toward her as I run, half intending to slow down or stop to see if there is something I can say or do for her, but as I draw closer, she looks me right in the eye and spits hard onto the concrete at my feet. I speed away, trying to deny the injury. People can take care of themselves. Why do I always suppose they can't?

When I return, she is gone from the bench, but there is a crowd in front of the Napoleon. With one hand the manager of the cafe is holding both the woman's wrists behind her back, which she submits to passively. A police car swings quickly around the corner and parts the crowd, and within seconds she is maneuvered into the back seat behind mesh-wired windows and locked doors. She hangs her head and does not look up as people gawk at her while the manager shows the police that one entire panel of his storefront is shattered.

"Someone could have been hurt bad," he says. In the front booth, a plateful of egg yolk has congealed around a triangular fragment of glass.

"I guess she threw a beer bottle through it," Eric tells me, expressing relief that it was not his own plant-filled shop window. The police drive away with her, and I notice from upstairs that within a half-hour a truck has arrived with two men to install a fresh pane of glass. I wonder where Bobby is this morning.

By noon the sky has transformed itself into brilliant blue, and the sea has reverted from gray-brown to the blue-green that people demand of it for "a perfect day at the beach." The crowd descends, and the mood and noise level ascend throughout the afternoon. I stand in line at the little grocery store next door, waiting to get my bottle of beer stuffed into the small brown candy sack that is supposed to shield it from the eyes of the Sunday cops, some of whom wear bermuda shorts and T-shirts and are conspicuous only because of the billy clubs and pistols at their waists. No one really believes they will arrest you for having an open beer in your hand, and yet I see people hold bottles under their shirts and turn the other way when the police approach. I do it, too, and decide it is part of the fun.

Outside the store I catch a whiff of marijuana that seems to come from several directions at once, and a ways up the walk an elaborately mustachioed young man is doing a pipe demonstration with parsley. His spiel has the exact tone and pace of the Vegematic salesman at the last Illinois State Fair I visited, but the main selling point for his clear plastic gadget is that while you may be too stoned to roll a joint or clip a roach—I am startled at the phrase—you are never too stoned to dump some stash into the miraculously enclosed pipe. "No muss, no fuss," he promises, "and nothing gets wasted but YOU!"

Across from his stand, a large crowd has lined up along a wide strip of smooth concrete where roller skaters are weaving intricate patterns among carefully spaced beer cans. The real attraction, though, is a row of six trash barrels that have been laid together on their sides, for every few minutes, two or three young male daredevils take turns jumping over them on skates. I find a place to stand among people at the end of the strip. The crowd seems excited and tense, anticipating the jumps, but seeing two successful ones is much less a thrill than I expected. The third guy removes his shirt and adds an extra barrel, and people applaud as he skates back to get a speedy start. I sense that we are all waiting for him to crash—that's what the excitement is about. The others just barely cleared six, and now he has foolishly added a seventh, and we are all standing here not exactly wanting him to miss or get hurt, but wondering, wondering if he won't lose control, and fascinated that he is willing to take that risk. It comes as no surprise when his skates clip the last barrel as he sails over it, flipping him a little sideways so that he lands on his back with a sliding thud at the edge of the concrete. He picks himself up quickly, acting as if the ugly scrape between his shoulder blades does not exist. His friend hands him a beer as the crowd applauds again and begins to disperse in favor of the blue-grass band that has started to fiddle away a few yards down the boardwalk.

"Don't be sad, lady." Suddenly at my side there is a curly-haired boy of eight or nine whose features have been expertly transformed into those of a white-faced clown by the man at the face-painting booth. "Come and see the bubble man." He grabs my sleeve, and I skip with him toward the bushy-bearded man in the silver jacket who, with his big hoop and pan of suds is waving into existence shiny bubbles the size of basketballs and bigger. A whole crew of adults and children tag along behind him as he walks, and everyone is smiling.

"See?" The little boy grins at me, revealing tiny pointed teeth behind the huge red mouth. Then he runs away quickly, chasing after the highest floating bubble, and I lose sight of him in the crowd that has gathered around two singers not far from the sidewalk cafe. A guitar case lies open at their feet waiting to receive whatever price people are willing to pay for a song these days.

"We're gonna do a very special Venice song for you now," one of the performers is saying. "You might say it's the city anthem of Venice. It's called 'The Dogshit Blues.'"

The crowd roars appreciatively, and I feel an odd sense of community in not being the only one who daily expends a good deal of concentration watching where I put my feet down in this neighbor-hood.

> There is dogshit on the sidewalk,
> Dogshit in the sand,
> Dogshit in the parking lot, Lord,
> There's dogshit in my hand,
> So I'm singin' them dogshit
> Them lowdown dirty Venice dogshit blues.

"Tell it like it is," people call out, and there is laughter and much mock checking of shoe soles as a police car comes easing through with its bull horn blaring, "Lost juvenile, lost juvenile, age six, hair blonde, eyes blue, name Dennis. Lost juvenile." I see the boy's tear-streaked face pressed against the back side window. He has a sucker looped around one thumb but shows no interest in it. I scan the crowd, expecting, I suppose, some frantic rush of mother toward him, but none occurs.

"Have you ever seen a roach lookin' like an ocean whale?" the next song begins. The lead singer looks my way, and for a second I'm afraid he may dedicate this number to me, but several voices respond with cries of "Yeah," and "You better believe it."

> If you never seen a roach
> Lookin' like an ocean whale,
> Then you never spent a night
> In the L.A. County Jail.

The crowd claps time, and one of the younger black winos rolls to his feet from the grass beside the singers.

"Tha's right, brothers, I can testify to that." We all laugh and applaud him and toss coins at the guitar case.

I wonder if that's where they took the woman who broke the window, and whether she'll have to stay there or if Bobby, or some-body, will bail her out. I wonder if she feels better or worse in there. Maybe she broke it because something in her wanted to go to jail. Maybe she broke it because something in her was breaking. She is the only person who has ever spit at me. I glance around for the little clown, wondering if I still look sad to him, but he has not reap-peared. Sun feels good on the top of my head. I get another beer and then stop to look at the used clothing an old woman has spread out before her on a cotton blanket.

"How much for the sweater?" I ask, feeling the two dollar bills in my back pocket. She sizes me up with squinted eyes, scrutinizing my worn flannel shirt and thin-kneed jeans.

"Two dollars," she says.

"How about $1.50?" I ask.

"No." She does not elaborate or defend her price, merely cancels out mine. I give her the two dollars and slip the big, bulky rust-and-gray sweater right on, pleased with the bargain and wanting to wear it, despite the small voice in my head that chants, "Wash it first, wash it first, no telling where it's been." I stroll some more, ignoring the musty odor of it for as long as I can, then head upstairs and put it to soak.

I am sitting on my bed printing a letter to my father when the rumbling starts. It sounds at first like a very large, very low-flying plane, and I lean toward the window to locate it before I realize that the sound is all around me, not outdoors. The windows begin to rattle loudly, and for a moment my body is frozen on the mattress, unable to move, although my mind knows I must get away from flying glass. The bookshelves begin to shake, and I imagine all my books sliding to the floor as the plaster cracks and descends from walls and ceilings. Get to the basement. No, that's tornadoes. The sound of the rumble intensifies, and when my little hand-carved wooden devil falls from the high, corner shelf onto the bed at my feet, I spring up in total panic.

I want to get outside but what if the building crumbles while I'm on my way? At least if I stay here I will be on top of the rubble heap. I dash to the bathroom and kneel down in the tub, feel it sway and sway my body with it, lowering head to knees and hearing myself begin to moan with sheer fright. I will not scream, I will not scream. I make myself breathe deeply and try to think rationally. How long do they last, how long do they last? I must have read it somewhere. And what am I supposed to be doing? Christ, please let it stop, let it stop, let it stop now. I put my fingers in my ears, unable to stand the noise of it, wish I had not seen the movie. Such a bad movie, such a bad movie I thought at the time, because a real earthquake would be so much worse than anything they put on the screen. Tidal wave. If the earthquake doesn't get you, the tidal wave will. I won't die, I won't die, even if the roof collapses. But maybe I should try to get outside.

It stops. It simply stops, and then I do not know what to think. I am shaking but have the presence of mind to see the absurdity of kneeling in this old bathtub, situated right beneath a window and offering no protection from anything, really. My knees are weak as I climb out and look around the place. Everything is just as it was except for the devil on the bed. I look down to the pagoda but see no signs of panic from anyone on the boardwalk. Maybe outside you don't feel it that much. I have a rush of diarrhea but stifle it, unable to stay inside another second. I scramble down the fire escape on very shaky legs and start to feel better as soon as I mingle among the crowd on the boardwalk again. The musicians are still playing, the skaters are still skating, a man on a tall unicycle rides high above it all. I am glad to see my neighbor from down the hall.

"How'd you like the quake?" she grins, leaning against the muscular, blonde young man at her side.

"Well, actually, it scared the shit out of me," I say, managing a nervous laugh. "I was inside and didn't know what to do."

"Oh, you shouldn't worry about it," she says lightly. "It happens all the time. Stand under a doorframe or something."

"Oh," I say. "This was my first one. In the midwest it's tornadoes." This talk is calming me, transforming the terror into chat about the weather.

"Well . . . welcome to California," she says as they move on down the walk.

Mr. Andrews is sitting in the parlor when I go through on my way up to the bathroom. He smiles his usual serene smile.

"I guess this building has lasted through a lot of earthquakes," I say conversationally.

"Oh yip, yip, quite a few of 'em. Plenty of 'em a lot worse than this 'un was."

"Did you get scared?" I ask. "I got scared."

"Oh nope, nope. I'm not scared of 'em anymore. Used to be, but not anymore. I've lasted this long and this building's lasted this long. Ain't no use to be scared of 'em now." He gets up slowly and we move to the elevator together. I want to take his hand. Really, I want him to take mine and pat it and tell me again how there is no reason to be afraid.

"You ever get you any Bug Death?" he asks as I slide both the old doors to and push "3" for him.

"No," I say. "I got some Roach Motels."

"Say what?" he says, slipping his large, gold watch from his back pocket by its chain and snapping it open for a peek at the time.

"I say I got me some Roach Motels. Traps. They seem to work pretty well."

"Oh," he says, replacing the watch and giving the pocket three gentle pats. "Hmm. That's all right, I guess. Bug Death suits me fine m'self." He shuffles out onto the third floor. "Well. . . Be seein' ya," he says, lifting his smooth white hand in a little wave. I have to suppress an impulse to hug him.

"Be seein' ya," I say.

Within a few weeks, all four of the traps are full, and I put out fresh ones. This time the roaches seem to be accumulating much more gradually, and I am unsure of what to make of it. I hope it simply means that there are fewer around now, and this is what I choose to believe on optimistic days. But it could mean—yes, given the cockroach's history, it could very well mean—that they have wised up to the smell of the glue or the location of the traps. Roaches can't learn their way through a maze as well as ants can, the encyclopedia said, but they have better memories for avoiding electrical shocks in the lab. Maybe crawling up to the entrance of a trap and being confronted with a whole box full of your own species' carcasses could serve as shock enough to activate that memory for avoidance.

I don't know. Sometimes I feel as if I have lost my perspective when I realize I'd almost rather see a roach than not see one. I have clipped the newspaper ad for a new "doomsday powder" that is out now which is supposed to *eliminate all roaches and prevent reinfestation for years.* It costs $8.00 a can. I guess I can always get some if the motel business doesn't pick up soon.

Chapter Three

Waitress

There is a woman that I watch across the way. I suppose this is spying, but she's newly moved in and has no curtains. It is an effortless sort of spying, really, with a certain innocence about it. In this tiny apartment I can face my wall of books or my over-full, doorless closet. I can turn to look at my kitchen sink. But mostly, if I am not reading or writing, I choose to stare out my window; and when I look straight out, quite often there she will be, alone in her place, doing the things one does to recuperate from a day of hard work, doing the things one does to get through evenings. Once in awhile, not often, she will hang a large, turquoise towel across the bottom half of her living room window, which gives me an odd sense of relief at no longer being able to see, even as it arouses my curiosity. What prompts this sudden concern that she might be on display, I wonder? And what does she do differently behind the towel?

I have no curtains, either, but there are shades to pull. She has ample opportunity to watch me back, but I don't think she ever does—her eyes are more readily drawn to the television screen that dominates her inside wall. Sometimes I find myself gazing over her shoulder at the quick, jerky, silent images, grasping from memory the texture of programs designed to fill time-slots. At this distance the shows all run together, broken only by commercials that give the woman a chance to move to the kitchen for a little more whiskey. No one seems to visit her, and she goes to bed even earlier than I do.

It is some time before I realize the woman is a waitress at the Napoleon, whose kitchen is situated just below her own. One sunny afternoon I see her for the first time outside her apartment—she comes out the white-boarded, side-rear door of the cafe in her white uniform and shoes, is delineated against the white brick of the building only by her bubble of dyed-black, slightly teased hair. It is too black not to be dyed, too black for a woman in her fifties. She colors her eyebrows that dark, too, so that, as she stands for a moment against the white brick, digging into her purse for keys, her pale, thoroughly powdered face takes on a somewhat ghostly quality, which dark red lipstick accentuates.

She is weary. She will go right upstairs and take off the uniform and put on her pale orange nightgown and matching peignoir, pour herself a drink, turn on the television, and sit with her tiny bare feet propped up on the straight-backed, white wooden chair opposite the one in which she sits. I already know this and merely wait for her to play it out.

Sometimes it takes awhile for her to reappear in the kitchen from the back room, and I think she must be taking a bath. There are days when I come in from work and head straight for the tub, too, feeling a need to wash away the day's typing or sweat from the drive home through congested streets. This cleansing becomes a ceremony that separates secretarial days from private nights. The cleansing and the exercises—I know I will feel better all evening if I do ten minutes of moving and stretching. Yes. I undress and try at least to do some exercises before I pour myself a drink. But the waitress has been on the move all day, needs to be still, needs to elevate her feet. Her uniform and hair must smell of frying food and cigarette smoke, and I wonder if all the odors from the Napoleon don't drift up through the floors and windows to fill her apartment. It is convenient to live so close to your job, but in this case there may be some disadvantage.

When she gets situated by the window with her drink, she lights up one cigarette after another. Such long, white cigarettes they are, out of all proportion to her small face and diminutive hands. She keeps an oversized ashtray on the table and taps at it much more than necessary, three taps at a time always, so frequently that the ash never has a chance to grow. This gesture fascinates me as I sit with my own whiskey, and I imitate it, discovering that it has the power to make me intensely nervous. The waitress sits perfectly contained and still, her weariness evident in the set of her shoulders.

She sips slowly on her tall, iced drink, but is otherwise unanimated except for the sheer energy of that tap-tap-tap—something inside her seems to flare up with each repetition.

Like me, I think she has a tendency to skip supper, or maybe she eats at the cafe before leaving at 4:00. I seldom see her cook anything, though sometimes she will bring a small brown sack of tidbits home with her and arrange them on a paper plate for nibbling throughout the evening. Once when she was out of the room a tricky gust of wind snatched her empty plate from the table by the windowsill—sucked it outward, lifted it skyward, and then dropped it straight down into the street below. I could not help but laugh and wonder how she would react when she got back, but she gave no sign at all that she noticed the plate was missing. I had to suppress a brief, maniacal impulse to shout across at her, above the television, "Hey, your plate blew out the window!" But perhaps she keeps track of dishes all day long and refuses them any more attention at night. At home she will *not* worry about breakage, and perhaps she uses paper plates in order to escape not merely the washing and drying of them but also the incessant rattle and clatter of the Napoleon. Perhaps, too, that is why whatever it is she brings home with her to eat never requires silverware. This all makes good sense to me—sometimes I get in from a day of work and refuse to typewrite anything, preferring the slow, quiet journey of pen across paper, however inefficient.

I do not cook much, either, although every few weeks or so I will get seized by some fit of economic good sense on my way past the meat counter at Lucky's, and I will broil myself a steak or bake some porkchops or chicken breasts. I have always been one of those competent, very plain cooks with a limited but quite edible repertoire. (Once a neighbor who loved to experiment in the kitchen tasted my porkchops. "These are wonderfully seasoned," she said. "*What* did you put on them?" I could answer only "Salt and pepper," never having considered any alternatives.) But, unfortunately, I always regret giving in to my impulse in the grocery store, because although I cook the food the same as ever, by the time I get it home and get it prepared and get it cooked and get it served at my single place-setting, it tastes funny. Somehow it goes bad on me between the store and the plate—or between the plate and the mouth.

At first, I tried to lay the blame for this on California. I thought, well, no wonder they're all vegetarians out here—they can't get any good meat. But the meat I get in restaurants here does not taste funny. I tried to lay the blame on Lucky's then, but the steak from Safeway or Alpha Beta is just the same, and I have had to face the fact that sitting down alone to eat what I have cooked for myself tends to flavor the food with pain. It's not just that the steak comes pre-wrapped in cellophane instead of the pink paper from Paul's Market around the corner, weighed and packaged by Paul himself and presented like a gift across the top of the huge old meat case. It's that I'm buying one instead of two, and as soon as I begin to smell it broiling, something in me thinks this must be a summer Saturday night—my inner ear begins to listen for the sound of the hand mower clicking away in the back yard, the sound of the screen door opening and banging shut as he comes in to shower, the tinkle of ice cubes in those special, frosted gin-and-tonic glasses, the smack of the cork from the pinot noir. I want to get just a little drunk and then savor the food and watch him savor it, linger over ice cream, laughing, drink coffee and B & B, go upstairs.

But not really. There is no going back, and I don't want to go back—even those nights had their own kind of desperation toward the end. I do not want to go back, and yet halfway through my steak I stop eating, can't clear the table fast enough, panic over what to do with the grease in the broiler, feel a wave of nausea when I glimpse the red juice on the styrofoam container in the garbage sack. I dump everything in and head down the fire escape with it all. I think about Kentucky Fried Chicken for the next day and usually end up eating it in the car, feeling strangely like some little animal in a cave, except that I have my radio on.

I should learn to cook some new dishes—that might do the trick. But the truth is I don't have the heart for it, have never, except on a few special occasions, viewed cooking as anything but a chore. My *Better Homes and Gardens Cook Book*, a wedding gift, now resides on my very top bookshelf, and access to it requires both a climb onto the bed and a long stretch. I used to stand in the kitchen doorway and watch him knead dough, envying the pleasure that seemed to come up through his hands and into his face from it. I would feel like a child leaning there in the doorway, hands clasped behind my back, a woman who hates to cook but loves to be fed. Some mysterious, automatic guilt attends all this for me, making it feel almost like a character flaw, like a refusal to grow up somehow.

As a bride I would cry with shame if I didn't get his eggs right. It was some funny way, the way he liked them then, that involved pouring water and keeping the lid on the skillet as his mother did—or was it his ex-wife? For me the whites would cook too fast and stick, already tough, to the cast iron, or the yolks would harden all the way through, or else I would panic and take them up too soon, transferring runny failures to the plates and trying not to sniffle as he assured me they were really all right, really all right, *really.*

Sometime during that period the local paper reported a suicide in unusually vivid detail. A woman in her thirties had gotten up one morning and fixed breakfast for her husband and son and sent them off to work and school. Then she began to fry an egg for herself, even had her toast in the toaster. And then, apparently, she just turned off the burner and walked into the bedroom and got the gun from under the bed, lay down across it in her yellow bathrobe, and shot herself. Everyone thought the story, the timing of the act, so strange, but I felt I understood it perfectly. I kept seeing the image of that solitary egg in the skillet, wondering if maybe she'd broken the yolk when she started to turn it. Cooking herself that egg required more determination, more devotion to staying alive, than she had in her that morning. She needed someone to feed her.

"I could eat out every day for the rest of my life and never cook another meal," I finally got around to admitting after six or seven or eight years of marriage.

"That's incredible," he said. "I find that very hard to believe."

But I meant it.

Somewhere along the way he began to fix his own breakfast on weekdays, and I began to frequent Boyd's Coffeeshop a few blocks over on South Main, just up from the post office, just around the corner from City Hall, where a waitress named Doreen always took good care of me. Boyd's was a long, narrow, yellow-walled room crammed with orange vinyl booths and formica-topped tables, and most mornings the mayor himself could be found sitting right in the center of it all in shirt-sleeves and tie, talking football and real estate and crops and politics with his cronies, occasionally reaffirming his manhood and good-ol'-boy status by telling a slightly off-color joke. There was a little half-booth at the very front of the restaurant that was either an architectural mistake or a stroke of genius, squeezed in as it was with only one seat and a tiny table, almost right up against the storefront glass. I came to consider it my own private spot, would look up from my book or magazine to see people go into the Corn Belt Bank across the street and come out guardedly counting their money or watch drivers of large cars fail miserably and hilariously at parallel parking on the meterless street. But I think I sat there mostly because I was sure to get Doreen that way.

She looked to be in her late forties and seemed a born waitress in the sense that she took to it so gracefully. I admired her efficiency, her dignified posture, her fresh, white uniforms, her surefootedness, her poise under pressure, and her easy manner with the customers. I envied what appeared to be contentment in her face, a lovely sort of contentment, devoid of stupidity. I always suspected she must be divorced or widowed, that she must have raised some kids on her own.

I liked her a lot partly because she never asked me any chatty questions—she seemed to respect that I came there to be alone. Maybe something in my manner gave her a clue that a simple, conversational question like "What do you do?" might send me into instant identity crisis. *Housewife* stuck in my craw and would have made me feel doubly guilty that I hadn't gotten up early to fix his breakfast. *Faculty wife* implied that I should be planning dinner that night for the department chairman or buying hot dogs to cook out for the student picnic. *Secretary* would have done all right except that I was between jobs (and why was I between jobs, anyway, when I had neither swollen belly nor little ones at home?). *Writer* seemed tenuous at best. But Doreen, bless her heart, had sense enough not to inquire. And yet she liked me, too, I could tell.

"You gonna have a stack today?" she would ask me cheerily. "You gonna have some extra butter on that?"

I had once asked for extra butter, and she always remembered. I never failed to be touched by the graciousness of her asking me instead of my having to make the request, even if she sometimes got a little carried away and plopped what seemed like half a cup of soft butter on top of three small pancakes, and even if there *were* little brown flecks of toast in it off the spreading knife at the grill, and even if, in fact, there was (by law) a carefully printed sign over the counter that said, "This establishment serves oleomargarine." It was a genuine honor to be served by Doreen, and sometimes I would get to feeling ecstatic sitting there in Boyd's over coffee and saturated hotcakes, as if that were the one place in the world where I belonged. I always carefully overtipped.

"The female *what?*" she asked one day, surprising me by putting down her carafe of coffee and picking up Germaine Greer's book from my table.

"*Eunuch,*" I said.

"What in the world is a *eunuch?*" she asked.

"Well," I said, "it's a man who's been . . . desexed, you know, castrated."

"Hm," she said, and then her brown eyes began to twinkle and dance with knowledge. "A female eunuch. Could be the dullest book in the world, am I right?" We laughed a good laugh, woman-to-woman.

The last time I was there I paid my check and then walked to the back of the place, where Doreen was on break with her cigarette in the last booth. "I may not see you again," I said. "I'm moving away. I'm getting a divorce." I heard my voice crack in the middle of the word.

"Welcome to the club, honey," Doreen smiled, taking a last deep drag. "Don't worry. Me and my boys have always made it fine. Where you going?"

"California I think."

"Well, I sure do wish you the very best of everything," she said, getting up to walk with me, pulling her order pad out of the deep pocket at her waist and taking the long yellow pencil from behind her ear in response to a gesture from the businessman who was already occupying my seat. "It's supposed to be awful pretty out there, I know that much."

One morning I wake up suddenly at 4:00 for no discernible reason except that moonlight is shining full on my face. Everything is unusually still except for the sound of waves tumbling in, crashing against rocks just up the shoreline, and receding. They roll in, crash and recede; roll in, crash, and recede. This is a perfect sound to sleep with. I sit up to look for the moon, expecting to see it out over the water, but no, it is much closer than that, perched precisely atop the palm tree across from the Napoleon, so huge and so near that it is almost dreamlike. I reach my arm out the window to feel the soft, damp air, and from a certain angle it looks as if my fingertips are touching the moon's upper edge, just as its lower edge is touching the top fronds of the tree. It is a harvest moon, only not quite such a vivid orange (*and* there is no nip in the air, *and* there are no hayrides scheduled, *and* it is, after all, late winter and not autumn).

This must be why I came here, I think to myself, so that I can lean out my open window in late winter and see the moon sitting on a palm tree while the waves roll in behind. Maybe this is what I should say when people ask me what brought me to California, what brought me to Venice, since I never know how to answer these questions. I came here because I couldn't think of anywhere else to go, but why couldn't I think of anywhere else to go? Things fall apart and you move to California—it's taken for granted, an American cliché. You read Joan Didion, and then maybe things fall apart for you, and you begin slouching towards Los Angeles. "The country is on a tilt," Frank Lloyd Wright is supposed to have said, "and everything loose is sliding into California." Mostly when I am asked I keep it simple.

"I came to get away from those awful winters," I say, and it's as true an explanation as any.

One recent afternoon the psychic I was interviewing for a free-lance article turned to me suddenly over our pina coladas and said, apropos of nothing, "How did you feel about all that cold weather back in Illinois?"

"I always *hated* it, ever since I was a child," I replied, a little surprised at my own emphasis. "I would start shivering in November and not warm up until April."

"Well, no wonder," she said. "In your last incarnation you were an Indian brave who died trying to cross the prairie with his wife and child in late October. The snows came early that year, and you all starved and then froze to death. But you are a very American soul—three times you have been here as an Indian and once as a Puritan woman in Salem."

I cannot believe these things, and yet I cannot disbelieve them, they feel so right. I will not freeze to death in California, and I know this is one reason I feel good here, have even said so to old friends and relatives. And my arrival has at times felt like the completion of some more than ordinary journey. If I have not travelled to other countries, it is, most essentially, because I have not wanted to, already knowing I like America best, as surely as I know I like corn better than asparagus or endive, though I have never tasted either of the latter.

The moon is sinking slowly until the trunk of the palm dissects it, low enough now to shimmer on the water, illuminating the waves as they travel in. All at once I am ravenous, the kind of gut hunger that renders me weak and shaky. I get up for a snack and discover, to no great surprise, nothing on the shelf but some club crackers. What I want is some of my mother's cornbread crumbled into a glass of milk, to eat it with a spoon. I will not freeze out here, but I could starve to death before the Napoleon opens at 8:00. The waitress's kitchen light is on, though she is nowhere in sight. I am going to have to watch myself in the grocery store, make sure I put some food in the cart—not just coffee and wine and toilet paper and toothpaste. I nibble crackers and watch the moon go down, watch how the darkness that it leaves behind gradually yields to soft, gray half-light. Then I doze deliciously, on and off, among the cracker crumbs.

By seven o'clock, when I begin to think about staying awake, a thin fog has rolled in, imparting a certain heaviness and gloom to the morning which intrudes upon my lingering high from having touched the moon. I hear the unmistakable sound of water splashing on pavement and sit up to view the scene I know I will find below: the smallest of the three young Mexicans who work at the Napoleon has attached the short, green hose to the spigot concealed in the rear doorway and is washing down the two long sections of wooden slats that fit behind the counter, designed, I suppose, to cushion the feet of the cook and waitresses from the linoleum-covered, concrete floor. He performs this task diligently and with obvious concentration every morning but Thursday, when the place is closed, and when he finishes the slats he will hose the doorway clean of the night's piss, and then he will go in for the bucket and the long-handled brush-broom with which he will scrub the large plateglass windows, inside and out.

The waitress (did she mean to leave that light on all night?) appears at her kitchen window above him, dressed for work. She is wearing little half-glasses on a chain around her neck, and as she leans out over the sill with her styrofoam coffee cup, the black frames dangle just beyond the white brick ledge.

"Mornin', Freddie," she calls down.

"Good morning," he replies.

"It's another day, I reckon, even if it's a foggy one." Her voice is deep for her size, low-pitched and throaty, and she has a slight Southern accent. *Reckon*, she said. It is not deep Southern, maybe just Kentucky or even the southern tip of Illinois or Indiana. Maybe it's just a midwestern twang that has begun to *sound* Southern to me out here. What brought *her* to Venice? Freddie looks up but does not interrupt his scrubbing.

"I guess so," he says. "Another day."

By 7:30 the wide-striped bamboo curtains in the Napoleon have been rolled to the very top for the window cleaning, and I can see the waitress scurrying around the empty place, filling salt and pepper shakers and creamers and sugar jars, arranging them just so at each table. When Freddie finishes with his brush-broom, she wipes off all the tables near the windows, where he no doubt dribbled soapy water, and situates the curtain cords securely so they will not violate eating or sitting space. The cook stands behind the counter, arms folded across his white t-shirt and apron, waiting, I suppose, for the griddle to warm up.

After the waitress fetches herself a cigarette, she returns to the window, glancing at her watch. By ten to eight, several people have gathered outside the front door, and among them is a bearded young man in khaki shorts who is holding a toddler in his arms. He and the child are wearing identical red baseball caps. When the waitress spots them, she quickly deposits her cigarette in an ashtray on the counter, disappears, and then reappears with an old-fashioned, dark wooden high chair—nearly as tall as she is—which she sets up beside one of the rear booths. In a moment, she is back with a bib, which she folds in half and leaves on the table.

Just at 8:00 a pretty young woman in levis and a purple tank top comes tearing down the street, long hair flying, and nearly falls as she skids around the corner to the front of the restaurant. She is the other waitress. (Actually, I once overheard her tell someone that she is an actress looking for work—she pretends to be a waitress the way I pretend to be a secretary.) When Freddie unlocks the door for her, the waiting customers follow her in, and soon the back section, which seems to belong to the waitress in the white uniform, is nearly full. I notice that the first order she takes is from the man with the baby, and both of them remove their ballcaps when she appears at their table.

I grow nervous as I approach the cafe and resolve not to sit in her section. There would be something unfair about it, sitting at one of her tables like any other customer after I have seen her a little tipsy in her nightgown. I need to be fed with no guilt attached, and one lovely thing about waitresses is the way they can nurture you without expecting any return beyond the tip. And yet with this woman I feel a desire to turn things around and do something for her. I am not saying I would cook for her, but certainly I could bring her a cup of coffee and a Danish or something while she took a load off her feet at the last counter stool. Already, this early in the day, I see that she is resting one knee whenever there is an empty seat as she takes orders, bending over the table and donning the little spectacles to check prices on the menu, then removing them and sliding an absurdly long gold pencil from the teased hair just above her tiny ear. The pencil has an oversized eraser which weighs it down nearly to the middle of her well-rouged cheek when she returns it to its nest. As she scurries by my small central table, I see DELLA carved in white letters on the black plastic pin on her lapel.

A stout young man with short, curly, tousled-looking blonde hair sits at the counter, rubbing his face with both hands. He looks as if he just woke up or as if he might have worked the graveyard shift somewhere—he is wearing soiled gray work-pants.

"Coffee?" Della asks him, already pouring. "What's it gonna be this morning?" The young man mumbles, hesitates, finally says a cheeseburger with lettuce and tomato and onion, which Della writes down.

"No, no. That's not what I want. I don't know. Come back later." Della erases the order carefully and smiles at him.

"We're just gonna have to wait 'til you perk up a little bit, I reckon." When she comes back by he orders a tuna sandwich with tomato, which she doesn't write down. "That'll cost you another 20¢ to have that tomato put on there," she warns him. He hesitates, thinks it over.

"Oh, well, what the hell?" he says. "I'll go for it."

Della writes the order down and carries it straight to the cook, and then she pulls a huge white coffee cup from beneath the counter and fills it for herself. "Old waitresses never die," it says in large black letters. "They just keep their sections closed." She comes around the counter and rests her right knee on the vacant stool beside the young man, sips coffee, lights a Marlboro 100, begins to tap-tap-tap it against the ashtray.

All at once there is a very loud burst of music behind me, and I turn to see one of the women regulars from the pagoda standing in the doorway with a big portable radio, which she is more or less aiming into the cafe at top volume. She is heavy-set with long, ratty-looking hair, wearing, as usual, army-green shorts and what might loosely be called combat boots. Now Della plants herself firmly beside the counter, hands on hips, and yells the entire length of the room.

"Don't stand in the door with that damn noise. Get out of here. Go on. Take that damn noise out of here." She retrieves her cigarette as the young woman stands her ground for a few moments and then retreats, letting the door come to. "Stands in the door like that with that damn radio," Della says scrappily, loud enough for anyone in the place who wants to hear her. "She's been eighty-sixed out of every cafe in Venice."

"She's nutty," the blonde man says. "Don't pay any attention to her. I saw her try to beat a guy up out on the boardwalk. She's nutty with dope."

"It's her own damn fault, too," Della says. "Her own damn fault."

The door reopens and the young woman comes back in, this time accompanied by a yellow-haired woman a little older than herself and in much worse shape. Her clothes are filthy and her hair matted with bits of dried grass in it, obviously uncombed, let alone washed, for days or weeks. They take two stools near the cash register right by the cook, who turns around to face them.

"Don't serve those two, Thomas," Della calls up to him. "I already told her the last time she was in here not to come back."

The woman in combat boots sets her radio carefully upon the counter. "I want some toast and she wants some cottage cheese," she says, as if Della did not exist. "My money is as good as anybody's."

"You sit there and behave yourself and eat quick," Thomas says. "And then I don't want you in here again. I don't like to have you around, it's always trouble."

"Well, that's too bad," the woman says sarcastically. "Really. I have to be around people I don't like all the time, all the time. You bother the shit out of me, but I can still be around you." Her companion begins to pick at the cottage cheese, holding a cigarette in her other trembling hand.

The blonde young man finishes his tuna sandwich. "She's nutty," he says softly to Della. "She gets a welfare check or a social security check for doing nothing but being nutty. I wouldn't give her the debris off my plate. I wouldn't give her the sweat off my skin. Then somebody like you who works hard. Who gives you a check for nothing?"

Della looks him straight in the eye. "I've worked ever since I was seven years old," she says. "Ever since I was seven years old."

The waffle that the actress brought me has gotten cold during all this, but my hunger has passed anyway, and to tell the truth, she overcooked it, neglecting to heed the timer-bell on the little round iron behind the counter. Now as I gesture for my check, I have to struggle to draw the young woman's attention from the man she is flirting with at the next table.

"What's your name anyway?" he finally asks. "What's your sign?"

"Dawn, but I'm thinking of changing it to Aurora. What do you think? I'm an Aquarius."

Waffles. Aunt Lucinda's waffles, her special treat for me ever since I was a little girl, and then she gave me that waffle iron as a wedding gift, but I never used it much. On my last visit I told her she should set up a little waffle house in her kitchen and make herself a fortune at the age of 82. She shook with laughing.

"There's been times when I was just about up against it enough to do somethin' like that, I can tell you. I never had done public work 'til your Uncle Nute died, you know, and then there I was with three little 'uns to feed."

Public work, she calls it, and I think she must mean working for the government or something, but she means work outside the home, outside the cotton fields of western Tennessee in the late thirties.

"That's when I got me a job waitressin' at the Southern Hotel there in Jackson, a real nice coffeeshop there where all the business people and higher-ups ate. 'Course, they didn't pay nothin' for the waitresses. They paid seven dollars and a half every two weeks, and I had to depend on tips. But for that day and time I was a good waitress. I worked at it. I needed the money and I give good service and I got good tips. A lot of days I'd make $10, and in them days that was good money, good money."

I try to imagine big old Aunt Lucinda moving jolly and generous among the tables at the Southern Hotel. "Ain't you gonna have you a little dessert?" I can hear her saying. "We got ever' kinda pie you can think of." I want her to tell me what it was like.

"Well, I never will forget one time I like to got scared to death," she says. "'Course, down there then they did have such segregation, and they fed the colored people in the kitchen, the ones that wanted to eat there. They had a li'l ol' table in the kitchen where they fed 'em at. So I was in there one day and these two colored men drove up in a big car and they were army officers. So they come in the front door and nobody there but me. They walked in and set down there at the table in front. Well, *that* was something they just didn't allow *anywhere* there in Jackson. So I told 'em I couldn't serve 'em, they'd have to go to the kitchen, and they resented it. I just walked out there and told 'em 'bout as nice as I knew how, you know, and they resented it. So I walked back behind the counter where we kept a li'l ol' pistol. 'Course, the only other time I'd ever picked it up, just to mess with it, it went off and put a hole through the counter and like to have give me heart failure. But I went back there where they kept it. But then that colored boy who worked in the kitchen—man, I guess he was, he weighed 200 pounds—he come out of the kitchen and just told 'em they didn't do that down here, you know. He said, now if you want to come back to the kitchen, I'll feed you back there. But they left. They knew I went back and got that gun. They never said a word. They didn't like it, but they left. Now that kindly scared me up good. I didn't really know what to do. I wouldn't have shot 'em. I wouldn't have shot 'em. But I guess I was agonna bluff 'em."

"I would have resented it, too," I say as neutrally as possible. "Especially if I was in the army."

"Why sure," Aunt Lucinda agrees. "Just about anybody would, I reckon. But anyway I made enough for me and them kids to live on."

I jump as the rough woman at the counter snaps her radio back on full blast. Della scoots the length of the counter to face her up close, containing her fury as best she can and keeping her voice down. "Take that damn noise out of here and don't you ever come in here again," she says, pointing her index finger nearly in the woman's face. For a moment I am afraid there is going to be an actual fight, but Della backs off and returns to her own section, and the woman turns off the radio. As I go to pay my check, she is speaking seriously and intensely to her friend, who is staring into the cottage cheese bowl and gives no sign of hearing.

"That waitress is out of her mind," the woman says. "She's out of her mind. Don't pay any attention to her. She's not out of her mind, she's out of her heart. A lot of people aren't out of their minds, but they're out of their hearts. I try not to put her down for it, though." Della stands at the rear of the room, arranging near-empty catsup bottles on a plastic contraption that holds them tipped so that they can drain gradually into newer, fuller containers.

Going home I fall into step behind a ragged, filthy young man whose hair is as matted and repulsive as that of the blonde junkie in the cafe. As we approach the back of my building from the alley, I slow down, not wanting even to get close enough to pass him along the way, but then he stops to rummage in the large brown metal trash bin at the foot of my fire escape. A surge of shame and embarrassment washes over me, and I can watch only out the corner of my eye as he uses a stick to dredge up potential food from the garbage. That steak, that last steak I had is probably still in there somewhere. I feel slightly sick with the thought that he might find it and eat it with his grimy hands, and yet I want him to if it has not gone rancid by now. I could tell him it's there, I think to myself, maybe show him which side of the bin I tossed it into. But no, I cannot speak to him.

I could hand him the dollar in my pocket, but he does not ask me for money, and something in the way he holds his head tells me it will be easier for us both if I just pretend not to see what he is doing. I feel some deep shame in the face of him, not because I have wasted food but because he has wasted himself until this is how he lives, how he takes care of himself. This image of what can happen to a person frightens me. In the elevator I decide I will take something down to him before I remember that I have only the much dwindled supply of crackers.

"It's his own damn fault," Della would say, and my old friend Leona would agree with her. Many things about the waitress make me miss Leona—her teased hair, her toughness, her respect for hard work and survival, her loneliness, even her bitterness. The two women are about the same age, and Leona even worked as a cocktail waitress for awhile right after her divorce ("The men all brought their *cocks* in, honey, and wanted me to be the *tail*. I had to give it up.") She raised her three children alone working for minimum wage as a hospital receptionist after she walked into her bedroom one Saturday afternoon and found her husband in bed with her cousin.

"I grabbed him up outa there and threw his pants at him and pushed him right out the door, kiddo, and then I threw everything else of his out in the driveway. He never set foot in my house again, but you know what?" Her eyes begin to twinkle. "I went to that bastard's funeral last year and forgot to wear my underpants." She laughs a long, hearty laugh. "But as for *you*, I think you're sittin' around mopin' too much in that apartment. If you're gonna be divorced, you might as well practice up—let's go out on the town."

To Leona, going out on the town meant going to little neighborhood bars that had concrete floors and country music on the jukebox. "Just remember my name is Yvonne if anybody asks," she would wink at me.

"OK," I'd say. "Then call me Bunny."

We would drink a lot of 35¢ draft beer and act silly and call each other "Yvonne" and "Bunny" and let whoever offered buy us drinks, and then we'd dance to Charlie Rich or Freddy Fender or Johnny Paycheck. "Take this job and shove it," he'd sing, and the place would go wild with hoots and applause. The slow dances Leona called "belly-rubbers." As she would head off to the dance floor with whoever in her low-cut, hot pink blouse and her beehive of bleached-blonde hair, she would turn to me with a lusty gleam in her eye and whisper, "Uh-oh, Bunny, it's a belly-rubber. I hope he don't get too excited." We would dance late, and then, to the disappointment of Chuck and Dean or Sammy and Don or Herb and Carl, we would leave together to negotiate the bleary-eyed drive home. "You're gonna have to loosen up some, kid," Leona would say. "You're actin' too goddamn married, if you ask me."

One night at the Hickory House she met Lonnie and fell in love with the tattoo on his arm. Just below the roll of his white t-shirt sleeve was a little boy sitting in a bath tub with a mischievous expression on his face. "I hold my own," its caption read. So she and Lonnie, who was 41 to her 56, got together, and something in her face softened, though it was weeks before she told him her name was not Yvonne, and I doubt that she ever told him about her grandchildren. He had spent most of his life in the Navy, and he would take us to the V.F.W., where he and Leona seemed to know everybody, and we would eat a fish supper and dance to a live country band.

"My heart is breaking, like the tiny bubbles," they'd sing. "She's actin' single, I'm drinkin' doubles." Every time I'd dance with somebody, he'd buy me a beer, and there would sometimes be three or four lined up at my place at the table, and I would feel good. Once during intermission I played "Hotel California" on the jukebox. "Who played *that?*" the barber I'd just danced with asked the table at large, and I didn't quite have the nerve to 'fess up. By the time the band quit, everyone was supposed to be paired up with somebody to go to the Dixieville Trucker's Home for breakfast, but I always declined these invitations, so Leona and Lonnie and I would part company for the night.

Before too long, she found out he was two-timing her with a 35-year-old platinum-blonde beautician. "I just told him to go straight to hell," she said, anger masking the hurt. "Go on over there, I told him. I bet she's got your box lunch warmed up for you right now. Just don't forget to pick the hairs out of your teeth." We stopped going out after that, and for quite awhile Leona was coming into work hung over and looking her age. "Men," she said. "The bastards. I'd rather watch TV."

When I stopped by the hospital to say goodbye I found Leona in the basement coffeeshop sharing a back table with Jodie the waitress, who was telling about an obscene phone call she had gotten the night before. "Said he had a long, stiff dick for me. Said he knew I'd like it. I just hung up, but I like to never got back to sleep. It's awful for somebody to call up a divorced woman with something like that." Leona and I laughed a lot.

"Well, listen, Bunny," she said with her old twinkle. "Don't do anything I wouldn't do out there."

One day a white phone appears on the table where Della eats and drinks and smokes, but it is weeks before I hear its ring float out from her window across the street and into mine, and even then, the conversation is so brief that I suspect it must have been a wrong number. I wish, actually, that she had installed it in the bedroom, because to me there is something automatically poignant about a woman sitting for hours every evening that close to a phone that does not ring. But she does have a new friend—every day now she puts out little tidbits of food on her kitchen window ledge, and within a few minutes, a large white pigeon appears for his late afternoon snack. Then Della leans against the refrigerator with a drink as she watches him peck up the food. Once, the bird lights on the ledge before Della has had a chance to change into her peignoir and lay his feast, so he waits patiently for her to appear. When she does come into the kitchen and see him, she smiles a beautiful smile that transforms all the hard lines in her face into tenderness and makes me wonder what she looked like as a girl. A few days later at the Napoleon, I hear someone who lives in her building ask how her pigeon is.

"Oh, that damn nuisance," she says, pouring coffee into five cups and managing to carry them all at once. "I don't know why I fool with that damn pest."

One night late a woman's scream pierces into my sleep and I sit straight up, instantly wide awake. "Stop it, stop it," I hear a woman crying. "Stop it. You're hurting my arm."

A man's voice pleads, "Come on baby, come on, come on with me now. It ain't that far." They seem to be somewhere on the street between my building and the Napoleon, too close to the store next door for me to see them. Suddenly Della appears at her kitchen window in her nightgown.

"No. Stop it. Let me go," the woman is saying.

"Let her go, you son of a bitch," Della calls down, sounding angry and fearless. "I'm gonna call the goddamn police if you don't let her go right now."

"Shut up, bitch," the man answers.

"LET ME GO," the woman screams. "You're hurting my arm."

Suddenly the young woman two floors up from Della appears at her window, backlit by a small nightlight in her kitchen. "Let her go," she calls down, and then her German Shepherd appears beside her, puts his paws upon the window ledge and gives out one deep, resonant bark. "I'm gonna bring this dog down there and let him loose if you don't let her go," the woman threatens, sounding as if she means it.

"I'm calling the police right now," I yell, shocking myself. I have never yelled anything out my window, have never wanted to make myself conspicuous that way here. I feel concerned about it and fearful even now, and yet I go on. "I'm watching you," I lie. "Let her go right now."

"Let her go, you son of a bitch," Della calls out again, and the dog begins to bark nonstop.

"LET HER GO,," all three of us yell at once, and then I see a woman scurrying in high-heeled shoes across the street and around the corner of the Napoleon. The man does not pursue her, and I breathe a deep sigh of relief. I lean out my window and give a little wave to Della and her upstairs neighbor, and both lift their hands gently in my direction. "Is he gone?" I call across.

"Yeah," Della says. "The son of a bitch is gone." We all go back to bed, though I doubt if my neighbors get back to sleep any sooner than I do, tossing and turning, full of anger and strength and fear and triumph and pride all at once.

I begin, on the days I work, to eat breakfast at a drugstore near the university. I marvel at the place, for stepping inside is like stepping back twenty or twenty-five years in time and 2000 miles in space—to the middle of the country in the middle of the fifties. You walk past the magazines and the postcards and the candy and tobacco, through the perfumes and cosmetics, past the prescription counter, all the way back to the long, S-shaped soda fountain, and the most significant sign of the times along the way seems to be that the Trojans, ribbed and unribbed, are out on display instead of in some locked drawer. You can still get a cherry phosphate or a chocolate Coke here, and you can still get a malt or an ice-cream soda served in just the right-shaped glass. But I come for the breakfasts at first and then, more especially, I come for the waitresses, and then, most specifically, I come to be taken care of by Alma.

Alma and Dot and Billie are all in their fifties and a little on the plump side, but they orchestrate themselves like dancers behind their respective curves of the big S. Things are arranged compactly, so that nothing they need is really very far away, and it is a slow and graceful dance they do, even in the busiest of times—none of them ever hurries, and yet service is quick and efficient, beautifully paced. Every Friday they decide together what color uniforms they will wear each day the next week, and then their extraordinarily ordinary faces are cast together against pale yellow or pale pink or pale blue polyester as they move with their generous bellies and breasts to and fro between customers and provisions. There are two ancient, drawerless cash registers along the edge of the S where the waitresses punch tickets with the totals they have added up from their order pads, and you can always tell the new customers, because they try to pay at these registers. "You pay that up front, hon," Alma or Dot or Billie will say patiently and kindly and smilingly many, many times a week (if one of the regulars doesn't inform the newcomer first). After eating here a few times, something in me calms down at the mere thought of these women in this drugstore. There is something intensely sane and peaceful about it all, and I become one of the most regular of the regulars.

I try out Billie first and then Dot, finally settling loyally with Alma because she most quickly recognizes me as a new regular and bothers to remember the precise details of my "usual" order. She performs her duties consistently with innocent dedication and no trace of resentment. By the third time I appear in her section, she gives me a cheery good morning and recites my order for me with the pride of a child who has just memorized a new poem. "One over medium, hash browns, English muffin and coffee. And you like strawberry jelly, don't you?" She takes time to go through the whole box of little jelly packets to find me a strawberry, emitting a small cry of surprised delight when at last she comes upon one. I thank her and say that grape would have been fine, but she says, "Oh no, oh no. You should have the kind you like best. It makes everything better." And she is right. I eat these breakfasts with deep pleasure and always walk away from them nourished.

Sometimes I feel self-conscious about the peculiar attachment I begin to have to Alma, how irresistible I find her clear blue eyes and her coarse gray hair and her sloping double chin; but then I see that she treats her other regulars specially, too, and I sense that they must feel something of what I feel for her. And then I find myself embarrassed at the twinges of jealousy I have. Watching Alma wait on the others has its own beauty but reminds me of how I felt when I first discovered that a therapist I was seeing actually did have other clients. I guess the way Alma mothers us all automatically makes us sibling rivals, even while it gives us a sense of family as we sit together along the counter.

There is a middle-aged mailman who stops in every morning about the time I do, and I see that by the time he reaches the perfumes on his way back, Alma has already placed his order: "Poach one in a bowl," she calls out in the direction of the kitchen window. "Wheat toast, hold the potatoes." She pours his coffee. "And here's your Sweet-n-Low," she says, just as he picks up his spoon. He grins. "And here's the sports section." She hands him the newspaper, sees me watching, and asks if I want part of the paper. I say yes, that would be nice, say it not because I want to read but because I want to accept the gift. And every morning thereafter, she sees that I get the section that contains the movie and book reviews.

One day I go in a little sickish, a little anxious, a little shaken up by an accident I saw on the way to work. I go to the drugstore, even though the idea of a fried egg makes me queasy. "No, not the usual," I say before Alma asks with her eyes.

"No?" she asks, already concerned.

"I'm not feeling so well," I say. "I don't know what I want, really."

"Well," Alma says soothingly. "I know what. How about some oatmeal? I can have Katie fix you some oatmeal. I bet that would make you feel better, wouldn't it? Some nice hot oatmeal? Be good for your stomach."

"Yes," I say, "yes," and then Alma gently calls out, "Katie, I need a bowl of oats," and she stoops and reaches to the very back of a small white refrigerator, brings out some half-and-half, and pours me a little glassful. "This'll be better than milk," she whispers. "The boss keeps it here for his coffee, but he won't miss it."

When I mention the accident, she says, "This traffic out here is something, isn't it? I'll be glad to go back to Illinois and see my sister and get away from this place for awhile." It turns out that Alma is from Pleasant Hill, Illinois, which seems like the perfect place for her to be from. We talk about all the roads and towns we both know in southern Illinois, and I get through the day's typing just fine.

When she goes on vacation for two weeks, I have to make do with Dot or Billie, neither of whom ever gives me a paper or remembers about the strawberry jelly, but I think it may be because they know I am Alma's and unlikely to switch. The breakfasts begin to lose some of their power, and I am surprised to admit to myself how much I miss her. When she returns, we greet each other warmly.

"How was Illinois?" I ask.

"Hot and humid, like always," Alma laughs. "But it was nice to be where there aren't any freeways."

"That humidity is really something, isn't it?" I find myself saying. I have had this inane conversation a hundred times before, and yet I *want* to talk about it with Alma. "At least the heat out here is dry. But you look tired. Did your trip wear you out?"

"No, but I didn't get much sleep last night. I kept hearing a noise, you know, a noise in my apartment there and I just knew somebody was in there. The police came out and checked all around and said there wasn't anybody, but I think there was, you know? I think there was somebody. But you know how it is when you live alone." She looks at me directly to see if I know how it is when you live alone.

"Yes," I say. "I get scared sometimes for no reason."

"That's it," she says. "Sometimes it's for no good reason, really, you just do. But I did hear that noise. More coffee?" I finish my meal thinking how I never want Alma to be frightened, and I never, ever want anything bad or ugly or painful to happen to her. I wonder for the first time what she does when she gets home at night.

"Where do you live?" I ask her as she slips my ticket just beneath the edge of my plate.

"Culver City," she says. "Where do you live?"

"Venice Beach."

"Oh, my. I don't think I'd want to live there from what I hear," she says. "Too much crime. Do you like it?"

"I do," I say. "I love it. I love the ocean and the fresh air, and there are so many different kinds of people."

"Hm," says Alma. "Well, you be careful now."

The next afternoon as I head for the store, my porch is crowded with black men who have sought refuge from the spraying and sweeping of the street crew at the pagoda. They hang out here sometimes in defiance of the "No Loitering" sign recently attached over the doorway. I hear them laughing and cutting up and see them pass the bottle before I get to the exit, feel the familiar uneasiness rise in me at having to pass out through them—not fear, exactly, but just some deep-seated uneasiness at having to pass through a crowd of men, and especially black men. But all five of them seem to be in the best of moods.

"How you doin', mamma?"

"All right," I say. "How you doin'?"

"I bet you Jewish, ain't you?" says the tall one who likes to shadow-box himself in the plateglass of the Napoleon.

"Nope," I say.

"Puerto Rican?" he says, laughing at his own joke.

"No," I say, straight-faced. "I'm Negro." There is a brief moment of silence during which I wonder tensely whether I have offended them, and then they all burst into deep laughter.

"You *Neegro*, huh?" the tall one laughs. "Well you sho make *my* knee grow."

"You all right, mamma," another man says, and when I return, they all greet me like an old friend.

"Here come back the Queen of the Afternoon," one of them says, smiling and bowing as he holds the door open, then shutting it carefully behind me. I laugh and feel good and friendly, too, but am still relieved to get back inside.

A few nights later some of these same men have a late party at the pagoda with Mojo, who is in rare operatic form for the occasion, decked out, as usual, in his three-piece white suit and Panama hat. "Ah-Ah-Ah-*AH-AH*-Ah-Ah," he travels the same scale over and over. By now this has become for me one of the familiar night sounds of the boardwalk. I am accustomed to it in the way one gets accustomed to the sound of a furnace going on and off or all the quirky creaks of an old house, so that if I wake to it at all, it is only for the few seconds it takes for familiarity to register. Tonight tuning out takes a little more concentration, because the revelers are getting a kick out of imitating Mojo, so that his frequent musical impulses are followed by drunken, off key echoes. Still, I manage to sleep until Della's voice rises above the others about three o'clock.

"Shut up, you stupid son of a bitch," she yells down at Mojo, who is now performing on the street just below her window. "Take your goddamn noise away from here."

Mojo stops for a moment to look up at the woman in curlers leaning out her window, then resumes his song, which the others join into as loudly as possible. They all link arms and face Della to deliver a slurred, operatic serenade. I wonder how she can keep from laughing, even in her anger, but she is scrappy and feisty.

"You're keeping everybody down here awake with what goddamn noise," she calls out. "People have to work tomorrow, don't you know that?"

"Why don't you come down here and suck my dick?" the drunkest of them yells back. "That's all you good for. Gimme some pussy, white bitch."

"I've heard your goddamn noise all night, and I'm sick of it," Della persists, and I begin to wish she would just close her window and let the men move on up the street before they turn even meaner.

"Listen, baby, this is *Venice*," the one leaning against Mojo says, shaking his finger up at her. "This is the way it is, an' you got to coincide with it. If you cain't coincide with it, then get out. 'Cause this is *Venice*. I been pissin' down here before you ever even seen the Pacific Ocean."

Just then a squad car cruises by on the boardwalk and slows down to check out what's happening on the street. At first it passes by the intersection but then backs up and turns, headlights suddenly illuminating and silencing the serenaders. "What's going on here?" the driver says calmly, not getting out of the car. He has no doubt played through scenes like this more than once before with Mojo and his pals, is probably well-versed in the futility of arresting them.

"Right here," Della calls down. "Right up here, officer." The policeman switches on the spotlight on his dash and aims it straight into Della's face so that it appears, from my perspective, as if she must be the offender. She squints and shades her eyes with one hand but does not flinch.

"They been howling out there all night," she says. "Keeping everybody down here awake. Can't you make 'em take their damn noise somewhere else?"

"She been makin' more noise herself screamin' out that window," one of the men informs everyone at large, carefully not aiming his comment at the squad car.

The officer turns off the spotlight and suggests very calmly and quietly that the men continue their party somewhere other than out on the boardwalk or beneath this woman's window. "Go on home," he tells them. "Time to hang it up for the night now."

As they begin, at their own pace, to move off up the street, Mojo turns back to Della, bows, and lifts his hat. "I hope you have a very quiet evening, Madam," he says, no trace of malice in his voice, then retreats backwards with his Panama over his heart. "A very quiet evening indeed."

The next time I stop in the Napoleon for coffee, there is such a crowd that I have to sit in Della's section at the counter, which makes me feel very shy. I can't tell by the way she greets me whether she knows who I am or not, and I decide to leave it that way, not wanting to feel any more self-conscious than I do already about knowing who she is.

"You think you'll be out on the 30th, then?" the man next to me asks her. I recognize him as the manager of her building.

"You bet," she says firmly.

"Where did you find a place?" he asks.

"Mar Vista," she says. "Looks like a nice, quiet little neighborhood."

"I hope you like it," he says.

"So do I," Della replies, resting one knee on the stool next to mine and sipping from her big "Old Waitresses" cup. "So do I."

"Well, so do I," I think to myself, taken aback at my strong reaction to the news that she will move. Something in me feels queerly threatened by it, as if it might mean that I will have to move, too, just when I've begun to settle in here. My new desk is arranged now the way I want it, and the plant I've nursed for six years is finally flowering in the sea air and sun. The idea of putting who I am into empty boxes again, carting them down in the old elevator and driving to some unknown place is terrifying, almost unthinkable.

By the time the 30th comes around I am resigned to Della's leaving, but this does not make seeing her pack any easier. She seems to have acquired only small boxes, so that none of them will be too heavy for her, and by mid-morning, wearing old-fashioned black peddle-pushers and a bright red halter, she has already made many energetic trips down to her old white Chevy. I try to concentrate on what I am reading, but a peculiar emptiness dwells in the room with me, and my eyes are drawn back again and again to Della.

She begins to clean out her refrigerator, which does not take her long and makes me wonder if it stayed as empty as mine. At the last she picks up a quart of milk, sniffs it quickly, then dumps it into the sink. Something about this pierces me, this lifting up of the milk and then the quick, private little sniff, the pouring down the drain, the rinsing of the porcelain. The milk goes bad before you can use it up by yourself, and I buy pints now when I buy it at all.

I am seized by a sudden, shocking desire to cook something for Della. It is a crazy idea, but before I have time to squelch the impulse, I climb onto the bed and pick from the top shelf *The I Hate To Cook Book* with its yellowed pages and its greasy, gunk-stained cover. That stew I used to make, that "Stayabed Stew"—that will be just right if I can get it down before she makes her final trip to her new place. It says five hours at 275, but I've cheated on that before. I make a list and hurry to Lucky's for the meat, the carrots, the onions, the potatoes, the mushroom soup. You can use canned peas, but, for the first time, I buy fresh ones.

Early on, I began to ignore the quantities called for in this recipe—I always just keep putting things into my one large casserole dish, the one I have used only for popcorn these past many months, until it is chock-full. Now I remember barely in time not to use quite the whole can of soup, and I omit the bay leaf, as always, adding extra salt and pepper. I keep glancing out my kitchen window to see how Della is progressing as I trim the fat off the meat, and within an hour, by the time she has driven off with her second carload of belongings, my apartment and the entire corridor smell delicious. I read and pace around, can't help opening the oven door once in awhile, although I know it's foolish.

Della does not return for nearly two hours, and I am at first relieved that the stew will be done before she leaves for good, but then the idea of actually taking some over to her starts to make me very nervous. After all, she doesn't even know me. What if she is insulted or suspicious or just plain embarrassed? What if she won't even accept it? And what ever possessed me to make enough food for five people, anyway? By 4:30 it's done, and I've decided I can't take it over, but then the absurdity of the giant dish sitting on my tiny counter more or less shames me into action. I spoon a huge portion onto a plasticized paper plate and cover it with foil, wait until Della appears back in her kitchen, then head down the fire escape.

The door that I know must be hers stands open as I reach the top of her stairs, and I feel a wave of renewed shyness about what I am doing. How difficult it is to make a simple, neighborly gesture. I knock lightly on the doorframe, and in a moment Della arrives, broom in hand.

"Hi," I say. "I live across the street and noticed you're moving out. I just cooked myself too much stew, and I thought you might help me eat some of it so I won't have to throw any away. It's Stayabed Stew." I extend the plate and Della looks pleased, not at all hesitant.

"That's awful nice of you," she says, her red mouth easing into a smile. "That's just awful nice." She props the broom against the door, takes the plate and lifts the foil. "MMMM. Doesn't it smell good, though? I can really use it, too—I've about wore myself out. You wanna come in for a minute?"

"Oh no," I answer quickly. "I really have to get back. I just wanted to drop this by. You want me to carry anything down for you?"

"Oh no, honey, I'll manage the rest all right. I sure do thank you."

"I hope you like your new place," I say. "Will you still work at the Napoleon?"

"No, I've quit. But I'll find me another job pretty quick. That's one thing about bein' a waitress, there's always plenty of work to do."

"Well, so long," I say, and she thanks me again, and I almost regret not going in for a bit, but then again I don't.

I get home and dip myself a big bowl of stew and sit down to it with a glass of wine, and then Della appears at the table by the window and begins to eat along with me. It is the best supper I have had in months, and I eat a second helping as generous as the first. Pretty soon Della sees me and comes to lean out onto her kitchen ledge with a cigarette.

"It sure was good," she calls across.

"I think so, too," I call back immodestly. "I'm glad you liked it." She waves and disappears once more, and I stop keeping track of her then, notice only that by sundown the place looks dark and both windows are shut tight.

For a week or two the white pigeon keeps appearing on the ledge in the late afternoons, but the young couple who move in put up curtains right away and take no notice of him, and so he gives it up. Dawn (or Aurora) has her actress friend Sarane working with her now, and service at the Napoleon is not half what it used to be.

Chapter Four

Pissing

It looks as if, after these many months in Venice, I am beginning to take public urination for granted. Walking today behind a well-dressed young man in an upper-middle-class neighborhood near the university, I was suddenly sure he was about to piss. He slowed down ahead of me and got that certain hunch into his shoulders as his right hand disappeared from view. I thought sure he was unzipping to piss against an upcoming palm tree, but my immediate reaction was not a shocked "Why doesn't he find a restroom?" so much as a casual "Why doesn't he find a *doorway?*" I think I was more surprised when he kept on walking than I would have been if he had relieved himself, and so my shift in perspective has become rather graphically apparent.

"I been pissin' down here before you ever even seen the Pacific Ocean," one of the winos had told Della, declaring outright his territorial imperative. The regulars are good about not using the side-rear delivery entrance to the Napoleon between 8:00 and 4:00, when the place is open for business; but otherwise that doorway belongs to them as surely as my right rear tire belongs to the huge, tan Great Dane who seeks out my car no matter where I leave it in the dusty, glass-ridden parking lot. This particular dog stands waist-high to me, nearly window-high to my Volkswagen, wears a blue bandana around his neck, and carries himself and his enormous scrotum with unmistakable male pride. He lifts his leg and aims at the top of the tire so that, by the time he finishes, the rubber, the wheel rim and the hubcap are all thoroughly doused. Rust has begun to eat away at the metal, and I have come to accept this as a fact of life the way

Freddie must accept having to scrub down that doorway every morning.

The black wino I call Preacher-Man once christened every bench at the pagoda as his own, the desire to claim territory obviously overriding the inhibition against fouling one's own nest. Preacher-Man, who manages to stagger with as much dignity as Mojo, loves to shake hands. He shakes hands with nearly everybody he meets, holding onto the extended hand with both of his while he talks earnestly, reminding me of all the Southern Baptist ministers from my girlhood who stood at the doors of churches making concerted efforts to clutch at every hand as the congregation headed home for Sunday dinner.

Preacher-Man, in his best shabby gray suit, simply took a notion one evening at sunset to piss all over the pagoda. The regulars who were present for the occasion protested at first as they scattered out of his range, but then, as it became apparent that he was going to do such a careful and thorough and deliberate job, they began to laugh and encourage him. They lined themselves up along the low concrete wall that surrounds the benches and cheered him on, and when the ceremony was complete, they showed no signs of repulsion at the condition of their public home, and none deserted the area. Preacher-Man had claimed it for them all, and when he had finished and tucked himself away and patted his fly, he went around to shake hands with each and every one of them, probably receiving congratulations not unlike those offered clergymen after a rousing sermon. These men, who barely own the clothes on their backs and have small prospect of ever owning much more, do own the beach-front in this peculiar way. I never sit on any of the benches along the boardwalk now, knowing full well that any one of them may have been recently christened. Weekend tourists invade the pagodas, and in their ignorance may sit for brief periods until blatant insults from the regulars (or perhaps sometimes the reek of urine) drive home the message of "No Trespassing." They move on, then, to the sand or the grass or some cafe.

The first time I glanced down and saw a man pissing in the Napoleon doorway in broad daylight, I did a literal double-take and then turned away, outraged and disgusted. I wanted to shout something and disturb his flow, showing him the same disrespect and contempt that I felt his urinating "in front of me" showed for me and for anyone who would involuntarily see him or inadvertently walk through the spreading puddle at his feet. I thought he must be crazy or perverted, was grateful to be across the street from him, even more grateful to be four floors up. The "lady" in me could not help but be offended and the woman somewhat frightened, even while good sense told me that this man was neither crazy nor perverse but merely full of beer and too lazy to walk to the ill-kept public toilet several hundred feet from the pagoda. If someone had pissed on our lawn or sidewalk in Illinois, I suppose we would have considered calling the police. Not nice, not nice, just plain not nice. And yet now that this has become a daily phenomenon in my life, I find that, whatever feelings it arouses in me, I no longer turn away.

I wonder why they all face west. Is there some deep pull that the ocean has on these human streams, or is it simply an act of caution, to face the direction from which the police are most likely to appear? Some of the men keep a wary lookout for passers-by, while others stare straight ahead, turning neither right nor left. The rest look down to keep precise track of what they are doing. Some hold onto themselves with one hand, some with both, aiming the jet high or low against the wall, while others let themselves hang free, keeping hands at their sides or leaning with both palms against the wall, relinquishing to gravity directional control.

One extra-tall fellow who uses this technique never stands close enough to the wall but releases straight down the length of his legs to concrete, making a noisy splash and a foamy stream much like beer poured to the bottom of the glass instead of down the side. Watching him, I am forced to recall that desperate summer after the first separation, living in Janet's attic, a complete emotional invalid. Late one night, numbing my pain with an excess of television and beer and not wanting to risk waking anyone with a trek downstairs to the john, I began to refill the clear-glassed Miller's bottles I was emptying. I did this carefully and precisely, putting the mouth of the bottle right up against myself, was fascinated with watching the whole process and feeling the warmth rise in the bottles. In my tipsy state, I was wonderfully proud of not spilling a drop, and when I got one full, I would recap it and replace it in the carton, highly amused by the fact that it looked just the way it had before it was ever opened. By the time I turned off the TV, I had a brand new six-pack, which worked out beautifully except for the repugnant, early-morning task of carrying it downstairs, twisting open all the caps again, and pouring seventy-two ounces of cold urine into the commode.

But this tall fellow always splashes on his shoes, though most try not to—and not to step in their own puddles. I wonder why some of them shake themselves afterward and some don't, that quick flick of the dick to rid it of the final drops. Is this something their mothers taught them, or their fathers? Does it have anything to do with circumcision or the lack of it? I never had a brother.

Pants down, squatting beside the front porch when I was four or five. My mother grabs me and then points to my wet shoes. "Little girls don't do that," she scolds. So I don't do it until I am seven or eight or nine, down in the woods with the boys, not understanding why I have to squat and they don't. Even George, the sissy I can't stand, climbs to the top of a rockpile, unzips, and pisses a high, wide arc all the way out beyond the rocks. He infuriates me by refusing to swing at my strike-zone pitches, keeping himself at bat in an umpireless softball game until I actually storm to the plate and spit in his face. But even George commands respect for the way he can piss. My father watching "What's My Line?" declares that Bennett Cerf "squats to pee," which delights me no end, although the deeper implications of the remark are many, many years beyond my comprehension.

The one they call Louis is my favorite to watch. He is dark black, of medium height and very stocky. Everything about him is thick and dense—even his words, because of two missing front teeth—and he has the walk of a weightlifter. Out of his mind on some drug, he once attacked two of the other regulars over a crap game, pinning one to the ground and threatening to slit his throat with a knife. Yet I am not afraid of this man when I meet him on the boardwalk, because he pisses with such delicate style, often wearing a jaunty, feathered black hat cocked to one side. He unzips slowly and holds himself in his right hand, eases forward until he is nearly touching the wall, and aims toward the rear corner of the entranceway so that his exposure is hidden from passers-by. His left hand slips into his pocket, and then as he begins to pee he does the most remarkable thing of all: he lifts his left foot ever so slightly to let the stream run under it. Balancing himself perfectly on one foot throughout this performance, he gauges the direction and pressure of his flow so precisely that it does indeed run beneath the uplifted foot and never beneath (or upon) the planted one. He shakes himself gently, puts himself away, zips carefully, hitches up his pants, improves the tuck in his shirt, straightens the set of his hat, and walks away with a studied casualness that never fails to make me smile. A man pissing can be funny and touching, sexy and scary, delicate and clumsy, messy and repulsive, manly and boyish, mysterious and wondrous. It can be many things, but so far I do not think it can be boring.

Jogging down my alley one morning early, just as the sun is beginning to clarify things, I see a man up ahead relieving himself against the back brick wall of the sidewalk cafe. I have to admit that within seconds of sighting him I could turn off the alley and head toward the boardwalk, or, given the inability to make that quick decision, I could still turn around before reaching him. But I want to see him, want to run close by him while he is doing it, see what he will do as I approach, feel the power of my running against the vulnerability of his having to stand there and piss. I move to the far side of the alley, and he turns not really his back toward me as I approach but his backside, placing buttocks between me and the hand that grips and aims his flow, forceful and uninterrupted, against the brick. He is an older black man—wrinkled brown pants, thin red sweater, salt-and-pepper hair.

"Excuse me, I just had to," he says, truly apologetic, not looking my way. That he speaks at all shocks me, and I concentrate on keeping a steady stride. "I couldn't wait no more," he says with such sincerity and sheepishness that I have to empathize and smile. " 'Scuse me."

"It's all right," I call back over my shoulder, suddenly embarrassed, not because I saw him, or even because I wanted to, but because he apologized.

My face flushing red-hot with that cousin in the bathroom. Something I have almost forgotten, never forgotten. How was it that they all went over and left us there in the house alone? I never needed a babysitter. Me watching some cowboy show when he calls me. "C'mere, I wanna show ya somethin'." I think he's in the kitchen, but no. I hesitate at the half-open bathroom door, see him standing in front of the toilet. "C'mere," he says. "I wanna show ya somethin'." I know I shouldn't, but he's sixteen and everybody's favorite boy, sings funny hillbilly songs, has never visited this far north before. "C'mere."

His stream is just about eye level for me. He wants to show me how he can move himself around and hit different sides of the toilet bowl. I watch in silence and then he finishes and takes my hand in his and squeezes it around his penis, and the blood rushes to my face. I close my eyes as if this will keep him from seeing me. It feels so soft and firm and warm, like the smooth part of my puppy's belly. He squeezes my hand hard and moves it back and forth, back and forth. "Watch this," he says, "look how big." But I won't open my eyes. He jerks fast for awhile and then takes his hand off mine and I run outside, stay out until our folks come back.

"Did you and Philip Wayne have you a big time?" his mother asks me, all smiles.

"I guess so," I answer, looking down, knowing I will never tell. I don't talk to him anymore before they leave, won't even sing along when he picks the guitar, won't take his dime for an Eskimo pie.

I cut the morning's run short, begin to feel a little weak and out of breath, sense, with resentment, a heaviness settling in my legs.

Just at dusk a tall, slender dark-haired woman dressed in black boots and skirt and turtleneck leans casually against the Napoleon doorframe while a man pisses in the entranceway. They are not regulars, not even especially seedy looking, which makes me think there must be something special about this particular doorway that draws people to it for relief. The man faces the west wall but turns his head slightly to speak to the woman, who arches her neck in his direction as she listens over her shoulder. I am feeling that this is a curiously intimate scene to watch when it suddenly registers on me that she is pissing too—her stream is travelling across the slight incline of the sidewalk to converge with his. I gape in disbelief. How can she be doing that? She must not have any pants on. She's going to ruin those boots.

Her posture against the white brick takes on a sensual cast as she spreads her feet a little farther apart and bends her knees just perceptibly, both hands clasping the soft cloth of her skirt to hold it forward and backward, clear of the flow, and still she is looking at him as he finishes and turns completely toward her—and me—to put himself away. They must love each other. She smiles and straightens up, shakes her skirt and moves into his arms for a long kiss that sends deep pangs of desire shooting through me.

No pants. Maybe they are French. She looks French, whatever that means, with the pixie cut and the black sweater. French-kissing. Why is it called that? Under the back hedge with the boys, we would sing, "There's a place in France, where the women wear no pants, and the men go 'round with their hm-hm's hanging down." On the grocery store wall around the corner from where the couple stand someone has scrawled in red spray paint, "Don't wear Underwear." In Venice, I think, even the "don'ts" are uninhibitive.

Such a rare sight, a woman pissing. The stalls, the doors. In bus stations the free toilet is the one with no door, and I have seen coinless women crawl on filthy floors beneath the partitions to avoid the lack of privacy. The only other woman I have seen in Venice was dirty and stuporous and barefoot on a chilly morning, squatting on a patch of grass at a busy intersection, oblivious to the fact that traffic was slowing down to ogle her in her nastiness and depravity, in her bare-assed, total loss of dignity.

That high school graduation party where all of us Southern girls got so drunk and lost our dignity, and my best friend Audrey Lee ended up peeing on me in the car. Not graduation, but the end of the summer after it, when we were all about to go away to school and knew that things would never be the same. We were a club—the principal wouldn't let us call ourselves a sorority—and we all loved and hated each other. We were all going away, but I was the only one leaving Mississippi to head north, and so the party was to send me off, and I said, "Why don't we get some vodka and have VD's?," which was the name we had made up for our favorite mixture of vodka and Dr. Pepper. And we all said we should go out to Pemberton Lake and there couldn't be any boys, but of course a few showed up for awhile before it was over, and we all pretended to be mad.

"Yall've just spo-ilt *ever'thing*," the Homecoming Queen scolded them as they piled out of Bubba Day's car, sugary voice conveying that we, or at least *she*, had been waiting all night for them to arrive.

Mississippi was a dry state then, and Audrey and I had been

unanimously nominated to drive out Highway 99, past the Star-Lite Drive-In and onto a narrow dirt road that led to an old, unpainted shack where Boonie, a big-bellied man in overalls, would come down off the porch and sell us any kind of Alabama-stickered booze we could pay for. And so we got six fifths of vodka for the twelve of us, and we all got drunk and silly in the way that only seventeen-year-old girls can do it.

Someone brought a radio, and we were doing The Twist barefoot in the sand and singing loud and doing the class yell about every ten minutes: "We're the best, We'll *always* be; We're the Class of '63!" Just around an abrupt curve in the lake, behind a couple of trees, was where everyone went to piss. There was no light except from the meager fire we had built, and so we went two or three at a time, and about the third time Audrey and I made the trip, she was fooling with her General Robert E. Lee High School class ring as she squated and somehow dropped it into the lake.

"Oh NOOOO!" she shrieked, and everyone came running. I pulled up my pants and stumbled to reach her in the darkness, afraid she'd been bitten by a snake.

"My ring, y'all, my RING!" She started to cry.

"Don't worry, don't worry," I said. "I'll find it, I'll find it." I waded into the lake, courageous with vodka, forgetting I couldn't swim. Soon all twelve of us were breast-deep in the muddy water.

"You cain't go off to school without your class ring," we all agreed, some of us drinking now directly from the vodka bottles, having run low on Dr. Pepper. When we got out of the water— without the ring, of course—we all started to giggle because we were such a mess, bound to ruin the club's reputation, which we had protected so sacredly for the past three years but which now seemed so irrelevant.

All of us packed our dripping selves into Betty Kay's huge old Plymouth—five in the front and seven in the back—and the giggles escalated all the way into town until we didn't know if we were laughing or crying, and then Audrey Lee, more or less lying on my lap, say, "Y'all, we got to stop this or I'm gonna pee," which made us laugh all the harder, so that, by the time she did it, I could hardly tell if it was her or me, the hot wetness streaming through her jeans and soaking into mine, saturating my hair, feeling very, very strange and at the same time wonderful and exciting; and still we could not stop laughing. Audrey was trying to apologize, but she couldn't get her breath. I reached my hand around for hers to let her know it was all right, and then suddenly we were pulling up in front of her huge, white-pillared *ante-bellum* house. Betty Kay didn't quite stop in time to avoid ramming into the bumper of my old '49 Chevy, which sobered me up considerably, but Audrey could hardly stand up when we got out.

"I got to spend the night at your house," she whispered loudly. "Mamma'll kill me if she sees me like this. You go ask her." We sat in my car until my hiccups stopped, and then I went to knock on the imposing white door, still dripping wet.

"Where's Audrey Lee?" Mrs. Tyler said as soon as she saw me.

"Oh, she's in the car," I said, trying to sound casual. "She wants to spend the night with me but she said if she asked you you'd say no but if I asked you you might say yes."

Mrs. Tyler smiled. "It's all right with me if it's all right with your daddy. What did you do, go swimming with your clothes on?" She surveyed me head to toe, amused and trying not to show it. "Y'all have a big time?"

"Yes ma'am, we sure did," I said, unable to do anything but grin and back my way off the porch, hoping she wouldn't try to get Audrey to come in for pajamas. She stayed out on the steps in the late August air and watched us pull away. When we got down the block, the laughter overtook us again.

"*Please* don't wet on my car seat," I begged.

"Oh, I won't," Audrey assured me. "I don't have to go anymore." We giggled all the way to my house and into bed, managing not to wake my snoring father, and then Audrey turned toward me and scooted over. "I really love you, and I'm gonna miss you," she said. "Let's always be friends."

"I love you, too," I said, hugging her, smelling woodsmoke from the fire in her hair. "I'll miss you, too."

And I do. I still have to call her once in awhile. The last time I saw her we sat by her pool in Meridian watching her incredibly grown-up children frolic in the water while we sipped good whiskey. We sat there late into the night, when her husband finally went to bed and left us alone.

"'Member that night I peed on you?" Audrey Lee said. "That night I lost my class ring? Lord." We laughed in the same old way, except that we both know what it means not to be seventeen any-more. But we also both know what it means to have been seventeen together. In the last letter I got from her, she wrote, "If I were dying, you'd be the one I'd want with me," which made me cry, because I know it's true.

"You know I would come," I wrote back. "You know I'd come if there were any way at all." Sometimes I wish she could walk the boardwalk with me, wonder what she would say about the way things are here.

On Sunday afternoons lately, amid all the hubbub and commotion of skaters and jugglers and singers and fiddlers and hawkers, there is one man who commands more attention than any other act merely by standing perfectly still. Sometimes he costumes himself in what looks like a Revolutionary soldier's outfit, complete with tri-cornered hat and dull but authentic-looking sword. Or sometimes he decks himself out in a pale blue top-hat-and-tails ensemble with white gloves and a shiny black cane. In either case, he assumes some formalized but natural-looking position on his feet and freezes him-self there, his face waxen and expressionless, eyes dull and focused on some distant point in outer or inner space, every muscle appear-ing absolutely motionless. When the temperature breaks 90, and even the most modest and obese of the beachgoers have stripped to bare essentials, this man in his early thirties stands in his heavy clothes and, as far as I can tell, never exudes a drop of sweat. Nearby, a blue-velvet-lined violin case lies empty to receive coins, and inside it is a small stack of tastefully printed business cards that say "HUMAN MANNEQUIN FOR HIRE."

I fall into a certain kind of trance myself watching him, fascinated both by what he is doing and what he is not doing. I wait with mounting tension for him to show some sign of life, and when he does not, after three or four or five minutes, I find myself moving on, unable to keep still enough to go on gazing at someone who keeps that still. It becomes too eerie, too much like staring death in the face. Mostly the crowds he draws shift constantly. People stroll up and give him the once-over, exclaim over him a bit, stare at him a little, and then move away. There is a queer sort of triumph or conquering in his art, for he can be a mannequin much longer than anyone can bear to see him be one.

Sometimes, though, in response to some mysterious chemistry, the crowd will turn hostile and will not only refuse to be conquered by the mannequin but will set out to conquer him. They push in too close, violating even the space we allow each other as ordinary human creatures, much less the space it is taken for granted we will allow performers, who carry with them an invisible stage. They make fun of him ("Hey, pretty boy"), snap fingers just in front of his vacant eyes, even jostle against him if there is a sudden movement of dog or child in the throng. Through it all the mannequin stays flawlessly composed.

"I hope my dog doesn't mistake him for a tree," one young man says, tightening the leash on his Collie. The crowd roars with laughter, and then one of his freakier looking companions extends a brown-bagged quart bottle of beer toward the mannequin's face. "Want some of this piss, man?" The crowd roars again, but the mannequin does not move a muscle, his posture remaining as rigid as the tophat on his head. Then Preacher-Man pushes his way through the mass of people and pretends he is going to unzip his fly.

"I'm gon' piss on this po' mothafucka's leg," he declares, which simultaneously causes everyone to laugh and back away, automatically making room in case he isn't joking. But he is, and when the mannequin does not flinch, Preacher-Man has to smile at him with a kind of angry admiration. "You the coldest mothafucka I ever *did* see," he says and retreats to the edge of the boardwalk. The crowd falls silent with a growing sense of awe and tension, and then a long-haired, ample-breasted blonde of sixteen or seventeen, wearing a very skimpy bright red bikini with bright red skates to match, rolls up within inches of the performer. She will kiss him, of course, I think, and then he will at last have to respond. She puts herself face-to-face with him and looks directly into his eyes, and then, slowly, she raises her right hand with its long, bright red nails and inserts her first two fingers just inside the mannequin's nostrils. It is a bizarre gesture, shocking and quietly violent, calling up for me the grotesque vulnerability of corpses—"The worms crawl in, the worms crawl out.''

The mannequin jerks away from her, looking more stunned than offended, and everyone begins to applaud enthusiastically—for the girl who enlivened him, I suppose, as much as for his coming to life or for his remarkable talent. The crowd is generous with its coins and disperses cheerfully, but the mannequin begins to appear about once a month instead of once a week; and when he does come to Venice now, he brings an oversized ''bodyguard'' with him who skillfully lifts him up and carries him to a new location on the boardwalk when the crowd gets too intrusive.

In a newspaper interview—every public figure on the boardwalk eventually gets interviewed somewhere these days—the Human Mannequin claims to be able to stand motionless for up to three-and-a-half hours at a stretch. He lowers his heartbeat from 78 to 32, which helps him achieve the waxy, ashen tinge to his face. And he wants to make a career out of being a mannequin but says, ''It's difficult for me to have a social and public life. Women find it hard to relate to me and what I do. I just wish people would understand that I'm really just a normal person with a normal life.''

So was the funeral director's son I went to high school with, but I never would go out with him. He was studying his father's trade, and they lived right in the big old house with the mortuary. Audrey Lee and I used to laugh and cringe over what it would be like to date him—up until my mother's death, that is. I supposed then that Otis had helped lay her out, and I would blush every time I even passed him the hall at school, not knowing whether to feel grateful to him or despise him for what he knew.

Even that young I always preferred to go to the cemetery alone, which was a source of wonderment and concern to my Tennessee aunts and cousins. ''Don't you want some of us to ride out there with you, sugar? We could wait in the car. It's such a long drive by yourself.''

''No thanks,'' I would say, wanting the twenty miles of country roads to myself, wanting my mother to myself.

''Well, go on then. You're the curiousest thing.'' The one time I relented, two cousins who went with me got into a dispute over which was the head and which the foot of the grave, sending me back to the car in angry tears they took for simple grief, which they understood and approved. It was years before I realized that they could talk that way because they no longer thought of their aunt as inhabiting that grave, while to me she was still there in some way, whatever else had happened to her.

The family cemetery, nestled in backroads among obscure little farms and shacks, dignified by the tiny brick church with the forty-foot picnic table beside it, big enough, maybe, to seat the entire congregation. Truehope Baptist Church. Hope true, hope true. Maple and pecan trees and mockingbirds, the lush smell of ripe corn blowing across the fields on a hot breeze that last time I went, all grown up supposedly, in the same awful summer of pissing into beer bottles in Janet's attic. Unable to write anything for months and then suddenly beginning, grotesquely and passionately and against all editors' advice, to gather material on—of all things in the world—ostomies. Gathering hours and hours of tape from people who could no longer urinate or defecate the usual way, people with holes cut in their bellies so that urine or feces could drain out into plastic bags worn constantly beneath their clothes. Stories of brutal but life-saving surgery, shattered and reconstructed self-images, impotence, phantom urges to piss, suicidal thoughts and attempts, daily small secret humiliations, astonishing adjustments to a new and peculiar way of getting on with life. Untold stories, I thought, that must be told, must be told by me. Immersing myself in cancer and death and shit—or the outwitting of all three.

Picking one yellow rose to take to the cemetery that steamy August afternoon, bathing but already sweating through my clothes by the time I get into the car for the narrow and winding, dusty drive. I stop for a six-pack at a small shack of a tavern near Atlee's Crossing, where the oversized air conditioner in the window turns my trickles of sweat to shivers. The three overalled men at the bar stop their conversation while I make my purchase—a stranger, and a woman at that. They wonder about me, which sets me to wondering, too—it is crazy to drink beer and drive these roads in this heat, but it tastes good and I finish several by the time I find the last gravel turnoff up to the church.

Under nearly every rock here is somebody kin to me or kin to my kin. Things are very, very still except for the birds and the occasional slight breeze. Once in awhile I hear a car pass on the road below,

watch the cloud of dust rise in its wake. Aunts and uncles and great
aunts and cousins to the nth degree, most of whom I never knew.
My grandfather, Reverend Will, born the year the Civil War ended.
He died in 1925, but once when I was here an old and distant cousin
in white shirt and suspendered pants walked up from his farm down
the road, kicked at the tires of my car, and asked me who I was.
"Oh," he said. "Well, then you're Reverend Will's grandgirl, ain't
ye? Now there was a good man, your granddaddy, and a wonderful
preacher."

I am glad no one is here now. I stroll among the tombstones,
carrying the rose in one hand and a beer in the other, feeling the sun
beat down on my shoulders, feeling my hair frizz up in the humidity, aware of the copious sweat between my breasts. Some of the
more recent stones have plasticized color photographs set into them.
I find my mother's grave and stare vacantly at it for a long time, put
the already wilting rose first on the rock, then move it to the grass in
front where it will look less like debris when it withers altogether. I
can see her sitting in that shabby green swivel rocker, waiting for me
to come in from school. She wouldn't approve of the beer. How she
did scream at the last when they put the catheter in. I have to piss.

Both the front and back doors of the church are locked, so I head
down a weed-lined path toward the ramshackle outhouse—or
shithouse, as my father would call it—but its rusty-hinged door is
double padlocked, too. I consider squatting in the weeds, but my
ankles are already itching and burrs cover the calves of my jeans. I
can wait. I sit down on a flat slab of granite one row below my
mother's and finish up the beer, and then, of course, I can't wait any
longer.

I peer all around me carefully, then scoot to the edge of the
tombstone and ease down my pants. The rock is hot, almost too hot,
against my buttocks. I watch the urine sink into the red earth. That's
when I got pale and began to sob at the funeral, when they lowered
the coffin into the red clay and shoveled the first clods of dirt back
onto it. The dirt was wet, and the coffin was covered in terrible pale
lavender velvet, and the clods didn't make any noise when they hit
it. That brutal silence. That coffin more a piece of finery than anything she had in life. I begin to cry as I piss and then to think "Piss
on death" over and over. "Piss on death, piss on death, piss on it." It

feels good to say it out loud. I look around me and up toward the stones on the hill. "Piss on death," I tell them. "Piss on all of it. Piss on it." Then for the first time I see a fresh grave, a mound of red dirt completely covered with dead and artificial wreaths. At the far end stands a large plastic display of red and blue and yellow tulips on a tripod of wire, and at the center of the arrangement—I look twice to make sure—is a little yellow plastic toy telephone beneath which, in homemade, gold-glittered letters, are the words JESUS CALLED.

The crying slides right into laughing—laugh-until-you-cry in reverse. JESUS CALLED. Sit in a cemetery with your pants down and piss and cry and laugh. I look down to discover a trickle of blood slowly descending the side of the tombstone I'm on. Well, bleed then, too, I think, pulling up my jeans and then standing up, stooping to collect some leaves and grass to clean off the stone. One day the phone rings, and it's Jesus, dialing direct. I wipe my nose on my shirtsleeve and head for the car, unable to think when I've felt so good; and the wet, sweaty, bloody, snotty, slightly drunken drive back through the country feels clean and glorious all the way. The next week, back home in the attic, I put away the manuscript on ostomies.

These past few days at dusk I have found myself keeping some kind of deliberate watch over the Napoleon doorway, hoping the French-looking man and woman will return for an encore performance. Something so nasty and wonderful and sexy in the way she stood there with him and how they talked to each other as they pissed, and then the tenderness in the way he turned to her, exposed, so that she could watch him put himself away before they moved naturally into each other for the deep kiss. The lovely, tender, sexy things that movies never show us. How there will sometimes be a drop or two of piss just at the tip when you first take him in your mouth.

That afternoon in bed when the phone rang. Important call, had to be answered. How he stood there naked talking, with that wonderfully stubborn erection, turning toward me still in bed, being so serious on the phone and so erect for me until I began to giggle and had to put the pillow over my face so the caller wouldn't hear. Rolling off the mattress then and crawling over to kneel in front of him, wanting to tease, not wanting him to forget me while he talked. Him torn between pushing my face away for composure's sake and pushing himself into me for pleasure's sake, between laughing into the phone and feeling perplexed at his predicament until he could endure no more and had to hang up. How he pulled me to my feet then, slowly, smiling, and led me back to bed. Such an important phone call, but who can remember now what it was about? How hard it is to tell always what's important as you go along. All our fierce and tender times. I never thought we would have to grow old without each other.

The man and woman do not return, but the doorway is busy as ever. Louis shows up with all his daintiness, and then a very young couple edge their way up the street quarreling as a little blonde boy of five or six alternately runs ahead of them and then back to push his way between them. As their voices rise, they stop near the doorway. "That's nothing but a goddamn lie," the woman says, hands on hips, glaring at the man. As if in response to this, the child begins to dance about and clutch at his pants, and then, without any apparent instruction, he darts into the doorway to piss. The mother gets pissed off, the child has to piss. I think of those bladder infections I used to have before I learned to be angry outright. The boy is unable to finish before his parents move away, and he zips up on the run to catch up with them.

One noisy and crowded Saturday afternoon I see a very yellow-haired, shirtless young man who could be a grown-up version of the little boy stumble quickly around the corner of the Napoleon to reach the doorway, penis already in hand. Sloppy drunk, he wavers as he stands there, careless with his aim, apparently oblivious to the puddle spreading under his bare feet. A man in tennis clothes walks by and glances innocently into the doorway as he passes. "Hey buddy, you wanna see my dick?" the young man yells after him, turning toward me, still pissing. "You wanna look at my dick? C'mere. Here it is." He waves it around and then steps back into the doorway. The man in tennis clothes does not look back. "Damn faggot," the boy spits out over his shoulder, finishing and heading toward the boardwalk before he even covers himself up. I am repulsed and titillated at once by his crudeness and embarrassed for the passer-by—how careful men must have to be all the time at urinals not to look at each other, or at least not to get caught.

Pissing

This same afternoon, as I watch an unusually tall and rough-looking black man in the doorway, he stuns and frightens me by suddenly looking directly up at my window, fixing his gaze on me in such a way that I feel more exposed, undoubtedly, than he does. Our eyes lock for a few long seconds, and then I pull my shade down, feeling shaken and a little ridiculous. Caught in the act. Guilty as charged. It's somehow more permissible to piss in public than to watch somebody doing it.

Some weeks ago as I came in from work, a chic young black woman was more or less pacing at the foot of my fire escape. As I approached, I could see that she was "keeping guard" for her man, who was pissing against the high wooden fence near the trash bin behind my building. I looked neither right nor left, letting the scene register only in the corner of my eye until I had the first-floor door open, just adjacent to where the man stood, at which point my curiosity got the better of me. He didn't catch me, but she did, and her expression froze with contempt and cut me to the quick—not just another woman trying to get a peek at her man's cock, but a white woman at that. I came upstairs wondering if I deserved all that anger, wondering if it's really perverse to be so curious, wondering if I will ever feel that kind of possessiveness about a man again.

On a hot night not long after this at the close of a fiery sunset, I find myself drinking gin-and-tonic and contemplating the possibility of taking myself out for a drink. Then, somewhat unexpectedly, I find that I am dressing up and putting on the expensive perfume I'm usually so stingy with. And then there I am walking down the boardwalk with an odd sense of purpose, past the sidewalk cafe where I would ordinarily go, on down to Sammy's, where the drinks cost half again as much. I know exactly what I am doing, except I don't know what I'm doing, having never done it before, not wanting to think too much about any of it, not quite admitting it and therefore not quite having to be so self-conscious and afraid, although just inside the door of the place I get butterflies that two more stiff gins served up at the bar barely dispel. It is crowded for a week night, and I am lucky to have a seat. The silver-haired man on the stool next to me does not speak. But then why should he? I decide I will play a round of music on the jukebox, finish the second drink and go home before this craziness proceeds any further. Ray

Charles' "Georgia on My Mind" is the only thing I'm in the mood for, so I press it three times. You can barely hear it, anyway, above the noise.

When I get back to the bar, a curly, black-haired young man is standing beside my stool. "I saved your seat for you," he says with a confident grin. "What's that you played?"

"Ray Charles" I say.

"*Who?*"

"RAY CHARLES," I shout, thinking he didn't hear me.

"Oh, oh," he says, looking blank. "Yeah. I think I've heard of him." He is wearing a silky, flowery shirt, unbuttoned to show off the thick black hair on his chest, which I immediately want to touch as he moves in close beside me and begins to talk about music. I have to lean my head toward him to hear.

"Can I buy you a drink?" he asks. "What is that, anyway, Perrier?"

"Gin-and-tonic. But you have to let me get you one next," I say, not wanting to be ungracious, but not wanting to feel bought, either.

"Great," he grins, draining his beer, launching into a tale of how he went to Woodstock when he was not quite fifteen and how it was probably the greatest experience of his life, no kidding.

"I saw the movie," I say, deciding not to tell him how I had to stuff little wads of Kleenex in my ears to bear the amplified sound-track. He looks about twenty, can't be over twenty-three. "Remembering the '60s makes me feel a little old, you know?"

"Yeah," he says. "I know what you mean. But I like older women. Really. They're more interesting. *Really.*"

"So how old do you think I am?" I can't resist this, can't help wondering.

He hesitates, looks me over, grins. "I'd say, oh . . . twenty-seven. Maybe twenty-eight." He means it. Six years off, but he doesn't ask. In the dim light my graying hair must look frosted. We laugh. He talks. I don't have to worry about a thing except listening and nodding and laughing with him, and then he borrows a dime and excuses himself to go call his mother in New York because it's her birthday. This makes me feel very safe with him, the fact that he is calling his mother on her birthday. I watch him walk across the room. Tight jeans, muscular thighs. I want him, don't know if I can let myself have him or not—or let him have me. My virginity feels at stake. He would be the first without love. I don't know if I want it, really, truly. I should leave while he's on the phone or in the restroom.

He comes back in a more serious mood. "I quit my job today," he says somberly. "It was a real hard decision, but I guess I'm glad." I feel such sympathy, figure he is going through some kind of agonizing career change.

"Wow," I say. "How long had you worked there?"

"Oh, three days," he says innocently. "Construction. Guess I'll look for something else." I burst into laughter and he laughs, too, not quite understanding what's funny. Things can be simple, I tell myself. Things can be simple and easy and uncomplicated. Things can be inconsequential. I touch his chest with the backs of my fingers, feel the warmth of his skin through the hair.

"Would you mind walking me home?" I say. "It's just up the street a bit." He smiles and takes my hand and we walk the few blocks slowly in the soft night, both glad to be out of the noise, glad to hear the waves rolling in.

As we approach my door I feel a failure of nerve, can decide to invite him up only after he makes it clear that he doesn't take it for granted that I will. He gives me a gentlemanly goodnight kiss on the cheek, but as he starts to back away I turn my mouth to him, grazing his soft thin lips with a kiss that surprises me in its tenderness, since I don't even know who this boy is. "Why don't you come in for a minute?" I say, and his dark eyes light up like a child who has just heard the bells on Santa's sleigh.

Upstairs with the radio on, drinks in hand, there isn't much to say. There isn't even anywhere to sit except on the bed. We look at each other, look away. "So have you ever done it on the beach?" he asks finally. "You live so close here."

"No," I say. "No, I haven't. Have you?"

"No, not really," he says, getting up, unbuttoning the shirt the rest of the way. How strange it is to undress all at once, and yet I am grateful to have it over with. His body is lovely, young, hard, eager. He doesn't know it can be slow and delicious, enters me right away, moves too quickly in every way, and yet it's all right with me, so good to have someone warm and close in this narrow bed, good to have someone inside.

He lights my cigarette and keeps the ashtray for me on his firm, hairy belly. "You're great," he says, patting my thigh. "You're pretty. Boy. Sometimes it's weeks before you meet someone, you know?"

"Yeah," I laugh. "Weeks." My body is humming with relief and pleasure and desire, and so he stays, pleased that I want more of him, finally falling asleep in the middle of the bed with me scrunched up happy against the wall. I listen to him breathe, listen to myself. I can smell his sweat, can feel his semen as it seeps out of me onto the sheet.

At 6:00 I awake with a start, confused for a moment about where I am. He has hardly moved at all. The morning light makes his skin unusually white beneath the black hair. I stare at him, wondering what in the world I will say when he wakes up. He looks like such a boy sleeping. Twenty-five years younger than my husband. My early-morning mind grabs onto this statistic and won't let go of it, like the first song you hear on a clock radio. Twenty-five years younger. My husband. Us married for half of this boy's entire life. How thick his eyebrows are. How odd he looks and pale—corpselike really, because I can hardly remember how his face looked animated. I touch his cheek.

"Wake up, Jason, wake up. Wake up. I have to get to work." He opens his eyes, looks around, rubs one eye with his fist, reaches out to put his arm around me. "No," I say. "No. Really. I'm sorry. You have to go. I have to get to work." He sighs, gets up, taking his shorts into the bathroom with him, and then I hear him pissing long and loud. A wave of grief rises in me with the sound, such a married sound. I don't want to hear some stranger pissing, not in my place, where I've travelled so far to be alone. I hand him his clothes through the door. "Sorry to rush you off like this. I really have to get to work."

"Sure," he says. "Sure." He comes out dressed, shirt buttoned nearly to the top, and gives me a modest kiss that just misses my mouth. "Well, listen. Why don't you give me your number so I can give you a call?" He extracts a little red leather book from his back pocket. Midway through the number, I realize I don't want him to have it and change the last two digits. "Be seein' ya," he says in the doorway. "Thanks for everything."

I crawl back into bed and cry for awhile. I am glad he was here and glad he is gone, wish I had been direct instead of lying with the phone number. The sheets smell good. My body is relaxed and vibrant. I think that this may last me for awhile.

In the bathroom mirror I see that my face has softened, unspoiled by the crying. The toilet seat is up, and I stare at it for a long time, as if I have never seen such a thing before. Then I dampen a Kleenex and wipe away the drops of urine on the porcelain rim, put the seat down, and run myself a good hot bath.

Chapter Five

Tenants

There is Iris again, huddled up against the back corner of our front porch as she has been for the past several afternoons when I've come in from work. Today she is wearing her heavy, wide-sleeved, bright red coat—though the sun has been blazing since noon—and she has another coat, a lighter, black one, wrapped around her calves and ankles. I always speak to Iris, though often she will not acknowledge the greeting.

Lately her habit is to sit on her little green cross-legged canvas stool, elbows propped on knees, holding a large white handkerchief over her nose and mouth. If she speaks, she speaks through the cloth and does not look where the words are aimed. This afternoon Iris is crumpling the hanky in her lap with one hand while the other holds upon the crown of her head a dark green, quart-sized prune juice bottle half full of what looks like milk, flattening her yellowish-silver hair in a way that accentuates the bizarre sweetness of her face. The last time we spoke, she blurted out a long, involved story about her cousin Violet, who was killed in a Wichita tornado in the spring of 1951.

"Do you have a lot of relatives named after flowers?" I asked.

"Oh yes," Iris said. "My Aunt April named her girls May and June."

"Oh," I said. "After *months*."

"No, no, my no," Iris said. "Not for years. Not a word for years. All dead for all I know. I'd rather be dead myself than live the way I do now. That's an awful thing to say—I know it is. But I used to be queen of this beach. We better not talk anymore."

Iris does exhibit a certain regality of posture as she keeps the bottle poised in its awkward position, pretending she isn't catching me in the corner of her eye as I come up the steps. Her cloudy blue eyes gaze neither right nor left, but she lifts the handkerchief to her mouth when I set foot on the porch.

"Hello," I say, undecided whether to inquire about the bottle.

"It's my head," Iris volunteers quickly through the hanky. "I got something on my head for it. You're the one in 411, aren't you?" She still hasn't looked at me. "Well, there was a man yesterday afternoon who came in. I've been meaning to tell you this for a long time. He opened the door with a knife, not a key, you know. What could I do? He said he was going up to 411. He did. That's the number he said, 411. He had a big dog. Was he a friend of yours? He might've been a friend of yours."

"No," I say. "Maybe he knew someone who lived there before me."

"He *said* 411. You better put two chairs in front of your door. A couple of chairs and then you won't be afraid. Keep your door locked."

"I do," I answer. "I use the dead bolt all the time."

"Put two chairs, too," Iris insists, finally looking intensely at me over the hanky. "Under your doorknob."

"OK," I say. "I hope your headache gets better."

"Oh, honey, could you do me a big favor? Could you close that window on the second floor there at the top of the steps? I get a shiver when I walk by it. Just close that window and then I won't be so sick."

"OK," I say. "I will."

As I close the dirty-glassed window against the warm breeze, I wonder if Iris imagined the man or if it was all an innocent mix-up of some kind . . . or what. Anyone who wants to get in this building can do so with ease, and I wonder if Iris lives in constant fear. "I'll just use this handkerchief," she once told me. "Then I won't catch what you have and you won't catch what I have."

"What do you have?" I asked.

"It's a dying disease, honey," she said with resignation. "I'm afraid it's a dying disease, and I'd hate for you to catch it."

Mr. Andrews, sweat soaking through the underarms of his coarse gray workshirt, gives me an inquiring look as he descends the third floor stairs. "Iris asked me to close it for her," I explain. "I guess she gets too cold on the way to her room."

"That 'un's a mess if I ever saw one," he says, smiling pleasantly. "All winter she complained of being too hot. Kept callin' me to come down and turn off her radiator when it was already off. Get me down the steps an' then not even open the door. Act like she wasn't in there, you know."

"She's down on the porch in the sun now with two coats on," I say.

"Yip. She's a sight, all right." Mr. Andrews pauses on the landing to finger the heavily laden key hoop that hangs from his belt. "Still a young woman, too—not but seventy-three. The wife's eighty-eight and not that bad off yet."

"I hear you have a birthday coming up soon," I say.

"Ninety-four Fourth of July," he beams, and I am suddenly touched by the pinkness of his scalp in the wide part of his thick white hair. As I turn to go upstairs, I notice once again the huge red-white-and-blue banner that hangs between two palm trees across the boardwalk, announcing the July 4th celebration of Venice's seventy-fifth anniversary.

"Hey," I say. "You'll be ninety-four and Venice'll be seventy-five."

"Yip," he says, letting the key hoop fall the length of its chain to crash against his thigh. "Older'n the town. I guess *that's* somethin'."

Half way to the third floor—the ancient elevator has not worked for months—I hear the door of 302 click shut as Mrs. Andrews' head appears tentatively over the top of the banister, thick, rimless glasses magnifying her dark gray-blue eyes to the point where it's difficult to notice anything else about her face. "Clarence?" she calls out unsteadily. "Clarence, are you down there?"

Mr. Andrews stops his careful descent, leans slightly on the hand that clutches the railing, and looks up toward his wife, though I don't think he can actually see her from that angle. "I'm right here," he says, with just a hint of irritation.

"Oh, Clarence. You were gone so long I didn't know what happened to you. I got so scared."

"Oh for gosh sakes, I just left. I told you I was goin' to see about that lock on 308 and then check the mail."

"Well I know it, but Clarence, I got scared up here by myself." There is a long pause. "You're not mad at me, are you, Clarence?"

"No, Trude," Mr. Andrews says, softening his voice into a certain gentleness and a certain resignation. "I'm not mad at you. I'll be right back up."

I speak before I reach the top of the steps, not wanting to startle her, since I'm sure she hasn't seen me yet.

"Who is it?" She turns in my direction without quite focusing on me.

"It's 411," I say. She edges herself back across the hall, pressing the thick black rubber tip of her wooden cane heavily against the almost threadbare carpet.

"I got so worried about my husband," she says, sounding near tears. "I wanted him to zip up my dress."

I see that the zipper of her bright pink-and white cotton print dress is closed only to just below her brassiere, where it is caught in a pucker of cloth. A more than faint whiff of urine rises from beneath her skirt as Mrs. Andrews stands patiently while I work to free the material. "Thank you so much," she says. "I do thank you so much."

My room is unusually warm, having accumulated sunlight all afternoon. Sometimes I still forget that I need not shut the windows when I leave, since there is so little danger of sudden rain. I come into this second summer still unsure of what the seasons mean here aside from a change in the length of days. In fact, several times in the past two or three months I have momentarily lost all sense of season in my body and, with nothing concrete to pin the time of year upon, have been forced to trust abstraction—"It's May, so this must be spring." In the brief time span between realizing I don't know what season it is and making myself concentrate on what month it is, I feel lost and out of touch, as panic-stricken as Mrs. Andrews sounded. I suppose that moment of lapse is where Iris lives all the time, too, her body hot in winter and cold in summer, no longer respecting the names of months at all (something in her even perceiving them as flowers). I do not find this so difficult to understand in a place where weather reports can run unvaried for weeks and weeks at a time. Native friends tell me there *is* an autumn and there *is* a spring, but I have not yet caught onto them, and if Iris ever did she seems to have lost them now, perhaps having suspended herself in space and time somewhere between here and Wichita. My uncle Eugene was killed the same year as her cousin Violet when a tornado lifted the highway patrol car he was driving off some Memphis two-lane and set it down not so gently near a pecan grove a few thousand feet away. Some seasons do have the ability to make you sit up and take notice, while others simply blend together to make years. I don't know who will zip me up when I am old.

"Do you think you'll break a hundred?" I asked Mr. Andrews.

"Yip," he said. "B'lieve I will. Don't see what there is to keep me from it."

It is difficult to grasp that Mr. Andrews is only twelve years older than my father—me one of those change-of-life surprises, grandparents already departed long before my arrival, my mother always embarrassed by sales clerks complimenting her little "granddaughter." When I receive a snapshot of my father, tucked into a note written in his large scrawl that no longer heeds the dark blue lines of his grocery store tablet, I am jarred into the realization that he has, sometime in the past year, eased across the boundary between aging and being aged. Visit before last he took me out for our ritualistic early Sunday morning drive through hilly Tennessee backroads, then out onto the main highway where he suddenly confided—almost in a half-whisper, though we were alone—that he was losing his eyesight.

"My God, Daddy," I said, feeling my whole body stiffen with anxiety. "Should you be driving? Can you see that car coming?"

"I know it's a *car*," he said calmly. "I can see the outline. Rest of it ain't nothin' but a blur on me." He not only wouldn't let me drive us home but swore me to absolute secrecy. "Ain't nothin' but cataracts. You tell Rebecca, she'll cart me off to some of these ignorant doctors around here. Most of 'em don't wanna do nothin' but cut on you. I don't want none of 'em gougin' around in my eyes. I'd 'bout as soon be blind."

Rebecca of course did find out within a few weeks, when he barely missed a car pulling out in front of the Big Star Supermart. And she of course did cart him off to the doctor, but it's deteriorating retinas, not cataracts, and there are no surgeries or medicines or eyeglasses that will make any difference anyway. In the photograph it is the eyes that shock me and make him seem so old—it is how he is looking right where he thinks the camera is, how he is just off in his guess, how this lends an exaggerated vacancy to his expression. Something has gone slack in him now, now that he can no longer drive or work on his car, now that he is forced to depend on Rebecca for just about everything. They were married one month before I was—can it really be twelve years?—and she takes good care of him.

Their phone, although it is otherwise thoroughly modern, still rings two short instead of one long ring, and it takes eight or ten of these before my father answers. "It's Carrie," he calls out to Rebecca, stunning me with my mother's name, which I haven't heard him mention at all in years and years. It shakes me up so that I don't even correct him but spend the first minutes of the conversation distracted, hoping he won't say it again—for Rebecca's sake as much as my own.

"All our early tomaters have just about scorched in this heat," I hear him saying when I tune back in. "Don't do no good to water 'em. I told her she better pick some and fry 'em up green. It's good and cool out where you are, I bet. I b'lieve they said seventy-eight last night on the Paducah station."

"It's beautiful," I say. "I wish you could see the ocean."

"I was tellin' her I bet it costs you five dollars every time you fart out there, don't it?" He laughs heartily, which makes me laugh as much as the joke itself.

"Just about," I say. "That's why I try not to do it too much." This is how we can talk together. I have always resented his penny-pinching, only lately beginning to appreciate that this hereditary trait is probably what enables me to live on my current $500 a month. It is difficult for him to understand why, after all my high-falutin' education, some of which he paid hard-earned money for, I am working as a part-time secretary. Usually at least once whenever we talk he reminds me that my writing won't put bread on the table or get me any pension and suggests that I find myself a better job—go back to schoolteaching or maybe get in on these computers. But today I am spared all this. Today he just wants to tell me about the big ol' ham they got on sale at the Big Star and how good the great northern beans smell simmering and that Rebecca has made a whole skilletful of cornbread. And then before we say goodbye, he asks if I can still read his letters.

"Sure," I say. "I think you do real well. And thanks for the picture."

"Well, I meant to tell you you needn't to go to all that trouble writin' me with that marker pen and that big lettering and all such as that. It's got where she has to read it to me anyway, so you might as well just write reg'lar." He pauses. "You better come to see us while I can still make out who *you* are."

This hits its mark. Along with the guilt and sadness rise the anger and hurt that he has never been able to make out who I really am. "I can't afford the trip now," I say.

"That's what I told you 'fore you ever went way off out there in the first place," he says.

For several days Iris won't say hello to me on the porch, though I always give her at least a little wave in passing. Then one late afternoon she beckons me with the hand that isn't holding the crumpled hanky over her mouth.

"I used to live right under you in 311," she says in a low, confidential tone. "And I was healthy as could be. But since they moved me down to second floor I'm sick all the time it's so hot all the time and one thing after another. But they said I had to move down or else pay more." She lowers her voice to a whisper. "Is anybody in there?" she asks, pointing to the parlor.

"No," I whisper back.

"Well, I'm a senior citizen so they let me pay less, see. They let me pay a hundred and I know you pay two hundred. Excuse me. I couldn't afford it but still I kick myself sometimes because I could have just eaten less, you know. But the doctor can't do anything about it. He says to eat protein but it hurts my ulcer. And my stomach hurts and my head hurts and the hemorrhoids. Excuse me. But a terrible thing happened to me once when this man hit me on the back and everything fell out. Excuse me for telling you this but he did, he just slapped me on the back and everything fell out. I wish I lived under you you're such a fine, quiet person, I can tell. Shhhh!" She shushes me vigorously, as if I had been the one talking, and applies both hands to the handkerchief, covering all of her face below the pale blue eyes.

"Don't tell him what I told you," she says, and only then do I notice that Mr. Andrews is about to step out onto the porch wearing his customary work suit but with a somewhat astonishing red and silver and blue striped cardboard top hat held precisely straight on his head by a tight piece of elastic that is only partially visible among the folds of his chin and neck. After initial surprise at the fact that he is wearing such a thing, it begins to seem the perfect thing for him to be wearing—he smiles his serene hello smile and manages not only to avoid looking silly but even to project a certain dignity. It is the first time I have seen him use a cane.

"How was your birthday?" I ask.

"Oh, it 'as all right. Went over to the daughter's. I got thirty-five dollars, so I guess I didn't do too bad. Great granddaughter got me this hat." He pulls at the brim as if to straighten it, but it doesn't budge.

"It's some hat," I say. "It makes you look like Uncle Sam."

"Don't I wish I had some of *his* money," Mr. Andrews chuckles, peering around me at Iris, who has shrunken back into the corner with her eyes closed, refusing to acknowledge his presence. He talks only to me then but speaks up, as if to make sure Iris can hear him, or rather perhaps to make sure she knows he knows she can hear him.

"I was finally able to see how to flip that gismo on the elevator down in the basement," he says, obviously pleased with himself. "They could have put in a new one for $3,000 when they should have. Now it'll cost 'em three times that, an' I bet they never do it. Trude's gonna break her neck on them stairs. Take a little ride with me, I'll show you the trick to it." I start calculating what it might mean to get stuck and wait hours for the rescue squad or the repairman or whoever. But I don't want Mr. Andrews to think I don't trust him, and with this comes the realization that in fact I do trust him, so we make our way into the little enclosed cage with its printed scrawl above the buttons that says "Last Inspection 1915." I know this is someone's idea of a joke, that someone has rubbed out the top of the seven in "1975," but even that provokes second thoughts.

"Trick is to push four first," Mr. Andrews says as he slides the double doors shut. "Take 'er to four and then back down and she won't stick. But you can't stop 'er on four or she'll stick there. You got to hold the button in when you get there."

"I'll just go back down to three with you then," I say, as if I had a choice in the matter. "Who's going to take care of Iris?"

"I dunno," he says. "No real family out here to speak of, I don't think. 'Course there's not that much wrong with her except. . . ." Here he points to his temple just beneath the hat. "She doesn't eat right is about half of it." We reach four and he pushes three and, sure enough, we jerk our way back down.

At the center of his door is a small rectangle of clean, almost new looking wood where the "Manager" sign used to be. "Hey," I ask. "Did somebody steal your sign or what?"

"Nope," Mr. Andrews says, leaning on his cane. "Not the manager anymore." He reaches up with one finger to find the elastic and pull it out from beneath his chin, takes off the hat and hangs it on a nail that protrudes from the doorframe.

"Oh," is all I can think to say.

"New owner wants a younger man for the job," he says, and he is smiling his smile, though a hollowness in his voice belies it. "I guess forty-four years is about long enough, anyway."

There is silence while I try to think of what to say. "Well, it must be a relief to you in a way, though, isn't it?"

"Oh yip, yip," he says, not looking back as he starts through the door. "Yip. I'm glad to be shut of it all right."

I lie on the bed and try to read, but Iris's voice keeps insisting itself somewhere in the back of my head, and I finally have to give in to it, hearing again and again, with a shiver of revulsion, "Everything fell out. He slapped me on the back and everything just fell out." It's true or it's something she thinks is true, and I feel upset in either case and don't even want to know which it is. I don't even know what she meant, really, and don't want to know, but then I'm afraid maybe I do know and wonder if she has a "prolapsed uterus," a term I've transcribed many times in medical reports, never looked up, and won't look up now. I don't know if it's something that can happen to you after too many children or none at all or if that has anything to do with it. "Everything fell out." Surely an exaggeration, anyway. As vulnerable as we are and brutalized by time, surely we are fixed so that things don't collapse inside of us and fall out. I touch myself—soft but firm, moist folds of flesh. I want to keep my mind and I want to keep my sight and I want to keep my cunt. Iris and I aren't anybody's mother.

The vasectomy. I hope he doesn't regret it now. I hope he did it for himself and not me, but of course he did it for us together and now he's left with it. I hope his next wife doesn't want babies, either. Such a tenderness in the decision and in the following through. Me waiting in a cold sweat in the emergency room, and then how pale he looked riding home on the pillow and how we tried to joke, but it was all too delicate and serious a business. My relatives could never quite grasp that we really did not intend to reproduce, would look at me with equal parts disbelief and disapproval whenever I said as much, gave up asking only after so many years went by that the truth spoke for itself and it began to look as if we were, after all, family enough for each other. "You're the curiousest two I ever saw," Aunt Lucinda finally said. "But I reckon it's all right if that's what you want. People don't have children anymore like they used to."

It is late—almost 11:30 Illinois time—but I know she stays up reading light romances or Zane Grey or watching TV, and I suddenly want very much to hear her voice *now*, even if it's not on the cheap rate, even if it's an extravagance. She answers sounding hoarse and dispirited, unusual for her, and I think maybe I woke her up after all, but she says no.

"Well, how are you?" I ask. "Are you not feeling well?"

"Oh I'm just restin' up after the trip back from Tennessee," she says. "After the funeral and all, you know."

I feel my gut tighten and brace myself, knowing it has to be somebody I know. "What funeral was that?" I ask.

"Oh my Lord, child, didn't anybody let you know about your Aunt Opal? She had a stroke I b'lieve it was Sunday week ago and they takened her to Memphis three or four days and then she passed on real early Thursday morning. Her heart just give out on 'er, is what it was. I don't think she suffered any. Now you needn't to cry, honey. Some of 'em should've called you or wrote but I guess they knew you couldn't get back noway. But it was her time, sugar, you know that."

"I know it," I manage to say. "I know it."

"She was about to get down where her girls were havin' to wait on her ever' minute, and she couldn't stand that. She told me that herself."

"I know it," I say. "I know it. How was the funeral?"

"Oh Lord, you know there was a big crowd that come out for it. 'Course it would've been a big crowd with nothin' but just her own family. But I know most of Overton was packed in that church. It took all six of the boys to carry the coffin. But Cleo and Maurella fixed her hair up, you know, the way she liked it—all that mass of white hair—and she did look awful purty, just awful purty."

"Well, how are you?" I ask, thinking I can't bear any more details all at once now. "I know this must have set you back some."

"Oh, I'm all right," she says. "I'm goin' to a banquet at the lodge tomorrow night. You know I'm not gonna be settin' here mossin' over if I can help it. You be sweet now and take care of yourself."

"Yes ma'am," I say. "I will."

I'm not cold, but I get out Aunt Opal's flannel quilt to cry on, wishing I had answered her last letter. I hope she knew how much I loved her, even if I did go too far away. I guess I felt sure I would see her again, but then death must always come as a surprise, even when we expect it. My father probably didn't want to pay for a long distance call, knowing I couldn't afford to come. I will get a letter soon. I crawl into bed thinking of Aunt Opal's laugh and her wit and her biscuits and her snuff and her Folger's coffee spit can. I cry with an immense sadness and aloneness—not just over the loss, but at not having anyone who knew her to grieve with. Once when Aunt Lucinda and I were looking at old photographs, me on the stool at her feet, we came across one of a young woman with an almost humorously forlorn expression on her face. I was about to say something trite and obvious, that she looked like she'd just lost her best friend, but Aunt Lucinda beat me to it. "Looks like she 'as sent for and couldn't go," she said, and I rolled off the stool laughing. But it doesn't seem so funny now. It is one thing to be sent for and unable to go, and it is another thing entirely not to be sent for at all.

There is a soft but startling knock at my door. In the dingy light through the peephole I see a woman in a black coat and loud pink headscarf facing the door across from mine, and for a moment I think maybe the knock was not for me, but then she backs up and taps again, and I know that it must be Iris.

"Who is it?" I call out, and she answers without turning around.

"It's Iris Bing that used to live right under you in 311 but I don't have my senior's card with me but I am. Do you have any potato chips because if you did I thought I might want to eat some that I could borrow."

"I'm sorry, I don't have any," I say. "I'm not dressed. I'm about to go to sleep." I think I need to be alone to cry, but then as soon as Iris says, "Excuse me," and disappears from view, I don't want to be alone at all and dash to the bathroom for my robe. "Wait a minute," I call, leaning out into the corridor just in time to catch her at the top of the stairs. "Come on in. I've got some cheese and crackers. Come back for a minute."

For a few seconds Iris seems to be ignoring me, even descending a step or two before she stops, looks my way, takes off the scarf, covers her mouth, thinks it all over, and decides to return. She is wearing the black raincoat that is usually wrapped about her legs on the porch. She has it buttoned all the way to the top, and hanging several inches below it are the hems of two nylon nightgowns, one pale blue that stops just below the knee, the other faded colorless and reaching· nearly to the tops of her fluffy, soiled yellow dimestore houseslippers. As she makes her way down the hall hacking into the scarf I suffer a twinge of regret—I'm not sure I want her to sit on my bed. Everything fell out. Maybe she isn't so terribly clean, and maybe she really does have something I could catch.

"I didn't think I would wake you up, excuse me," Iris says as she perches herself on the very edge of the bed, almost as if she has sensed my not wanting her there. "The doctor said for me to eat potato chips every night or I wouldn't have bothered you. Trude stepped on Clarence's glasses and now neither one of them can see the television and the new manager is going to burn everything in Arthur's apartment—you know Mr. Hammond down on first—because there is too much. So I hope he stays away from my room because I think he's, you know, I shouldn't say it but you're such a fine person and I think he's a . . . what do they call it? I think he's a dope fiend."

I feel as if a whole crowd of people just filed into this tiny room. "How about some cheese and crackers?" I ask.

"Oh no, my no, honey. It might hurt my throat. I mean it might hurt my stomach."

"How about some milk then? How about if we both have some warm milk to help us sleep?" I heat the milk and top it with nutmeg, and Iris stuffs the scarf into her coat pocket before she takes her cup and we both sit perched on the bed, sipping. "I wasn't really asleep," I say. "I'm just upset because my Aunt Opal died. In Tennessee."

Iris looks straight at me for a long moment, saying she is sorry with her eyes and almost making me start to cry again. "We better have some whiskey in it," she says suddenly, and I have to laugh, not only with surprise but with the realization that she was sharp-eyed enough to have spied my bottle in the kitchen. I have never had whiskey and milk before, but after the first couple of sips it begins to taste fine, sitting on the bed with Iris. When she crosses her legs I see a third gown, a printed flannel, underneath the long faded one, and I think I smell Ivory soap.

"Was she old?" Iris asks.

"Yes," I say. "Almost 88."

"So it doesn't matter so much," she says, taking a long swig.

"It matters a lot to me," I say.

"I used to be such a worrier," Iris says. "Worry about this, worry about that and I would try to stop it and I would quit sometimes but then before I knew it I'd be right back on it again, same thing, worrying over it. But you know what? Not anymore. I quit seven years ago. And do you know how? How do you think I quit? I used to worry over everybody and everything. Not any more. And you know why? I found out *nobody ever worried over me*, that's what. Can you close that window for me, honey? I don't want to die shivering." I close the window, though I've begun to sweat a bit. I really don't mind Iris sitting on my bed anymore, and I get up to fix us another drink.

"Let's just play some hearts, then," she says. "Take our mind off things."

"I don't have any cards," I say from the kitchen. When I hand Iris her cup, she grasps it in both hands, holding it as if to warm them, and then I see that she really is shivering, so I offer Aunt Opal's quilt.

"I don't have any cards either," she says. "But you have the prettiest color of blue eyes I've ever seen."

"Thank you," I say. "But they're just the same as yours, you know."

"I *know*," Iris says, adjusting the quilt about her shoulders as if it were some kind of stole. "You're a girl after my own heart. I said that the first day I ever saw you and you are and you know what? I used to be just like you and you know what? I think I'm going to adopt you is what I think. What do you think?"

"I think that would be just great," I say, not meaning it, not wanting the responsibility of being adopted by Iris. But then she gives me such a smile—such a sweet, shining smile that seems to have her whole self totally behind it, which I've never seen in her face before—and I regret not having meant it. And then I see that despite the whiskey and the quilt and the coat and the three gowns and the window being shut against the midsummer air, she is still shivering. And then I begin to cry about everything at once, not the silent crying I was doing before she came in, but the noisy kind that starts way down in the gut and pushes itself up and out and over everything in the room. Iris takes my cup and her cup and sets them on the table. She sits right up next to me then and puts her arm and part of the quilt around me and holds me until I can stop. It feels good to be partly covered up, even though I'm hot. By the time I am finished crying, Iris seems to be finished shivering.

"Here. Stand up, honey, I got to tuck you in," she says. She pulls back the covers and guides me into bed in my robe. "You go to sleep now. Iris has to go home. You just go right to sleep now." I have to get up to lock the door behind her and blow my nose and brush my teeth. But when I get back into bed I still feel tucked in.

Several times over the next few weeks, while his glasses are being repaired, Mr. Andrews brings his mail to my room or asks me to come down to 302 to read it or catches me in the parlor, where I pull up a chair between him and Trude and read aloud the letters from their niece Clarabelle in Seattle or try to interpret the insurance balance from their last visit to the doctor. Once it is a three-page, single-spaced form letter from a radio evangelist that Mrs. Andrews listens to four evenings a week. She has written to the man twice, each time asking for a healing prayer and enclosing $2.00, and it takes some doing for her husband and me to convince her that this is not a personal response, that basically all the letter is saying is that the Reverend F. Walter Wyatt has had a vision while praying for the sick, a vision that told him he must continue his radio broadcasts (for which he will joyfully accept contributions of ten, twenty, fifty, a hundred, or even a thousand dollars). Trude gets so bewildered and agitated over all this and Clarence so impatient with her that I leave them quarreling in the parlor as the Rolling Stones begin to blare from the new manager's first-floor front apartment. (Ron looks to be in his late twenties and wears Hawaiian shirts and a fairly conspicuous gold loop in one ear. "I always thought a manager was supposed to dress like a manager," I heard Mr. Andrews complain to Iris. "He went off to Mexico all weekend. Whole place could have come tumbling down. Some manager.")

One late afternoon I come in from work to find Mr. Andrews snoring gently in the sunlight, head tilted back against the top of the ratty old overstuffed chair closest to the large center window, jaw just slack enough to make you look away, both hands clutching several white and pastel colored envelopes which I'm sure he probably wants me to read. I hesitate to wake him, consider clearing my throat or maybe sitting for a minute to see if he opens his eyes, but then one of the new tenants, the one they call Big Ray (who usually roars up on his Harley) comes barreling through with his heavy chain belt clinking and lets the door slam sharply behind him. Mr. Andrews jumps awake, wipes saliva from his chin onto his shirtsleeve before he realizes I am there.

"You're the one," he says, scooting to the edge of the chair so he can push himself up with both hands against the armrests. "Trude wants you to read 'er these. Anniversary cards." He hands them to me—all carefully slit open with his pocket knife—as we head upstairs.

"How long have you been married?" I ask.

"Quite a little while," he says matter-of-factly. "Long enough, anyway. Maybe too long. Seventy years." I let this sink in. Seventy years married. Of course, it computes with their ages, but still I try to imagine it.

"Now she's got to where she even wants me to put the stickum on her teeth," he says, and I think yes, this is what 'till death do us part' really means.

Through the door as Mr. Andrews fishes for his key we can hear Trude singing to herself—a little flat and a little wobbly but with feeling. "There'll be sunshine and laughter, just over the hill," she sings, sliding into a rather intricate yodel which she breaks off as we open the door. There is a thick, sour smell in the room that makes me not want to breathe in at first.

"Happy Anniversary," I say.

"I'm dreading it, really," Trude says, rocking slightly in the cushioned rocker. She is rolling a little ball of bright red yarn between her thumb and first two fingers, more or less in time with the movement of the chair. "Did Clarence tell you our preacher has it up to marry us on Sunday? He called to find out all about our courtship and how long we went together and how much money Clarence was making when we got married and just on and on. I should get a new dress, but then I don't see what the use of that is, either."

"I'm afraid to get too dressed up anymore," Mr. Andrews says, easing himself onto the couch. "'Fraid I'll feel *too* good." He chuckles and gives me a sweetly flirtatious look.

"You're so good to come up here and read for us," Trude says. "Our daughter's tired of us, I know. If anything ever happens to Clarence, I know she'll put me in one of those homes. Our preacher said if we sign over all our property to the Baptist Church he can get us into the Baptist home. But I don't know. . . ."

"Fella's full of ideas," Mr. Andrews says.

"Red velvet curtains in the parlor," Trude says. "And we'd pass out fresh linens every week. That's when the place was really something. And right next door to you—I bet you don't know who stayed there a lot of times. Shirley Temple's mother. And Charlie Chaplin stayed right over here above the Napoleon. They even had a night clerk. Oh, it was posh all right, with Lawrence Welk at the pavillion on Saturday nights to dance. And every place in this whole building had a Murphy bed."

"Charlie didn't walk the way you'd've thought," Mr. Andrews says.

"I'll be glad when it's all over. I'm already worn out with it," Trude says. "I'm too nervous to stand up in front of everybody."

"You're gettin' cold feet," Mr. Andrews tells her. "I was the one got 'em the first time."

"Oh *you*, Clarence!" Trude laughs a real ha-ha-ha laugh, then turns to me. "He says I must be getting cold feet. Isn't he something now?" She laughs some more while Mr. Andrews sits with his arms folded, beaming at the two of us.

I spread all the flowery cards out on the formica table by the window that faces the ocean. Two of them compare anniversaries to roses (they pass quickly and are to be cherished), and another says that marriage is the long and winding road of love on which we journey through life. One has a number wheel attached inside which has been rotated to 70 (out of a possible 75) in front of the word *anniversary*. And then there is a personal looking letter of congratulation from President Jimmy Carter. I read all of them aloud slowly and distinctly and probably a little louder than necessary, as if I'm giving a performance of some kind.

"They sure have some pretty cards now," Trude says, and for a few moments we listen to the steady squeak of the rocker. "They'll all forget about us, though, after this is over."

"Until next year maybe," I say.

"I don't know . . . I don't believe we'll make it for the next one," she whines.

"You're not thinking of getting a divorce, are you?" I ask, and we all laugh, especially Mr. Andrews. They are the only couple I know that I could safely make such a joke with.

"I just don't believe we'll make it for another one," she says. "I can't see to get around anymore, and Clarence had such a bad spell last week. . . ."

"Shut up, Trude. She doesn't want to hear all that." Mr. Andrews gets up and starts going through his wallet, something he does every time I read for them, finally extracting a very worn dollar bill from its "secret compartment." I refuse it again, and he insists again, and I refuse it finally, assuring him there will be some favor he can do for me sometime—and no telling what it will be. He usually brightens at this and lets me go, but today he moves to the table and begins to rifle through his heavy, black metal toolbox, eventually choosing a fine old wooden-handled screwdriver. "You take this now," he says, opening the door for me. "It's a good one. Made to last."

It's been years since I've looked at the wedding pictures. I dig into the back of the closet for the cigar box. The ring is in there, too, nothing extravagant—just a medium-thick band, but with stripes of varicolored gold I wanted because I'd never seen anything like it before and thought we were special, too, and different. It still fits and flatters my hand, heavier than all my other rings. When I take it off, I think I can discern, just barely, its outline in untanned flesh. Impossible, surely, after this long, but marriage permeates the cells.

Who made me wear that silly hat? It must have been my own idea. We didn't even want a church wedding, but everyone said we should and so we did, I was such a girl, voice quaking through all the I-do's. We filled only two pew's worth of that sprawling Baptist church. Brother Tinker let us know he didn't like the ex-wife business or, for that matter, the difference in our ages, but yes, he would marry us—for Aunt Lucinda's sake. My face all unlined innocence feeding cake to the groom—I'd never smeared anything on his mouth yet just for the pleasure of licking it off. Awkward kiss for the camera. I can feel his lips if I close my eyes. The best snapshot of the day is not even at the wedding but that morning after tennis, gone so long they thought maybe we had run off after all. He has me cupped under his arm and the smiles are real, still flushed from playing and then necking in the park. We look like brother-and-sister buddies. Relatives, we decided by the time I left—we must just be relatives of some kind. Some blood tie bound us and severed us at once. Oh Daddy, yes.

You taught me everything—how to compose myself on paper, how to lose my composure in bed. When I was a girl in your class, you came in one windy afternoon with your hair mussed up and your tie blown back over one shoulder. I wanted to signal you but couldn't manage. You spoke of Socrates for an hour that way, and I hardly heard a word for staring at that tie. Somehow it showed me you were touchable, could be careless, disarranged, drawn away from that first wife. I lured you to coffee with a poem and remember touching the tip of your tie with the back of one finger. I couldn't say your name without the "Dr.," but I could bring myself to touch that tie. Even when we got tired of each other, it still thrilled me to slide your tie loose and ease it off you with one hand. Sometimes from the bed I could see some dark silk tie hanging from a doorknob, would want to pull at it with you in me.

Snowed in at twenty below the day we realized I would leave you for good. We both got the shakes and huddled together in the hallway whimpering. I couldn't stop and you made soup. We hunched over the kitchen table in blankets and tried to laugh because we were afraid of the empty darkness in the dining room. We slept all night without untwining, like lovers are supposed to.

There is a boyish place at the back of your head that will not age. I would come up behind you and touch it as you wrote, and you would turn your head for the kiss. Do you still wake up bright-eyed and fling yourself into the new day? I don't really want you back. Would it be so crazy if you just hopped on a plane once in awhile and flew to my bed? I would make you laugh and send you home fresh to whoever waits. You could stay just till we remembered what was wrong.

Who else cares what's in this box? The ring, the pictures, the locket, the five or six best letters, the first "A" theme from English 101. Treasures to pass on to the children, I suppose. All those years he was the one who knew me, and now something about myself is lost. All the stories you had to be there for. Who cares if he read me Emily Dickinson in the bathtub or could tell if I'd enjoyed a meal by the way I put two fingers of one hand into the palm of the other? "After great pain, a formal feeling comes." I wonder when it was, exactly, that I stopped being able to breathe in that house. I wonder how a man and woman can live together for seventy years, how everything can fail to shift in all that time. And I wonder how many times they've wanted to kill each other. Something in me says I will not marry again.

I take everything out of the box and line it with aluminum foil, then refold the essay, seal the picture packet shut, tie the letters into a bundle. His business-size envelopes don't look romantic. I sprinkle some potpourri, tie the box with double dark blue yarn and put it all away. I will be divorced the day I stop automatically dressing him in the earth-tone shirts I see in department store windows—something to bring out the rust in his rust-gray beard or socks that might complement some muted tone in one of his old ties. I wonder what he is doing right this very moment. And when is it that he thinks of me?

Sometimes I catch a glimpse of his face in the weekend crowds on the boardwalk, and my heart will leap straight into the base of my throat before the brain has a chance to register the extreme improbability of such a sight. Improbable but not impossible, not absolutely. He could be here, except that I know he isn't, even though one early evening not so long ago I followed the concrete bike path down toward where it nearly touches the water and was suddenly sure the bearded figure seated alone on the low wall up ahead had to be him, just had to be him.

The shoulders, the erect posture, the balance lent by one leg out-stretched to the sand. Even the cut of the tan jacket. Moving slowly toward him I could hear my own heart beat above the sound of the waves, knowing that when I got there he would be somebody else, yet compelled to close the distance in case, just in case, he might stand up and face me with his perfect smile and open arms. I walked faster, preparing to run to him if that should happen, then had to rush instead past the stranger with the too-dark beard and the too-thick lips and the not-nearly-lean-enough belly, choking back tears of ridiculous, bitter disappointment. But it might have been him, I told myself, it might really have been him.

Considering all this sets me strangely in tune with Iris's blurrings of *is* and *was, might be* and *might have been.* I find her standing on the second floor fire escape landing, surrounded by several large grocery sacks full of clothing and trinkets and cannisters and magazines. She has a blue-cuffed white athletic sock tied tightly around her head with the knot protruding straight out over her eyebrows.

"There's a man in the garbage," she whispers, wringing her hands, then drawing me into the doorway for more privacy. "I have to throw this away before I get thrown out of here but he's in there waiting to get all my things. Don't look at him, he'll see us."

I look down into the trash bin expecting to see some wino or junkie or poverty-stricken Mexican poking around for food or aluminum cans or saleable cast-offs. "There's nobody down there," I tell Iris, but this sounds too harsh, the contradiction too direct. "I mean, I don't see anybody. Maybe he left while you weren't looking."

"They're going to burn up everything Arthur needs or else he'll have to move. He has a newspaper from 1929 and the firemen said it would burn up. It wasn't like that when Clarence was manager. And now that man down there is waiting for all *my* things. But my cousin says go to a home but I'm not going. They already made me move once and I said that's it, no more, but nobody wants me to live here anymore."

Arthur's apartment is filled very nearly to the ceiling with piles of newspapers and miscellaneous "collectibles," which I always try to get a glimpse of when I pass his door, though there is only room for it to open about a third of the way now. Apparently the new owner took one look in—or one-third of a look in—and called the fire inspector, who declared 106 an immediate safety hazard. I happened to be downstairs by the mailboxes the morning a huge fire engine pulled up on the boardwalk and three firemen trudged in to rap on Arthur's door. He did not invite them in.

"Mr. *Hammond*," one of the firemen said with what sounded to me like exaggerated friendliness. "Mr. Hammond, now, you've got such a unique situation here we'd like to get a few pictures if you don't mind. We're just here to take another look around after the first inspection, you know."

"I don't think so," I heard Arthur say, his high-pitched voice even more shaky than usual. "I'm going to talk to the manager about it first."

"We've already talked with the manager," the fireman said, less cordial now.

"There are too many things going on around here," Arthur said. "Too many changes too fast. Come back in a few days and I'll let you know."

Irritation rose in the fireman's voice—Arthur's refusal to cooperate had transformed him from a charming eccentric into a stubborn old man, a pain in the ass. "You're gonna have to store some of this junk elsewhere, Pop. You can let us in now, or we can go get a police order and come back this afternoon. You take your choice." Arthur wouldn't budge, and I felt a surge of admiration for him, especially since something in the fireman's voice sounded almost as dangerous as the idea of having a fire hazard in the building.

I try to explain to Iris, who keeps wringing her hands and sneaking looks down at the trash bin, that what is happening with Arthur doesn't mean she has to move or even throw anything away. "But I'll take this stuff down if you want me to," I tell her. "I really don't think anybody's down there now."

"He might have been under the garbage," she says. "He's waiting under there."

"I don't think so," I say, about ready to give up, afraid I'm agitating her instead of helping.

"But he *might* be," she says. "I'll just keep these things in the sacks and then if they come I can throw them out the window before they get in. Because they want the old ones out, you know. Excuse me for saying this, honey, but they do. They want the old ones out so they can get young ones and raise the rent." We each carry two sacks to Iris's door, which I expect her to open up, but she doesn't, so I set mine down nearby against the wall. "I have such a headache," she says, straining to touch one hand to the knotted sock across her brow, nearly dropping one of the bags in the process. "But I didn't have any milk to put on it."

A little later, when I walk up the alley to Spirits of Venice for a bottle of wine, I decide to pick up a quart of milk for Iris—maybe she'll drink some of it from her prune juice bottle when the headache goes away. I tap gently on her door, then a little louder when there is no response. I'm sure I can hear some rustling, but she doesn't answer an even louder knock. "It's just me again, Iris," I call out when I see she doesn't have a peephole. "I brought you some milk. I'll leave it here by the door."

I come upstairs feeling a little hurt, wondering what goes through her mind when someone knocks. But then, a couple of hours later as I sit sorting things out at my desk, slices of cheese begin to sail in under my door, four of them in all—individually wrapped slices of Kraft American processed cheese, three with thoroughly dried out edges where the cellophane is torn. I open the door quickly and catch Iris on the stairs holding the bottle across her forehead.

"There's the cheese I owe you," she says casually, not breaking stride in her descent.

"Oh," I say. "OK. Thanks a lot." I come back in and stare at the stuff for awhile, hesitant about throwing it away, unable to bear the thought of ever eating it, finally disposing of it, temporarily at least, in the refrigerator. I don't quite know if she is paying me back for the milk or if it's for the cheese she *might* have eaten the night she came to visit. But then, of course, it doesn't really matter.

The days shorten into October, and I notice a change in the quality of light on the sand and on the water, a kind of muted clarity that soothes and assaults the eye at once, creating an atmosphere of heavy, curiously pleasant nostalgia. On the days I work I go in early so I can come home early to catch the late softness of the afternoons and watch the sun descend with hazy brilliance into the sea. I spend hours sitting on the bed staring out the window (and feel annoyed when a friend informs me that smog is responsible for the most stunning of the sunsets). The waves never once stop rolling in.

I am fortunate to have this room, would never have moved into the first or second floor here, where the windows face only the walls of the buildings next door, which block the ocean breeze as well as the view. The apartments there are truly shabby, have not been fixed up for years, and the last new owner lured (or forced) several of the elderly residents down with the promise of low rents, which he made up for with increases for the top two floors. I started out paying $185 and pay $210 now, but new people coming into singles like mine pay $275 or $300, and the word is that since *Vogue* and several other magazines and TV shows have proclaimed Venice "Roller Skating Capital of the World" and ultra-chic "center of the universe," this new owner will charge $400 for the singles and $700 for the one-bedrooms with a full front ocean view. "GIVE A SPECULATOR A INCH AND THEY'LL BUILD A CONDO," someone has scrawled on the wall across from the sidewalk cafe, and if Iris is not entirely right that the landlords are "out to get rid of the seniors," she is certainly right that no one would be sorry to see them go. In last Sunday's crush of tourists and skaters and skateboarders and joggers and vendors and hot dog carts, an 85-year-old woman was run down and killed in front of her own doorstep on the boardwalk by a young man speeding through on his bike. "She got in my way," he told the police. "What can I tell you? She got in my way."

One afternoon I pull into the parking lot and have to look twice at my building—scaffolding surrounds the entire place, and there is brown paper taped over every window, giving the structure a bandaged, surrealistic tone in the autumn light. I knock at the manager's door—loud enough to be heard over Led Zepplin—and Ron answers without bothering to put down his joint.

"What's all this?" I ask.

"Far out, huh?" he grins. "What's happening?"

"That's what I want to know," I say. "What's with the scaffolding?"

"Oh, that. Yeah. They're gonna sandblast the place and squirt fake stucco all over it. Ain't that the shits?" He offers me the joint, which I politely decline.

"What's the matter with the brick?" I ask. "Why don't they fumigate the place or fix the elevator instead? And how long will the damn paper be on the windows?" I hear myself sounding bitchy but can't help it, am already dreading the closed-in room.

"Coupla weeks, I guess," Ron says, in a tone that lets me know I'm bringing him down. "No use getting all uptight about it."

"Right," I say. But when I get upstairs I feel claustrophobic and furious, and after three or four days of trying to write or read or do much of anything at all in the airless room against the noise of the sandblasting, I decide to spend my savings and two recent reprint checks on a plane ticket to Tennessee. It's time, anyway, I tell myself—it's time, even if you don't really want to go.

I come in from the library just after dark the evening before my early flight, and in the light from a first-floor window I see what looks like Iris's clear plastic shoulder bag just beneath the fire escape steps. When I squat down to check it, I see that the contents are scattered all around. I know for sure that all those handkerchiefs and the oversized brown-and-white rabbit's foot belong to Iris. The sight nauseates me with fear, and I run straight up to the second floor in a panic. Such an ugly, violent thing, to see someone's purse like that. I look all around the fire escape and the trash bin before running back down to collect everything, then back up to bang on Iris's door.

"Are you in there, Iris? Are you all right? I found your purse." No answer. "Iris? Iris? I brought your purse." The door opens halfway into a dark room, and Iris peeps around from behind it with a scarf over her mouth. "What happened?" I say, hearing the urgency in my own voice. "Are you all right or what? Did somebody grab your purse?" She won't say anything, looks slightly to the left of me as I hand her the bag. She takes it and then begins rubbing her shoulder with the scarf, as if it hurts. "Did he hurt your shoulder when he grabbed it?" I ask. "Shit. Let's call the police, OK?" With this the scarf flies back to her mouth as she shakes her head with a vigorous NO, closing the door to a crack just wide enough to speak through.

"I dropped it. I did. I dropped it. I must have lost my purse.

"Are you sure? I mean, are you sure maybe somebody didn't grab it off your shoulder? Doesn't your shoulder hurt?"

"It's my headache. I'm taking a nap for it," she says. "I don't see anybody." She closes the door, and I hear the click of two deadbolts. "Nighty-night," she says.

"Do you want me to call your cousin?" I ask, desperate to do something, wondering how much money must be missing, unable to let go the image of some faceless, driven man or boy jerking at the purse.

"No cousins," Iris says firmly. "She has a one-track mind. Nighty-night."

I stop by 302 to tell Mr. Andrews what happened and that I'm leaving town for a few days. "Oh Lord," he says. "She probably won't come out for a week now. But we'll see about 'er. We'll see about 'er all right."

I spend the evening packing and sipping whiskey for the jitters about Iris and about the plane ride and about going east at all—even though Tennessee is not Illinois—and about nearly everything else my mind can dredge up to worry over uselessly. I toss and tumble in bed until past 2:00, jarred awake by every little sound from the pagoda and the alley, twice bolting upright with the certainty that there is someone on the scaffolding outside the papered window.

I wake up taut with a bad case of the dreads. In order to fly with any sense of peace, I always have to perch myself somewhere between firm belief that the plane will of course not crash and some sort of neutral resignation to the fact that the plane of course may very well crash, and if it does, so be it. I try to reach this balance sipping coffee, finally doctoring it with whiskey, which goes straight to my head and calms me down considerably. Earth and air, fire and water. I am at home only with earth, with both feet firmly on the ground. The others inspire awe in me—or fear. Fire. The dreads rise again, and on notebook paper I print a sign to tape to the middle drawer of my filing cabinet, which contains nearly everything I've ever written: "Firemen: In case of fire, please save this drawer first." I giggle with my own absurdity and tear it up—if there were a fire the paper message would probably be one of the first things to go. But then, just before I close the door behind my suitcase, I come back in and make another sign, editing out the redundancy of the first and saying simply, in extra-large letters: "FIREMEN: SAVE THIS DRAWER."

Air travel is too fast to suit my rhythms—L.A. to Memphis in less than four hours, no time for easing into anything. I am grateful for the two-hour bus ride to Overton, stopping at every tiny town. Several people on the bus talk to the driver and to each other as if this is a regular trip for them, which may be so, or it may just be that I am back where polite and cordial chatter is pretty much taken for granted. The soft southern tones and turns of phrase soothe me along crooked, winding, hilly two-lanes beneath a shockingly clear blue sky. There must have been an early frost, since many of the leaves are already gone and those left have lost their brilliance.

"So this Yankee lawyer that comes in the store all time come in the other day," a balding, red-faced man in front of me is telling his seatmate. "An' me 'n' my son-in-law, we was talkin' 'bout somethin' or other, I forget what, bein' curious. An' this feller comes up 'n' says Jim Ed, he says, says I want you to tell me one thing. Says ever'where I go down here I hear this is curious or that's curious or this 'un's curious or that 'un's curious. Now what does it mean when you all say somebody's *curious*? An' I looked 'im right straight in the eye just as serious and said oh, I reckon it's somebody just about like you." I laugh out loud with them—having been considered curious all my life—and the red-faced man turns around to grin at me. "How you, ma'am?" he says, and I tell him that I'm fine, just fine.

I get there in time for supper, and once the initial excitement of arrival has passed and the dishes are done and we've talked about what time I left and what I ate on the plane and what time I got to Memphis and what time the bus left there and where all it stopped and whether I didn't just about freeze from the quick change in temperature, I rediscovered that Rebecca and my father have very little to say to me and I have very little to say to them. I am like a stranger in the house only worse, I think, because small talk might come more easily to strangers. At first the conversation is punctuated with lengthy silences, and then it seems more that the silences are punctuated with occasional words.

"Anything else you want to eat, just go grab it," my father says finally, rocking hard against the blonde wooden floor of the living room, his eyes directed straight ahead rather than across the room toward me. Rebecca switches on the big old upright cabinet radio in the corner, and a gospel quartet overenunciates how we must get on board the Jesus plane if we want to be bound for glory from the airport of life.

"TV's got where it ain't nothin' but a glare on me," my father says. "Have to put dark glasses on to stand it."

"It's not anything but trash on it half the time now anyway," Rebecca says. "They all talk ugly and prance around half nekkid."

"If it's not that, it's the niggers," my father says. "The niggers has just about took it over since they let 'em on. Takened over the swimmin' pool here, too, till they finally had to close it down to keep 'em out."

This is bait for an old argument between us which I am no longer young and foolish enough to engage in. Promptly at 8:30, when the gospel program ends, Rebecca turns off the radio and asks me where I want to sleep. I insist on the couch, knowing that if I take her bed and they have to share his, neither of them will rest. She is relieved at my choice, yet has to ask me twice again until she makes it clear, for appearance's sake, that I *prefer* the couch, even though I've been offered a bed like any proper guest. I do not mention that it is only 6:30 Pacific time, since this would present too difficult a dilemma in the little crackerbox of a house—the TV would keep them awake, the radio would keep them awake, even a lamp to read by would keep them awake, since my father swears that the closing of his bedroom door smothers him to death. I stretch out beneath two sheets and a woolen quilt, listening to the three of us breathing, and discover that I am sleepy after all. The dream I nearly always have in this house comes back, with minor variations, and I wake myself with little whimpering cries of pain from walking barefoot over broken glass. At least I'm having it the first night, I think, getting it over with. Four nights to go. The intense quiet of the house reminds me of how noisy Venice is and how I've grown accustomed to it, and at some point the sound of a passing car makes me aware that I'm missing the ocean.

Breakfast is at 6:45. It is always a bruising mystery to my father that I don't want to rise and shine and eat a heap of sausage and grease-laden eggs and Wonder bread toast with them at this hour. "I'll have juice and coffee after I run," I tell them, heading out into the crisp morning, fascinated with being able to see my breath as I exhale. By the end of Sharon Street three or four dogs are following me, snapping at my heels until I have to pick up handfuls of rocks to throw at them. Front doors open, and people peer out through glass storm doors to see what the commotion is about. It's a relief to reach the narrow gravel farm road that leads out north of town. I see cows, pigs, goats, and any number of mules before I return, all bathed in the pure sunlight that is gradually spreading its way over the blackness of the gently rolling fields. By mid-morning three neighbors have phoned to find out just who I am.

"Oh, that's my daughter," I hear Daddy tell them. "She's down here visiting from Venus—Venus, California." This pronunciation touches and amuses me so that I climb onto his lap and surprise him with a big kiss. I don't know how this man can be my father, and yet he is my father, even if he thinks of me as something from another planet. "Bet it costs you $5 every time you fart out there, don't it?" he laughs.

"Just about," I say. "That's why I try not to do it too much." We laugh and then it gets quiet, and I feel awkward on his lap.

"I'm afraid you've gone and got yourself up Shit Creek out there as far as money goes," he says then, and I move to the sofa. "Why don't you write comedy—something that'll sell, if you got to write?"

"I don't feel funny when I write," I say.

"How come *him* to get the house is what I want to know?"

"He paid me my part of it," I say. "And I have the car. I didn't need the house. I needed the car and some cash."

"Hmph. A house is somethin' you can hold onto. Your own place, that's what counts. Now you're out there up Shit Creek payin' rent and liable to get murdered on top of it, if the smog don't choke you to death."

Anger wells up with the force of all my insecurities behind it. "I'm doing fine," I tell him, retreating into the bathroom. "I like my life."

The days fall quickly into a rigid pattern. Dinner, the main meal, is at 11:30, and supper, the leftovers, at 4:45. The local TV news is at 6:00, the gospel program at 7:30, and we're all in bed by 8:45. I take to daydreaming a lot, sitting in the stale-aired living room and staring at the gold, plastic-framed prints of "Pinky" and "Blue Boy" on the wall or at the lively black stallion in the field behind the house across the street, imagining myself riding all that power naked, sending shock waves through Overton.

I miss Aunt Opal, can't even take any flowers because there's a bridge out on the road to the cemetery. Some of her daughters stop by to visit in the afternoons, not really so much to see me as simply because I am their Aunt Carrie's girl. How do I like California, they want to know, and do I ever see any movie stars, and how come me to be so skinny, and, mainly, have I got me a boyfriend yet? Divorced. I can tell they feel sorry for me and a little disapproving—even if I *had* to get divorced, looks like I ought to be married again by now.

Rebecca is sweet to me, has saved the last mess of blackeyed peas frozen from the garden because she knows I love them so much. She watches daytime game shows and reads movie magazines avidly, though she hasn't actually been to a movie in over fifteen years. She is in her late sixties, never had any children of her own and sometimes tries to baby me with the little energy she has left over from babying my father. On Saturday morning she goes up the street to Paulette Blurton's, to the tiny lean-to of a beauty shop where Paulette washes and sets her silver-blue hair, as she has done every Saturday morning at ten o'clock for the past twenty-two years.

By the last day I am biting at the bit to leave, feeling numb from understimulation if nothing else. I hate to break the news to Daddy and Rebecca that the only bus that will make my flight connection in Memphis comes through Overton at 3:00 A.M. This will throw off their routine for at least two days. "Dadgummit," my father says, and I feel as guilty as if the schedule were my fault. The mid-afternoon discovery that none of the alarm clocks in the house seems to work fills me with panic. What if I don't wake up in time? What if I miss that bus? What if I miss that plane? The thought of another twenty-four hours in Overton is almost unbearable.

From the kitchen doorway I watch, incredulous, as my father sits down in his long-johns and spreads the guts of three clocks out on Rebecca's best embroidered tablecloth, along with an assortment of magnifying glasses and miniature screwdrivers. I watch him hunch over it all, squinting and poking awkwardly, until I nearly weep with the tension and the sadness. He taught me to read a micrometer at our kitchen table when I was in the fifth grade, was proud to have his own and not have to use the company's, like some of the other tool-and-die-makers. He can't help it if I got too big for my britches, read too much, went to school too long and learned all the wrong things. I see him start to sweat with his efforts.

"You don't have to do that, Daddy," I tell him. "Rebecca said we could borrow her sister's clock."

"I've fixed a hunert of these," he says, still poking. "She don't have to go runnin' to her sister for ever' little thing." Just then the clock in his hands goes off. "*There* she goes," he says proudly. "Come here and see what it's set for." The clock is set for 8:00, and it is now 4:00 o'clock. "Well, let's see," he says. "Set 'er for 9:00 and we'll see if she goes off at 5:00, and if she does, we'll just set 'er ahead that way for whatever time you want."

When 5:00 o'clock passes without a sound, he goes back to the table while Rebecca and I eat chicken and cornbread off the stove, standing up, then retreat to the living room rather than watch his trembling hands. The minutes pass slower than cold sorghum with all three clocks ticking and going off at random and me constantly looking at my watch, feeling right on the verge of a scream. Time, tense, tension—linguistic truths. Finally Rebecca can't stand it anymore either. "I'll just run over at Sissy's and get that clock," she whispers, drawing on her bright white banlon sweater. "You turn the TV up loud and maybe he won't even know I'm gone." She returns in a burst of cold air before she's missed, with a small black clock and a conspiratorial wink. She sets the alarm for 2:00 and places it carefully at the very back of the lower shelf of the end table by the couch, and I am too relieved to feel guilty about the deception. Soon one of the clocks clangs insistently from the kitchen until he can find the button to shut it off and then Daddy comes swaggering into the living room, grinning broadly.

"I b'lieve I got two of 'em fixed up," he says, presenting them to me for a test. Both appear to work perfectly.

"Wonderful," I say, kissing his cheek. "We should never have doubted you."

"What's *that?*" he says suddenly, pushing me away as if he smelled something burning. "Whose clock is *that?*" I feel myself freeze like a child caught redhanded in some dangerous mischief.

"Oh, that's *hers*," Rebecca says quickly. "It's one she brought with her." I feel the blood rush to my face. She did me a favor, and now I have to do her one by lying.

"Why didn't you *say* you had one them?" Daddy says. "Save me all that work?"

"Well . . . I'm not sure mine works either," I say lamely. "I'm sure the ones you've fixed are more reliable." I don't know if he believes me, but at least this compliment gives him a chance to drop the subject while we all retain some measure of dignity.

"Well by God, we'll just set all three of the bastards then," he says. "Let all three of 'em blast us out of bed in the middle of the night. I know I won't sleep a wink anyway," He and Rebecca each take a clock to their rooms, and indeed, at 2:00 A.M. there are three nearly simultaneous rings.

Standing in the chilly kitchen, waiting for the instant coffee to cool down, none of us will admit to having slept a wink. My father's face is puffy, his pale blue eyes watery and out of focus. He looks all of his 82 years or more, looks older in a way than Mr. Andrews, and I am suddenly shocked again by his age as if I'm just arriving in his house rather than about to depart it. In the car we all huddle toward the heater and debate whether the temperature is below freezing or just above. We do not pass a single car on the way to the bus station, which is really the Amoco service station, situated on the main highway that divides the town. It looks bleak and deserted beneath the new fluorescent street light that arches over the road in front of it. A large-faced clock with a circle of green neon around it saying "BUS DEPOT" is the only indication that we are in the right place. Rebecca stops beside the bubble-top gas pumps, and she and I gaze first at the clock, then down the road for headlights to appear around the curve. It is 2:45.

"We'll burn up a tank of gas just settin' here," my father complains, which angers me more than I care to admit. This trip has cost me close to $500. "Motor quits we could freeze to death."

"Oh hush up, Robert," Rebecca says. I wish I were in the back seat instead of thigh-to-thigh between them. We sit silent until nearly 3:00.

"You want to write something, write Bible stories," my father declares suddenly. "Write something good Christian people can read and enjoy. People are tired of all this trash. Some good Bible stories'll sell, too, don't think they won't. Get in on the Bible story market and see if you don't make some money."

"I think it's been done," I say dryly. "I think all the Bible stories have been written. But you're right—it's been a good seller." The neon-faced clock inches its way around to 3:15, and I begin to fidget, wondering if the bus might have come by before we got to the station.

"Prob'ly already came," Daddy says. "Or else he's run it up in a ditch somewhere between here and Bardville." Just once, I think, just once in my life, why can't he say something comforting? I feel a headache beginning at the base of my neck.

"Isn't there a phone here?" I ask.

"Inside the station," Rebecca points. "Locked up. Who you gonna call?"

"I could call Memphis and see if it left on time at least," I say feebly.

"Ain't no use to call," my father says. "He's either run it up in a ditch somewhere or he's stopped to get hisself a drink of whiskey. These ignorant bastards don't care nothin' about a schedule down here." Rebecca begins to cry softly, raising a gloved hand to her nose and sniffling. Having lived so long up north, Daddy sometimes refers to people in Overton as rednecks, which always hurts Rebecca's feelings.

"Jesus, I have to get out," I say, more or less through my teeth. "Let me out. I'll wait outside."

"Freeze to death," Daddy says as I start over his lap. "That reminds me 'bout that insurance policy. Can't see to send in the premiums half the time. Hope they ain't done cancelled out on me. You die, you'll get . . . I b'lieve it's $1000."

"Why didn't you give me the policy, dammit?" I snap. "I told you two years ago I'd take care of it." Rebecca continues to sniffle.

"Quarter a week since the day you were born I paid on it. Kept it up faithful all these years. Oughta be enough to bury you at least. I can't see to keep it up no more."

"*Mail* it to me, *mail* it to me. I told you that two years ago. I'll take care of it. Just mail the damn thing to me and quit worrying about it. Let me out." I grab the door handle.

"Thirty-five years at a quarter a week. It adds up. You better not wait two more years to come back down here now. You don't know how long your ol' papa'll be around. But it's a good little policy. If you was even just to get *maimed* I b'lieve it'd pay half."

"Let me *out!*" I open the door and squeeze myself past his knees.

"Freeze yourself to death out there," he says. "Fix yourself up good with a cold."

I slam the door, regretting it instantly, then begin to pace at the edge of the empty highway. Nearly 3:25. The breeze is cutting as I stare intently at the curve in the road, as if sheer concentration might make headlights materialize. When I turn, I spot a phone booth lit up about a quarter mile away, and I start to run, glancing over my shoulder every few yards to check on the bus. Just as I reach the booth and dig into my coat pocket for coins, it looms up around the curve. I see Rebecca jump out of the car to wave it down as Daddy pulls the suitcase from the back seat. My side hurts by the time I make it to the steps of the Greyhound, but I feel like kissing the driver as he tears at my ticket.

I am already settled in the soft, highbacked seat before I realize I've not kissed anyone good-bye. They stand huddled close together just outside the door, which hisses itself emphatically shut. I wave, almost pressing my nose to the glass, and Rebecca lifts a now bare, handkerchief-filled hand. My father, collar turned up against the wind, hitches his pants up underneath his bulky overcoat as if he were about to swagger in from work a little drunk on Friday night. He stares off just slightly to the right of where I am and gives no sign at all that he sees me until Rebecca lifts his hand and primes it into waving. We pull out past them without hesitation. A short ways down the road, I let myself cry a bit in the dark, nearly empty bus, not quite knowing if it's from relief or grief.

The whole trip home feels like slow motion. By the time we finally descend through the smog layer into a hazy Los Angeles mid-afternoon, I feel as if I've been around the world. The disorientation of driving from the airport seems to right itself once I pull into my own parking lot and see the ocean, despite the fact that my building has been transformed from its lovely old blonde brick to a slick sort of stucco that Daddy would probably call "baby turd yeller." The paper is off the windows, and most of the scaffolding is gone. I am even half glad to see one of the regular winos who has been getting on my nerves as I run lately, yelling out "There goes my baby!" from wherever he is to wherever I am for whoever is around to hear.

"There's my darlin'," he says now, approaching with his best super-cool walk. "Where you been, baby? Let me carry that thing for you." Reluctantly, I let him transfer the suitcase from my hand to his.

"Oh . . . back east," I say. Never in my life did I think I would have occasion to refer to Overton, Tennessee, as "back east."

"I thought I miss seein' you these mornin's," he says, as we round the corner onto the boardwalk. "But listen, darlin'. I don' want you runnin' *too* much. I want you to stay fluffy for me now."

"You look fluffy yourself in that coat," I tell him, and he begins to pet the filthy, off-white, thick-furred woman's jacket as if it were an animal.

"Tha's right," he says with a grin. "Tha's right. Jus' call me *Mr. Fluffy*." He sets the suitcase on the porch, backs down the steps and struts off toward the pagoda.

"Well, thanks, Mr. Fluffy," I call after him, and he turns and tips his hat, though he isn't actually wearing one. Before I can get my key in the door, Mr. Andrews opens it for me.

"There's my favorite tenant," he smiles, picking up my bag. I give him an awkward hug. That he would call me his favorite tenant touches me much more deeply than he could possibly imagine: in fact, I feel myself go limp with it and nearly start to cry, which makes me realize what a strain I've been under for the past week.

"You're my favorite manager, too," I say as we both sink down on the sprung-out old sofa. "I'm glad to be home."

"How d'you like the new building?" he asks with a little snort of disgust. "It's a mess if you ask me."

"They've ruined it," I say. "They've taken all the character out of it. All that money just to make the place look cheap."

"I don't know what's gonna happen around here next," he says, sounding more discouraged than I've ever heard him. "I just don't know anymore." He fills me in on Iris, who apparently stayed in her room until yesterday morning when she brought all her grocery sacks down and sat on the porch, refusing to answer any of Trude's questions about what happened to her purse. "We took 'er some soup and set it outside 'er door an' it disappeared, so I guess she ate it. That cousin of hers has called here three times, but Iris never would talk to 'er 'til she threatened to drive out here in person. I guess she wants to put Iris away somewhere so she can quit worryin' about 'er." Mr. Andrews pauses and tugs at his chin. "I can't figure anymore what's gonna happen next."

On my way up I knock on Iris's door. "Just wanted to say hello," I call out when she doesn't answer. "Maybe I'll see you tomorrow. I brought you a souvenir."

"Bye-bye," Iris says.

My little room looks beautiful to me, the way the sunlight enriches the deep rust carpet and the oaken grain of my desk and filing cabinet. I take down the silly fire sign, unpack quickly, and luxuriate in being alone. I put classical music on the radio, have a leisurely bath, pop popcorn for supper, eat it in the comfort of my own bed, and by 8:45, Tennessee time, am very much ready for sleep.

The next day after work, I take Iris the cards I bought her in the Greyhound station in Memphis—a slightly oversized deck of bright red playing cards with a map of "The Volunteer State" on them. When she doesn't answer, I break the cellophane wrapping and begin to slip cards under the door five or six at a time. "Look, Iris," I say. "I brought you these so we can play hearts and take our mind off things. Come on down to the parlor. Clarence said he'd play with us." After a bit I can tell she's picking them up as fast as I'm sailing them in. "Come on now," I say. "We'll be waiting downstairs."

"OK," she finally says. "All right, then. Here I come, ready or not."

Mr. Andrews and I pull the low, scarred-up coffee table over to the couch and speculate whether Iris will really come down—and whether either of us will really remember how to play hearts if she does. In a few minutes she arrives, limping slightly but otherwise looking chipper, even almost dressed up in a shapeless navy blue dress and a rhinestone-covered, loud turquoise sweater that I have never seen her wear before. Only the dingy yellow houseslippers look familiar. She has her hair pulled back in a ponytail, which is flattering despite its lopsidedness. No scarf, no hanky, no prune juice bottle. Only the cards, which she immediately begins to shuffle like a pro, shoves over to me for the cut, and deals. "Excuse me, honey," she says. "You're such a fine person, but these aren't regulation size cards."

Mr. Andrews and I look at each other, and I have to stifle a laugh. "Just a durn minute," he says to Iris. "We don't even remember how it goes."

"Object of the game is not to take any hearts or the queen of spades. Hearts are against you, the queen's thirteen. Unless you take all the hearts plus the queen—then everybody else gets twenty-six against them. You can't lead a heart till one's been played or that's all you have. Start by passing three cards you want to get rid of. Two of clubs opens."

Mr. Andrews and I sit stunned at hearing Iris sound like *The Book of Hoyle*, and she looks at us both as if we are slightly retarded. "Let's play to a hundred," she says then. "Two cents a point, winner take all."

"Shoot," Mr. Andrews says. "You're crazy as a durn loon."

"Wait a minute," I say. "Just wait a minute. Why don't we play a few practice hands first, then maybe play to fifty at two cents a point?"

"Penny a point's steep enough for me," Mr. Andrews declares.

"Oh, Clarence," Iris says with a certain amount of real disappointment in her voice. "Where's your spirit? You used to have spirit, Clarence, you did. You used to."

"Not my spirit I'm worried about," Mr. Andrews says. "It's my money."

In the practice hands, with constant, pointed instruction from Iris, Mr. Andrews and I begin to pick up the rhythm of the game, and then we start to play for real. He plays intelligently, but slowly, and Iris tends to get impatient with him, drumming her fingers on the table when he ruminates too long over what to lay down. I find myself mesmerized by Iris's incredible transformation into card shark, fail to attend enough to my own game, and end up losing the first two hands. She is quiet and quick, sharp and lucid, strategic enough to minimize the elements of luck and risk, which actually figure quite heavily in hearts. I go up and fix us a couple of double-shot highballs, which Mr. Andrews declines. "Not stupid enough to get drunk and gamble with two women," he says.

By the time we're on our second drink, I'm having myself a grand time—can't remember, in fact, just when I have had a better time, even though I'm losing. People come in and out of the parlor, several of them new tenants I've never seen before, and stare at us. I suppose we do make an odd sort of threesome. Passers-by on the boardwalk mosey up to the window to read the "Apartments for Rent" sign that lists vacancies with the new outrageous rents.

"The roaches are free," I finally call out to a rather chicly overdressed young man, who scampers off, and Iris gets herself into a laughing fit that holds up the game for several minutes. "The roaches are free, the roaches are free," she keeps repeating hysterically, and Mr. Andrews and I laugh with her, though he tries to keep his inside, won't open his mouth and let it out the way we are.

The pay phone by the mailboxes rings three, four, five times. "If it's my cousin Rose," Iris says to no one in particular, "tell her I've gone shopping. I might've gone shopping. Or on a vacation. Tell her I went on a vacation. No, tell her I've gone to the doctor. No, no. Tell her I might be out shopping."

"You answer it," Mr. Andrews says to me. "I'm sick of talkin' to 'er."

"Tell her I died, honey," Iris says, tossing her head back with a laugh as I start to the phone. "Make her happy for once."

It is indeed cousin Rose, who speaks a little too loudly and abrasively for her undoubtedly kind intent to squeeze its way through the telephone wires. I feel foolish saying Iris is out shopping, but I say it, and Rose seems grateful that "at least she's out of her room."

"OK. OK. OK," I say. "OK. OK. I'll tell her. Yes. Yes. OK." I feel sober and embarrassed as I come back to the game, offended that Rose would speak to me, a perfect stranger, as if Iris's privacy didn't count at all. Iris looks at me straight on.

"She says to tell you everything's set up for you to go to Monica

Manor," I say. "Whenever you decide, all you have to do is give her a call and she'll bring the papers out for you to sign and help you pack up and move over there. She says for you to call her tonight—when you get back from shopping."

"It's your turn," Iris says, studying her hand. "Clarence led the ten of clubs."

We play in silence for awhile. Iris already has several hearts, and then she takes the queen of spades. She leads a diamond, which I've been out of all along, and I discard the ace of hearts one second before I realize she is trying to take all the points, risking everything in order to win big. I try to retract the card, but Iris gently places her moist, gnarled hand over mine.

"Excuse me, honey," she says sweetly. "But once you put it down, it's played." She has the lead and keeps it, can hardly contain her glee. I feign exasperation, though I'm feeling only amazement and admiration.

"Stop her!" I shout at Mr. Andrews. "Can't you see she's about to slaughter us both? Damn!"

"Nothin' I can do about it," he says, and he is right—the rest of the game is fated. Iris tries to keep her face serious, though her mouth starts to jump around some as she slams us with twenty-six points apiece, bringing the score to sixty-six for me, fifty-three for Mr. Andrews, nineteen for herself.

"All I have is a dollar bill," I say, sliding it across the table to her as Mr. Andrews counts out fifty-three cents from his coin purse.

"Don't worry, honey," Iris says soothingly. "I got change." She bends over, takes off her houseslipper, dumps what looks like a hundred pennies on the table, and carefully, cheerfully counts out thirty-four of them for me.

"Dumb like a durn fox," Mr. Andrews says as she scoops his change and my bill and her remaining pennies into the slipper and eases it back onto her heavily veined foot. "No wonder she came limpin' in here." We head up the stairs together, Iris in the lead.

"I'm not going," she says, more to herself than to us. "I don't care. I'm not. Iris isn't going anywhere."

Chapter Six

Muralist

The painter is back at his wall this week. I keep curious track of his work schedule, since from my north window I cannot see the north side of the one-story building next door. I know he is working when I see the top rung of his ladder just above the edge of the roof or when he steps back across Westward Avenue, brush in hand, to figure something out, or, of course, when he paints close to the top of the mural so that he himself rises head and shoulders above the wall, holding a brush in one hand and a can of paint in the other, arm looped through the ladder for security. His posture at these times looks terribly awkward and uncomfortable and precarious, but his face registers only a half-crazed blend of intense concentration and bliss. This is a man who loves his work, and when he is not actually painting, he often appears in the Napoleon doorway several times a day—either to admire what he has done so far or to envision what is yet to come.

He likes to catch it in all kinds of light and from every possible angle. I have seen him staring at it from way out in the sand at sunset and from the pagoda early in the morning. Sometimes he will sneak up on it from the alley and peer, smiling, around the back corner of the restaurant, and once during a real downpour, he sat himself down in the doorway of the apartment building across the street and watched for a good long time as—I suppose—the already bold, deep primary colors of his masterpiece darkened with the rain. I nearly ran into him as I hurried home along the sidewalk just past dusk one night, startling us both, startling me into speaking, in fact, which I would not ordinarily have done.

"I live up there," I told him, pointing. "I like to watch you work."

"Oh," he said, shifting uncomfortably, jamming his hands into the pockets of his spattered jeans.

"There's something inspiring about it," I said, which sounded corny as soon as it was out of my mouth.

"Oh," he said, starting to move away. If he wasn't embarrassed by what I said, he was probably embarrassed at being discovered looking at the mural in the dark (or at least with only a bit of light from the street lamp on the boardwalk and whatever was shining from the apartment windows above us). We said a clumsy good-night and moved off in different directions, and I felt sorry to have intruded and sorry that I spoke, but I meant what I said. I do find something inspiring in this man's willingness to pit himself against a huge, blank wall, armed only with a paintbrush hardly bigger than a pencil. He is a small man, anyway, and standing beside the mural, which must be at least 15 x 40 feet, he looks like a genuine dwarf.

So far the painting itself, crowded and crude and dense in color and design, does not inspire me, but the painter does. He has been working off and on ever since I moved in here, even having to repaint the wall and start over once when the local Chicano gang destroyed his original outline with spray-paint graffiti. I could tell him about some other abuses—the dogs I've seen pissing along the mural's lower edge, or the child who habitually bounces his black rubber ball against the crowd of large, dark faces situated closest to the boardwalk. Once I even saw Juanita, the Mexican-Indian who is the most pitiful of the women winos, lean against the mural to vomit, then turn around and slide down into her own mess. For her, as for the dogs, a wall is a wall and nothing more.

"That mural is a piece of shit," I heard one young man loudly inform another as they walked up Westward. "The *technique* is for shit, the *concept* is for shit, and the *effect* is for shit." I suppose he could be right—there is something off-putting about the painting so far, something that makes looking at it too difficult to sustain long enough to see what is there. But what inspires me is the way the muralist himself looks at it, with so much apparent joy and appreciation and respect. I can read my own writing, as Virginia Woolf put it, only with a kind of guilty intensity, and an 8½ x 11-inch sheet of paper must hold more terror for me than great walls hold for the muralist. I am inspired, I suppose, by his willingness to risk not merely private failure, but public failure, and I miss him when he lays off for a few weeks, sometimes even months, whether it is from lack of energy, lack of concentration, or simple lack of money and materials, which might force him to ignore his work and take a job.

Until a few days ago, I had not seen him around since a skater rammed into his shopping cart full of paints, across which his ladder was balanced, tipping over the whole shebang and scattering tubes and cans and brushes among the Friday afternoon crowd of feet on the boardwalk. You can still see a deep red stain in the asphalt where one quart can hit and splashed and soaked in before the artist could compose himself and cover it with cloths, the young woman standing sheepish beside him in her chic new skating togs, shrugging her shoulders, apologizing and telling him, I imagine, that she just hadn't quite learned to stop herself yet (which is the excuse put forth by every skater who has collided with me so far, as if negligence made all forgivable).

As the painter began to collect everything, a couple of the regulars from the pagoda retrieved the shopping cart, then grabbed Glory, one of the black street women who can outdrink, outcuss and out-signify most of the men, and dumped her into it seat first, proceeding on a Keystone Cop caper through the crowd with Glory waving her bottle of wine and yelling at the top of her lungs, "Go to yo' ROOOOOM! Go to yo' ROOOOOM! All you mothafuckin' tourists, go to yo' ROOOOOOM!" I found the scene hilarious and full of comedic justice, but the painter didn't laugh. He leaned patiently against the mural with his arms folded, paraphernalia in a pile on the sidewalk, waiting for them to bring back his cart, and when they did, he resisted letting them help him load it up. He resituated the ladder and, with angry shoulders, pushed off quickly through the circle of onlookers.

This week, sitting in a window booth at the Napoleon, I was surprised to see him sketch the shopping cart into the mural, which made me realize how he has been working on the project, sketching only a small portion at a time rather than having the whole thing laid out (as he did before vandalism forced him to start over). He has painted the far right and far left sides of the wall, but the center and various spots at the top and bottom remain empty—and free of any discernible plan. I watched him sketch the shopping cart with charcoal or pencil, the image much cleaner and more graphic than the rest of the painting, but by this morning, after he had worked on it for a couple of days with his bold and dense brush strokes, the clarity of the image was lost. There is a *something* there, with splashes of color bursting forth from it, the most predominant being a very bloody red which extends itself out into the spaciousness at the center of the wall. I don't know what I would make of it all if I didn't think I already knew what it was. I feel as if I know a secret now, whether I do or not. No doubt his other images would mean more to me if I knew what lay behind them. No wonder he proceeds so gradually on this painting if he has to try to capture the fluid life around him rather than some idea fixed in his head.

Very often people strolling on the boardwalk will stop in little clusters, gaze at the mural for a moment, then move on. Others stop, gaze at the mural for a moment, and snap a picture of it. And even more commonly, a group of people will stop, gaze at the mural for a moment, and then pose themselves in front of it for a photograph, figuring the colorful backdrop will make a suitable souvenir. It puzzles me why so very few people are willing to spend any time at all looking at the mural itself, while so many want to capture it on film. "And this is one of the murals we saw in Venice," I can hear them telling the folks back home, and I can see the snapshots being dismissed as quickly as the experience—or lack of it—that lies behind them.

Sitting on my bed one morning, elbows and coffee on the windowsill, I watch a man direct the two women he is with to cross the street and pose before the mural. He motions with one hand to get them positioned as he focuses the camera, then takes two or three shots before he catches sight of me up above the scene. I see him see me and adjust his lens for the longer view. I am tempted to get up and back away from the window, have to suppress an impulse to stick my finger up my nose or cross my eyes, but instead I pick up my cup, sit perfectly still and stare, somewhat disdainfully I think, right at the camera. He snaps quickly and the three of them disappear around the corner, and I sit here feeling strangely violated, even though I cooperated fully in the violation. I wonder what the picture will show? I wonder what the man wanted to capture or will think he has captured? Contemplative Woman with Morning Coffee? Contemporary Venice Resident? Or did some of the underside show— Contemptuous Photographic Subject?

There is an old man named Luke that I think of as the "professional" derelict of Venice. You can see him most days sprawled out on the boardwalk with his pint of Gallo Ruby Port and his collection of old magazines and bits of junk spread out around him. "You may have anything you see here at your own price," he politely rasps at passers-by from his reclining position. "Yes, the old man works everyday. The old man is not a bum. Old Luke earns his way in the world, thank you very much, and I hope you all have a beautiful, beautiful day this morning." It is his wrinkled magazines, which he salvages from trash bins, and his cleverness that distinguish him from the other winos, who try to intimidate or shame people into forking over spare change. Luke, with his open sores, grizzled beard and red-flushed, careworn face, never appears to ask for anything but manages to keep a fairly steady flow of coins coming his way. He even got to me once as, walking past, I let my eyes linger a couple of seconds too long on some of his wares.

"Hello my dear young lady," he said, slurring each word carefully. "You may have any magazine at your own price." He paused. "Or . . . if you're a little short today, just take what you want here and enjoy it. I'm going to be on the Carson show next week, so it's not as if I really need the money myself." He took a long swig of his wine, and I threw 50¢ into his crumpled, filthy white tennis hat.

One has to respect Luke as a survival artist who provides for himself as best he can in the process of self-destruction. Every few weeks he will drink himself comatose or get beaten up or start to choke on his own vomit, and the paramedics will appear, either to treat him on the spot or take him away, though never for more than a few days. He always returns with fanfare. "Yep! The old man is back!" he will shout again and again, and the neighborhood people greet him with tolerance, even warmth.

"Now let me see if I can guess where you people are from," he calls out to certain strolling or gawking passers-by, and most cannot resist stopping to hear what he will say about them. "Now you, sir, I would take to be from the fair city of Helena, Montana. Am I correct or am I correct?"

"North Hollywood," the man says, aiming his camera first at Luke's magazines, then at Luke himself.

"That was going to be my next guess, young man. You didn't give me a chance. Yes, you may photograph me for a very modest fee. I'm the most photographed man on Venice Beach, you know."

There are the stereotypical tourists with their instamatics who want to record mainly themselves at different locations along the beach, and then there are the hundreds of amateur and professional photographers, loaded down with expensive equipment, who turn to the "local color" of Venice in pursuit of art. Among these latter I suspect that Luke's claim of fame contains more truth than exaggeration. You can buy a 5×7 or an 8×10 or an 11×14 color print of him from at least two of the photographer's booths on the boardwalk any weekend for eight or fifteen or twenty dollars. Everyone who takes his picture, I suppose, thinks it's an original idea, and perhaps it is for all of them—he has such a face, such a face that allows the camera to capture in one second a lifetime of abuse and determination (or perhaps determined abuse).

Luke has a female counterpart named DeeDee who is probably the most photographed woman on the beach. I can never get over her name, which always makes me think of a suburban teenager, sitting on a pink canopied bed, talking on a white Princess phone. But DeeDee is probably about Luke's age, somewhere in the fifties, difficult to gauge—both no doubt younger than they look. Tragedy and comedy meet in DeeDee's wrinkled, toothless face, which makes her peculiarly "photographic." Unsmiling, she looks battered and burdened, full of anguish and yearning. But when she grins, baring her whole top gum, she looks just plain goofy, absurd enough to undercut, parody or redeem whatever effect her face was having before the smile. You cannot look at that face without wondering what her story is.

On a jammed-up Saturday afternoon I notice that there is a bigger crowd than usual around a couple of the regular street singers who are performing their fast version of "Sittin' on the Dock of the Bay." As I make my way into the semi-circle of clapping audience, I see that the real center of attention is not the musicians but DeeDee and Luke, who are dancing up a storm of a jig and singing along off-key and about two beats behind. DeeDee grins as Luke grabs her arm to twirl her, but he makes one misstep, and they both sink down in slow motion, laughing, ending up stretched out on the asphalt side-by-side clapping their way through the rest of the number. The crowd loves them and applauds for them as much as for the singers. This is the kind of scene people come to Venice for, I think, more than they come to be near the ocean. People come here to people-watch, knowing they are liable to see almost anything—from skinny-dippers to someone freaking out on PCP. The musicians take a break, and Luke and DeeDee sit up as he hands her his bottle of wine. "Let's get naked, DeeDee," he tells her, "and run all these people away from here." Everyone laughs, DeeDee most of all.

"Hey, old man," a guy suddenly calls out to Luke. His tone has a tinge of nastiness. "Hey, old man. When did you eat last?" Luke's face transforms itself from happy drunkenness to sheer anger.

"A half-hour ago," he spits out. "When did *you* eat last?" The crowd tenses up, backs away a little bit as the smug young man tosses a quarter at Luke and says, "Here old man, go get yourself a Twinkie or something." Luke picks the quarter up, not without some difficulty, and pitches it into the musicians' guitar case, where it no sooner lands than the man tosses another coin, this time hitting Luke on the forehead. With this, Luke reaches into his back pants pocket and pulls out a razor-like knife.

"Would you like to see what I shave with mornings?" he asks. "You little prick. It'll cut a lot of other stuff, too—like your throat if you keep hassling me." The crowd laughs uneasily, which doesn't cut the tension. I suppose the idea of Luke staggering over to try to carry out his threat is funny, but the anger and intent behind his words are deadly serious, and the young man eases himself back to the outer edge of the circle and disappears as the musicians launch into another song. More and more I move through the weekend crowds with a sense of dread because of the constant potential for violence. Someone snaps a picture of Luke sitting with his bottle in one hand and his razor, still open, in the other.

DeeDee gets up to dance again, this time alone, moving with a slower, steady rhythm, eyes closed, seemingly oblivious to the crowd. She is wearing navy blue and pale yellow plaid wool slacks with a navy blue turtleneck, and though the outfit looks like castoffs from someone's weekend ski wardrobe of several years ago, it snugly fits her petite, emaciated body and does her proud as she sways to the music.

> If I could read your mind, love,
> What a tale your thoughts could tell,
> Just like a paperback novel,
> The kind the drugstores sell.

There is something terribly poignant in her drunken, effortless motion—some potential for beauty that has been destroyed in her remains in the way she holds herself as she dances, transcending the stringy, thin brown hair, the sunken mouth, the blackened, scarred-up bare feet, and the reek of alcohol. It is as if, while she is dancing this way, she almost loves herself a little bit. "The feeling's gone, and I just can't get it back." DeeDee stops suddenly, just before the end of the song, and plops herself down on the grass, then curls up like a fetus, as if to go to sleep. But as the musicians make their pitch for money, she sits up again, scoots on her seat outside the circle of onlookers, pushes herself into a squatting position and, with the expression of a six-month-old infant, quite obviously releases her bowels into the plaid wool pants. I can feel my stomach turn over, and several people in the crowd groan and look away, but the photographer who was snapping Luke before pushes through to position himself up close to DeeDee, gets on his knees, and takes shots from all angles.

"You son of a bitch," she says, waving him away with one wild gesture of her arm, and I think yes, you son of a bitch, why didn't you catch her dancing? But maybe he did, of course, and this is one more thing he needs to capture. Cast a cold, cold eye. Use a machine to help you do it. I head home feeling sick as DeeDee rises carefully, smelling foul, seat darkening with brownish-yellow, and walks off with legs awkwardly parted so as not to smear herself any worse than she already has.

Within a couple of months one of the tiny art galleries around the corner carries an exhibition of Venice photographs by local artists— "Venice Looking at Itself." There are action shots of skaters, miscellaneous shots of crowds and sunsets, detailed shots of pagodas and old buildings and the boardwalk deserted in the rain. And then, back in one corner, hangs an 11 x 14 black-and-white of DeeDee squatting. It is a rich, brilliantly executed photograph—he captured the posture and the infantile expression perfectly, so that you can guess what she must be doing, though there is no visible sign of her mess. Seeing her frozen this way eliminates the I-can't-believe-this-is-happening feeling I had in the face of the actual scene. The brutality of form and texture and light here leaves no room for compassionate or self-protective denial. The picture leaves out so much and yet seems to contain everything. All the Venice stories I have wanted to write are beginning to weigh heavy in my gut. I envy the photographer his instant, icy art that requires no self revelation, figure I could write better stories if I could cast a colder eye myself, sit off to the side somewhere indifferent, paring my fingernails, as Joyce put it, while the characters lead their lives on the page. I keep having trouble with what to leave in and what to leave out, what to make up and what simply to record. How to spin a tale about DeeDee that would somehow go beyond the reality of her? The photograph tells one kind of story but not the whole story, so that to the extent it lies, it lies by omission rather than commission.

"To tell a story," my mother's expression for lying, one of the worst things a person could do. "You're not telling me a *story*, are you?" she would ask with eyebrows raised when as a child I would try to fib about this, that or the other. "No ma'am," I would answer, a fib in itself, of course, which really meant, "Yes, but I'll try not to do it again." To this day I blush and stammer around when I have occasion to lie, however trivial it is, however much to my advantage.

"Papa never whipped me but once, and that 'as for tellin' him a story," Aunt Lucinda has told me again and again. "I wasn't but eight or nine years old, and he sent me over to the field. I don't know how come him to send me by myself to replant that corn, but he did, over at that patch of new ground by John's Branch Bottom. He give me a little bucket with that corn in it, and he said, 'Now put two grains in a hill.' Well, I got over there, and I looked around, you know, and it looked like an awful big job. And I decided, well, I could just pretend I planted it. So I just dug a hole right at the end of a row—didn't even have sense enough to go out in the weeds and throw it away. So I just dug a hole right there, you know, and poured that corn out and covered it up. Then I went on back to the house, and Papa said, 'Did you plant all that corn already?' I said, 'Yessir, ever' bit of it, two grains in a place.' Well, the time passed on by and come one day I takened Papa a drink of water out in the field, and there he was down, you know—he'd stopped plowin' and was down lookin' at that green spot all around where I done my plantin'. I seen that, and I knowed right straight that ever' grain of that corn had sprouted twice. And he said, 'You told me a *story*, didn't you?' I said, 'Yessir.' And there was some little switches agrowin' there out of a stump, so he broke off one of 'em and he said, 'Now, Lucindy, I'm not whippin' you because you didn't plant the corn right.' He says, 'I guess I shouldn't have sent you over here to do it. But you shouldn't have told me a story, either, and I'm gonna whip you for tellin' the story.' Well, he whipped me all right. And I never did tell him another one, either."

How to create some fiction that nature won't belie? All the stories I've started about Danny and had to abandon because he became too stereotyped or maudlin or heroic. How to give the right form to the lie, so that it not only does not seem false but actually reveals the truth and something beyond? This must be what drives me to write and what keeps me from writing, this business of trying to lie perfectly in order to tell the truth.

Early one morning over huevos rancheros at the Napoleon, I see the painter arrive with only his ladder and a long-handled roller brush sunk into a slanted tray of paint. He sketches a crooked line of demarcation from the top to the bottom of the mural and proceeds to paint over everything to the left of it, covering a whole section of palm trees and waves and miscellaneous shapes of color, quickly restoring all the space east of the shopping cart to its original pale yellow blank wall of stucco. He steps back to examine what he has done, runs one hand through his thick black hair, crosses his arms, fingers his mustache for a bit, then disappears, leaving his equipment where it lies on the spattered sidewalk. Time for visions and revisions. I wonder if it was sheer dissatisfaction with the completed images or some urgency behind an image yet to come that pushed him to erase weeks of work in these few minutes.

I stare once again at the large, wide, dark, nearly identical faces which comprise the far western, upper portion of the mural, rendered in an almost child-like fashion which draws the eye to them as a resting place from the dense complexity of the rest of the work. Rising beside them is a thick, intricate knot of black, which commands its own kind of attention and throws that corner of the mural off-balance somehow, from where I am sitting. I try to concentrate on the painting for a longer time than I have been able to in the past but once again find this difficult, find that I need to look away often, that I keep losing interest, even though I don't want to. Then, as I get up to pay my check, I catch out of the corner of my eye that the black knot is a knot of *words* curling around on itself, printed in a hard-to-read, fancy sort of Biblical script.

Outside I lean against the corner of the Napoleon to cipher out the message, which begins to seem impossible until I realize that the words start at the center of the knot and curl outward in a circle: "Matthew and Marcus and Luke and Johnny, Matthew and Marcus and Luke and Johnny." In a flash the whole top right side of the mural becomes clear to me—these are the names of four of the regular winos. Matthew is the one I always call Preacher Man, and Marcus is the small black man with the withered leg who uses his crutch as a weapon when anyone gives him a hard time. Johnny is Mr. Fluffy and, now that I know that, I can see a suggestion of his furry coat at the shoulders below one of the faces, just as I can see that the grayness into which the chin of one head flows is probably meant to represent Luke's beard. I can make it out now—the dark brown crutch above one of the heads extending upward into a sagging, wilted sort of brown-black cross, which also resembles—or doubles for—the architecture of the pagoda roof. Several lumps of tan must represent loaves of bread, since I see that juxtaposed with each face is a brown paper bag with the top of, not a bottle exposed, but an intricately wrought, fancy silver goblet. I feel the thrill of discovery, though at the same time I am reminded of those puzzle pictures that ask "How many animals can you find?" and then list them, upside down, at the bottom of the page.

Upstairs a little later in the morning I hear a commotion at the pagoda. Mostly I don't rush to the window anymore for commotions at the pagoda, but these are female voices I hear, furious female voices, rising shrill and hostile. I look down just in time to see Glory slap the face of a skinny, butch-haired blonde who then pushes her backward with a forceful shove.

"You better not show your face back down here," Glory yells, taking off her glasses and handing them to Louis.

"I'll come back any goddamn time I want to," the white woman says. "You don't own the planet. I am a child of the universe, so I have more right to be here than you do. And if you hit me again I'll have you arrested for assault."

"Bitch," Glory says. "I'm not jus' gon' hit you, I'm gon' kick yo' teeth in. Who'."

"I ain't no whore."

"Well, you a bitch to me."

"You're damn right I'm a bitch," the blonde says, moving right up into Glory's face. "I *have* to be 'cause cunts like you live here." Glory moves quick—in what seems like one smooth motion she slaps the blonde's ear and tears her skimpy white T-shirt nearly all the way off one shoulder. They trade slaps then, and I can't tell from this far away how hard they are hitting each other. Mostly it looks as if they don't know how to put the force of their weight behind the blows, and this makes the fight seem more playful than it really is. The regulars sit watching, amused as the women try to pull at each other's hair, though the blonde has very little to pull. A fight between two men would not have been allowed to continue this long. Just bitches fighting, doesn't count, though I can see blood now on the blonde's shirt. When Glory grabs at it again and tears it a little further, the blonde pushes her down hard, and while Glory is recovering, the blonde, with defiance and an air of triumph, rips her own shirt all the rest of the way off and tosses it in Glory's face.

The crowd around them balloons now that it is no longer merely a scene of violence but of violence and sex (even though the woman is so small-breasted that she almost looks male from where I sit). "More, more," somebody calls out.

Glory draws back, as if she hadn't figured on having to deal with this much spunk. She makes the mistake of turning her back to her opponent, and the blonde grabs her round the neck and wrestles her to the ground, pins her, sits astride her like a lover and begins to bang the back of her head hard against the concrete. Glory lets out a series of piercing yelps, and only then does Louis jump up and pull the blonde off, restraining her while a couple of the other regulars help Glory to her feet and guide her to a bench, using the discarded shirt to soak up blood around her nose and mouth. There is hooting and applause, and a young woman who apparently knows the blonde throws her a beach towel, which she puts around her neck in the manner of an athlete rather than using it to cover herself up.

"I guess you won't mess with me again, bitch," she says as she starts up Westward. "See! I'm a child of the universe!"

"Fifty-cent who'," Louis calls after her. "Fifty-cent white bitch who'." The crowd disperses, and someone brings Glory a bottle as she lies stretched out with the bloody shirt over her face.

I turn away upset, disgusted, angry. These scenes are beginning to have an air of unreality for me—they seem like a movie, yet almost less real than a movie in a way. Senseless violence, craziness, ugliness. It wears on me sometimes. There have been three reported rapes in apartments on Westward in the past few months, not to mention the scores of robberies and at least two murders in the neighborhood at large. I run, don't walk, from my car to the building now when I come in after dark. Some weirdo banging on my door at 2:00 in the morning—don't I have any coke, man? Somebody gave him the wrong room number, not surprising since we have a dealer on every floor these days. Shivering with fright at being woken up that way I direct him, through the closed door, to Ron the manager, who is supposed to watch over the building. Dear Ron, the manager, who sold Jake down on third the magic mushrooms laced with acid that sent his fist flying through his back window, squirting blood all over the fire escape steps, blood that is still there weeks later, blood that I am always tempted to clean up myself but haven't yet, trying instead to overlook it, step around it, forget it. Venice of America, Where the Debris Meets the Sea. There is truth in the joke. So many lost and damaged souls. I have to be a little crazy myself to live here. I resent having my morning's concentration, my best writing time, shattered by a stupid, meaningless, nasty fight between two already battered women. I can't even feel sorry for Glory.

I decide to take a blanket and go out for some sun, not really to sunbathe, I guess, since I'm going fully clothed, but just to take in some light and air and get out of this room, where all the stories I'm not writing seem to be using up a lot of the oxygen. Luke has his magazines spread out now across from the Napoleon, and as a young Japanese couple move away from looking at the mural, he says, "Hey now, if you kids can tell me what that's all about, I'd certainly appreciate it, because I've been studying it and studying it, and I can't figure out *what* the artist is trying to say." The man and woman look at each other and giggle, and I can't tell if it's just because Luke is talking to them or because they couldn't figure the painting out either. "Also," he yells after them, "I'd like to ask for your support because, as you may know, ol' Luke has decided to run for the city council. All you need to join the campaign is a social security card and twenty-two dollars." They have passed him and aren't looking back. "And eleven cents," he adds, no longer to anyone in particular. "Twenty-two dollars and eleven cents. Or . . . if you don't have the twenty-two dollars today, you can just give me the eleven cents and we'll call it even. I'm going to clean up Venice, by God. I'm going to get rid of all the bums *and* the murderers *and* the tourists." He toasts himself with his brown bag.

I consider telling Luke that he is in the mural, just to see how he will react—he'd probably get a kick out of it. But if the painter wants him to know, he should have the pleasure of telling Luke himself, and if he doesn't want him to know—unless Luke can see it for himself—then I have no business telling either.

I head for the grassy area in front of the sidewalk cafe and search for a stretch of ground that is free of dog piles and large enough for my blanket, end up being able to unfold it only half way. I marvel at the barefoot young men throwing frisbees—how do they avoid the piles as they run? Almost as soon as I get settled, using my purse for a pillow, Suzanne, the most disturbed of the younger street women addicts, starts right toward me with her disjointed, out-of-rhythm walk, talking loud and angry to someone only she can see or hear. "Get the fuck out of here. I don't want to hear that shit. Shut the door right now. Where are my papers? *Where are my papers?*"

She is terribly disheveled as always, her thin red hair matted against her head, pale green eyes looking fiercely vacant. At first I think she is going to walk right onto my blanket, but just as I get arched to scoot out of her path, she makes a sharp right turn, proceeds for a bit, then turns again, proceeds, turns again, making a circle, more or less, in front of me. One leg of her jeans is rolled up above the knee. She takes her Levi jacket off and puts it over one shoulder, then starts to pull the jeans up some and discovers, apparently to her surprise, that she has a pair of shorts on underneath, so she tries to balance herself and get the jeans off. "You leave us alone. Get the fuck out of here. We can do it outselves. Take your clammy hands off." While she is managing this, the jacket falls to the ground. "*Now* what are we gonna do?" she says, glaring at the coat as if picking it up were an insurmountable task. "*Now* what the fuck are we gonna do?" It looks as if she may puzzle over this for awhile, so I gather up my things and find another spot, this time a little farther back from the boardwalk. People all around are laughing and talking and singing and eating and drinking and rubbing oil on each other. You can see the Santa Monica Mountains and Santa Monica pier, Venice pier and the Marina, even Catalina if you concentrate. It's what they call a perfect day at the beach. I seem to be the only one who can't ignore Suzanne, shrug her off with a laugh, or take her in stride.

Two of the frisbee throwers stop and spread a blanket out near mine. Both are good-looking, well built, shirtless. One of them, the one with curly blonde hair and the best tan around, asks me in a well-mannered tone what time it is and gives me a winning smile when I tell him, as if "2:30" were just what he wanted to hear and as if I had said it just right for him. This is the warmest thing that has happened to me all day, and it has a calming effect. I lie on my stomach, close my eyes, and settle into a kind of invisible cocoon in which I'm aware of all the sounds around me but don't really allow them to penetrate—at least not until I hear the blonde guy's voice again, sounding angry and threatening this time: "I'm gonna fuck her *ass*, man." My buttocks tighten automatically, before I can even look up to make sure he doesn't mean me. Surely, of course, he doesn't mean me? He stands facing the boardwalk with his hands in his back pockets, and it is "Babs" he has spotted just past the cafe— "Babsy" formerly Bobby, female formerly male.

Of all the bizarre characters that abound in Venice, none has quite the powerful effect of Babs. As she glides along the boardwalk, the dense sea of people almost literally parts for her, with those in the know informing their friends in not so muffled whispers: "Hey, catch this one . . . used to be a man . . . not that bad looking . . . silicone, I guess . . . check out that suit." She is wearing, as she often does, a rather extremely daring one-piece black swimsuit with a deep-plunging neckline, a diamond cut out at the center which exposes her navel, and leg openings that are cut to a sharp point high on either hip, lengthening her already long, slender legs and accentuating her crotch, making it impossible not to wonder what surgical mystery lies beneath the cloth. Usually Babs has a steady entourage of male friends swarming around her, but today she is alone, moving more confidently than I can ever hope to in a pair of red, opentoed, four-inch heels, carrying an oversized red leather bag to match, and wearing bright red sunglasses with pink tinted lenses. Her bleached blonde hair, parted on the side and turned under just a bit, bounces lightly against her shoulders as she walks with a studied sort of gracefulness. It is the way she holds and moves her elbows, as much as anything, that suggests femininity (or a caricature of it). Babs exudes a fascinating sort of perverse charisma that renders her attractive and repulsive at the same time, and I can't help staring at her, just like everybody else.

The curly-haired young man next to me lopes over to her and exchanges some words, sharing her spotlight, then takes her hand and guides her back to his blanket and his dark-eyed, hairy-chested friend. I close my eyes again and turn my head away as I hear them arranging to meet at Babsy's place at four o'clock. She speaks with a kind of coy hostility in an effeminate, not feminine, voice. "So how do you guys like it? How about a *sandwich*, one in each hole? *Whatever*. But do you guys care if Sean watches? He likes to watch, you know, and I told him he could sometime this weekend if he wanted to. I mean, if you guys don't mind. How much meat do you two have, anyway?"

"More than enough for a half-assed pussy like yours," the dark one says, laughing a mean-edged laugh.

"Listen," the other one says irritably. "I want to fuck ass, and I don't give a shit who watches or who sucks what." I feel my ears turn red with a burning sensation I can't remember having since the sixth grade when Steven Spain tricked me into looking up the word *teat* while he was watching from behind the librarian's closet door.

"Calm down, honey," Babs clucks sarcastically. "Don't get a hernia over it. Everything'll be fine. You know Babsy won't let you down. Ta-ta til 4:00."

I gather up my things again, not wanting to lie that close to the two frisbee players anymore. I have never heard such a blatantly sex-filled conversation that was at the same time so blatantly hateful and unerotic. What is it that these people loathe—themselves, each other, women, men, sex itself, what? Somewhere along the line something I don't understand has gotten twisted. I can understand the lust. I can understand the homosexuality. I can even understand something about the transsexual journey. But I cannot understand the desire for brutality over tenderness, and I cannot fathom the depths of anger and contempt and disrespect I felt in that conversation. My head is buzzing with it—the cock as weapon, ejaculation as a means of releasing hatred instead of love with Babs, *with Babs*, as the receptacle. Such a story to be written here. What can it be like to live a pornographic life?

I decide to walk for awhile and "windowshop" some of the craft and clothing booths that have become more numerous in the past few months. Right in front of the first one I come to is a hot dog cart with a huge red-and-white banner waving in the breeze that says, "Hot Dog Louie Does It In The Buns With a Weenie." I have to smile in spite of myself, though I can't really view it as harmlessly cute in the way I might have an hour ago.

Inside the tent I look at the Indian cotton print dresses and the coarse white, machine-embroidered blouses. There is a soft, filmy, sexy black pants outfit that I am tempted to try on. Twenty dollars, a very reasonable buy. But I'm not really in the mood, and besides, who would I wear it for? As I move on down the rack, another woman starts at the other end, and then Babs comes in, pulls out the black garment, and begins exclaiming over it immediately.

"Aren't these great clothes for the price?" the woman says to her.

"Oh, you *betcha*," Babs says, holding the pants suit up to herself on the hanger. "Don't you just *love* this? If I had the money, I'd buy it in a *minute*."

"Don't think I don't know what you mean" the other woman says.

"I've just *got* to try it on no matter *what*." Babsy's tone is pure girl-talk, though I've never known women who talked that way.

Jesus. It will probably look better on her, anyway. I am suddenly exhausted. What a day. I go straight home and collapse on the bed. Such an exhausting day, and I haven't accomplished a thing—I notice that in my absence nobody has completed the page I left in my typewriter. When four o'clock comes around, I find myself wondering just what's going on. I am relieved and grateful when Karen calls to see if I want to go to a movie.

"Yes," I say. "Definitely. A comedy. We have to find a light comedy that has next to no significance whatsoever." She offers to pick me up, but I decline, knowing how uneasy she feels coming into Venice at night.

We end up lingering over dinner with a second bottle of wine, deciding to skip the movie, and I manage to turn my day itself into comedy, which thoroughly entertains Karen and makes me feel altogether improved. There is something funny at the heart of most stories, and it's easy for me to catch this in the telling—an imitative accent or gesture, a turn of phrase, a shift in tone, the right embellishments. By the time we get to Irish coffee, Karen and I both find it utterly hilarious that Babs and I have the same taste in clothes.

"You've got to write some of these stories down," Karen tells me.

"It wouldn't turn out funny on the page," I say, remembering then that I haven't yet told her about Wendy, the new woman next door, one of Ron's friends and customers who is also a "writer," though so far I've been unable to get past the first two sentences of any of the single-spaced cosmic prose she keeps taping along our corridor walls. One evening a couple of weeks ago, Wendy knocked at my door, calling out "Hello, hello in there" in a singsong voice. I took a quick peek, recognized her face, then opened the door to find her standing there with nothing on except for a pair of low-slung, lacy black bikini underpants.

"Hi, I'm your new neighbor," she said, extra mellow, but otherwise matter-of-fact. "I was wondering if I could borrow some safety pins."

"Sure," I said, shocked into the same casual tone. If she could act as if she weren't naked, I supposed I could too, though her pendulous, much more than ample breasts made it difficult to find a neutral place to rest my eyes as we, or she, conversed. I didn't ask her in, but in she came.

"Wow," she crooned, looking dreamy-eyed around the room. "Oh, wow. Your place is beautiful. Oh, wow. What a beautiful place you have. I never used safety pins until I got these Chinese cloth shoes. Hey, *wow,* I love your typewriter. Now I have to. They keep ripping." I gave her a handful of pins to make sure she wouldn't have to return for more, then widened the door for her and stood by it until she picked up the not-so-subtle hint and stopped caressing the tiny stuffed dog that sits on my windowsill. "So anyway, wow," she said as she stepped back into the hallway. "Nature's children. We are all nature's children. You have to come visit sometime. Promise me, promise me, promise me you will."

"OK," I said.

"Promise? Do you promise?"

"Sure," I said, not letting myself close the door as quickly and emphatically as I would have liked. Later I heard her typewriter going, and when I passed by her door, there was a childishly printed sign taped up:

> WRITER AT WORK
> DO NOT DISTURB
> Please oh please
> I must have creative space to be alone.
> No one to disturb except
>   Punky, Breeze, Cosmos, Gwen or Ron,
>   PLUS Big Ray if you have something
>   for me.
> I love everyone who gazes at my message.
> LAY DOWN THY RAGE ALL WHO ENTER HERE.
>   Wendy

"It's the first time I realize that nature's children wear black panties that look like they came from Frederick's of Hollywood," I tell Karen, who is laughing hard, insisting I've made up at least part of this tale. She is a native Angeleno and thinks I'm poking fun at some laid-back L.A. stereotype. The story is great, but I wasn't laughing when Wendy came to call—she's a 45-year-old woman with silvering hair and acid as a way of life. I don't know how she pays her rent.

Muralist

"Venice is changing, a community in transition. People have been saying that for ten or twelve years," Karen says. "Why do so many of these stories still have that familiar, doomed late '60s ring to them?"

"I think maybe that's one of the constants of the place," I say, "whatever else may be going on around it."

I suppose every artist in Venice—writer, photographer, or painter—wants to capture and hold the place in some way up to the light or close to the heart. And if it eludes the grasp, like a teasing lover, this merely serves to increase desire. The St. Francis Hotel, one of the oldest buildings in town, is the site of a remarkable four-story mural which is a stunningly clear, nearly photographic mirror image of the street that leads up to the hotel, the reflection meeting reality at the far left of the mural, where a painted colonnade rises up right next to the actual colonnade of the building itself. The work is meticulous and wonderfully proportioned, but now, a few months after its completion, the beer-joint pool hall at the far end of the street has become a sushi bar; the clothing and liquor stores have both become neon-signed skate rental shops; the health food store has been transformed from the dull green of the painting to bright orange; and the craft shop, with its display of pots and weavings, has become an art gallery whose whole front window is covered with posters of the St. Francis mural, posters which reflect the mural across the street much more accurately than the mural now reflects the street itself. Such irony in the way the artist outdid himself by sticking so close to the truth in his work that he left his concept vulnerable to being undermined by reality, so that now the painting is as much a statement about change as it is a visual enlightenment of the actual. Within the next year, a three-storied apartment house will go up in the parking lot directly in front of the mural, both destroying and obscuring its mirror perspective in one fell swoop.

The building next door to me has been vacant since the Korean family who ran the market lost their lease. Now a "For Sale" sign is up, and I worry what this might mean for my muralist and his work. A few weeks after obliterating the eastern third of the mural, he has nearly completed a whole new section that is the "prettiest" thing he's done so far. Rising up out of a life-sized gondola, which floats on a patch of sky-blue water, is an androgynous nude figure that stretches almost to the top of the wall. The breasts are hardly more than suggestions of nipples, and the artist has extended the burst of red from the shopping cart until it cuts directly across and just past the upper thighs in place of genitals. The power in the figure, the intimation of its weight and strength, is in the upper torso and arms, which lean into pushing a long, thin, brown oar downward into blue. The facial features are not yet complete, but the close-cropped, yellow-tan hair is shaped exactly like that of the blonde who conquered Glory, and in an arc just above the top of her head, CHILD OF THE UNIVERSE is printed in very thick but clearly legible black letters, while VENICE OF AMERICA/VENICE OF THE UNIVERSE sits in a double arc at the base of the wall, in the water beneath the boat.

Even if I didn't know about the fight, I'd think this portion of the mural was romanticized. The canals of Venice of America, the brain-child of a man named Abbot Kinney who "invented" and named the town, are now stagnant green, littered with debris and pathetic looking ducks. One cannot gaze into that water without some sense of decay. The butch-haired woman did not just say, "I'm a child of the universe"; she said, "I am a child of the universe and have more right to be here than you." That would have to settle somewhere at the heart of the story for me, if I should try to write it, that saccharine philosophy cracking in two with rage right there in the middle of her sentence. Always a matter of what to leave in and what to leave out. And yet I admire what the artist has done— the simplicity of his image, the derring-do that resides in the posture of the nude. S/he is stabbing the water with a ferocity that makes me think yes, Venice is not merely romantic but ferociously so, which must be some part of what draws people here.

Before my alarm one morning, the telephone rings me awake. His voice is unmistakable, and this is not a dream. Getting married, he is, and selling the house, and there's a quit-claim in the mail I have to sign and send right back before the closing next week. Quit-claim, quit-claim. Getting married. He said no when I left, but I knew he would—he's the marrying kind. I will not ask what she is like. The top of my head begins to tingle. I don't want to cry on the phone. Selling the house—good, they won't be in our place. Selling the furniture, so do I want my desk? Yes but no. My racing heart, the sound of his voice, and all that lies beneath the words. That tension in his tone, I want to soothe us both somehow. I hate the tremble in my voice, just like at the wedding. Better not to say too much. I'm glad that he is well. Yes, I am well and feeling fine. How strange and familiar this man does sound, all we know and don't know about each other now.

"I'm happy that you've found someone," I say. "It isn't good for you to be alone."

"I never had your talent for that," he says. "And what about you, have you met anyone?"

"No," I say. "Not really, no."

"And the work," he says. "Are you writing a lot?"

"Several things at once," I say, "and none of them quite right. I guess I'm stuck."

"You've been through that before," he says, comforting. I can almost touch his face.

"So . . . anyway . . . ," I say.

"So . . . anyway," he says. "You'll sign the thing and send it right back?"

"Yes," I say. "Quit-claim," I think.

There is a long and awful pause. "I will always love you" sings back and forth over 2000 miles of wire. No need to say what we know would only hurt.

"I guess it's goodbye," he says. "Sometimes I've worried that you might think I stole your youth or something, you know?"

"Don't be silly," I laugh. "I was never that young. Does she want children?"

"No," he says.

"That's good," I say.

"Take care," he says.

"You too," I say, and then he's gone.

I am crying, but the top of my head is numb, as when our old garage door jumped its track and came crashing down on me. More stunned by the blow than hurt, I sat in the car feeling safe and relieved and grateful, even exhilarated at being struck from out of the blue and surviving it whole. I am relieved now and light, even in the sadness. Some weight has lifted I didn't know was there. I won't be going back, I won't be going back. I must have been afraid I might, and now there is no question left.

I don't know how I'll spend this day, but it won't be typing academic business letters. I call in to announce I'm taking a sick day, and Dr. Owen has the good sense not to press me into lying about my health. "See you next week," he says in his monotone, and it occurs to me that I could find a better job—more money and more interesting work, maybe even fewer hours.

The sidewalk cafe is empty, just opening up. I sit right down and order a bloody Mary, something I've never done before in my life. I wonder why I've never had a bloody Mary? The waiter writes it down as if he'd expected this all along and brings me a tall glass with an oversized, leafy stalk of celery standing up out of the red. It tickles my cheek every time I take a sip, which amuses me more the more vodka goes down. Maybe you're supposed to take it out. Maybe you're supposed to eat it, I don't know. I order a second one and examine the stalk in my empty glass—at the bottom the celery has soaked up some of the tomato juice, giving it a cast of pink. Miss Dawson showed us that in the fourth grade at Horace Mann—how plants drink. She pulled a stalk of celery wrapped in Kleenex out of her purse and emptied Jimmy Atherton's inkwell into a glass of water and stuck the celery in, and right while we watched, the dark liquid started travelling up inside the greenish white. Ink in the veins, ink in the veins. When I ask for a third one, the waiter just perceptibly raises his eyebrows. I know he's right and order breakfast.

After a long stroll down by the water, I climb over rocks until I find one flat enough for sitting cross-legged. I stare at the sea and feel as if the beach is mine, so few people are in sight. I really do live on the edge of the country, and this morning that fact seems newly remarkable.

I used to love to watch him walk, such erect grace and confidence, the stiffness in his back conveyed to perfect advantage. I never told him how, when we first lived apart, I drove past him on our street one day and watched him walk up the hill toward the house, slowed down to watch him walk that way, it touched me so. I sat in front of the post office then, blocking the drive-up mailboxes, weeping at the way he walked. It made me want to run after him, grab his elbow and nestle under his arm, plunge back into his rhythm thigh-to-thigh. I never told him how I loved the way he would shovel a vigorous path all around the house after heavy snow or the way he kept that ancient mower sharp and oiled to click and whir and sing through summer grass at dusk. That bright green bird feeder he set up for the winter cardinals, and then all the rigamarole he had to go through to keep the squirrels from taking it over. How the next fall he raked up all the leftover horse chestnuts and kept them in the basement to put out for the squirrels at Christmastime. I never told him how I loved the way he would smile at me as I walked toward him from somewhere. "You always look just right," he'd say and slip his arm around my waist. "You always look just right," and he would kiss my cheek and smile. I hope his new wife makes him glad. I wish them well. When she walks to meet him, I want her to look all right, but not *just right* — I hope she never looks just right, so sometimes he will think of me.

A huge wave suddenly crashes up and over me and all the rocks. "Hey!" I yell, as if some child had aimed his hose at me. "Hey!" It makes my throat feel good to shout, as if releasing something caught. "HEEEY!" I stand and yell at the surf through my hands, feel the wind and water drown it out. "Hey!" I walk back along the shore and remember that I've never been in the ocean. I toss my sandals and coin purse and keys into the sand, walk out a few feet, turn inland, sit down and let waves wash over me, hair and all. I really should learn to swim, I think. The water's warmer than I thought but still a shock, and so's the bitter taste of salt. I head home dripping in sagging pants, aware of hard nipples beneath clinging shirt.

A photographer I've never seen before has her pictures lined up on the sidewalk in front of the building next door. At the end of the row is a black-and-white of Danny—yes, it is Danny—curled up asleep on a large, flat rock with other rocks looming up behind. His sleeping bag is zipped all around, leaving only the side of his face and head visible. He's wearing a hat that's come half way off, and one shoe lies sole up on the rock right at the curve of his belly, while the other sits below among accumulated beer cans and litter from the beach.

"When did you take this?" I ask the woman. "When did you see this man?"

"Some time ago," she says. "A year-and-a-half, probably two years ago. I found him one morning about seven o'clock down by the water. That's the only print I did of it because it came out so dark. You can have it for fifteen if you like." She sees I'm more than mildly interested. But what would I do with such a thing? I wish she hadn't stolen his image while he slept that way. He looks so small and vulnerable in the center of his hard, cold bed. I don't want this photograph, but I don't want anyone else to have it, either. I can't decorate my place with it, but someone else might do just that.

"I've got nine-fifty here," I say, and the woman takes it without quibbling. She slips Danny into a clear, thick plastic cover and tells me to "Enjoy."

As I step into my apartment, it feels astonishingly small. A home without any living room. All this time and here I am still sleeping in that single bed. I slide the photo into the folder that contains my abortive attempts to make a story from what I knew of Danny's life. I slip off the soggy clothes and rinse brine from my hair, then sit in my robe drinking wine at the window. Nearly two o'clock already. The day's gone fast. These days go fast. The muralist is hard at work, one hand clasped around the top rung of his ladder. From the slant of his arm he's leaning right—maybe filling in the facial features of the gondolier.

The top three floors of the Napoleon building are glaringly white in the sun, though the structure casts a deep, sharp shadow in the street below. Suzanne is moving up the sidewalk in her halting, awkward way, hands constantly busy with her hair or with her nose or with the pockets of her jacket. She is not talking to herself today. She steps up to the line of light where the shadow of the building stops, and she stops too, freezes there, as if it were the edge of a cliff. She stares down at the line of light for quite awhile and wrings her hands, then takes one step backward, farther into shadow. Her hands fall unnaturally still then at her sides, and she looks as if she's concentrating hard. I guess she has to figure out if she will brave the light or go back the way she came. She stands and stands and stands, very still, as if waiting for the answer to appear, and then in three decisive motions, she eases herself back up against the shady wall of the restaurant, slides down it until she is sitting, and sinks into a nod.

Muralist

They tell me when I was five or six, they asked what I wanted Santa to bring. "A small basement with a light in it," I said. Now what kind of child is that? Some part of me inside has always lived in that small basement, but since I've been in Venice I think all of me's resided there, despite the ocean and these windows and the accident that I'm four floors up, not one floor down. A naked bulb that dangles from the center of the ceiling. This tiny cell where I've looked and looked at everything I could. I think perhaps it's time I gave myself some room to move.

The sun and wine have made me drowsy, and I curl up on the spread, not bothering to pull the shade. When I wake up, it is already dusk. Suzanne is gone and the painter's ladder. I scoot to the end of the bed and look east. Lights are beginning to twinkle across the cityscape. All those people in all those dwellings, I imagine them all getting on with their lives. I heat some tomato soup, eat crackers, and drift back to sleep, still with the smell of the sea on my skin.

For several days all over the beachfront shocking purple fliers have been circulating which announce in bold black letters THE CORO- NATION OF BABSY BABCOCK AS QUEEN OF VENICE to take place Thursday at 10:00 A.M. on the grassy knoll at the foot of Cordova Street. "*Come* one, *Come* all," it says on the crown crudely sketched at the center of the invitation. "Have a good old Venice time." Already when I jog by at 8:30, several of Babsy's pals are hanging tie-dyed lavender sheets across the concrete exterior of the public john, fussing good-naturedly over which part of the design should fall at the center.

"It's going to be her best birthday yet," says the one I think is Sean as he fashions a small platform from several rectangular blocks of wood. "God knows the girl could use a lift these days." A Chan- nel 18 camera crew unloads equipment from a plain white van.

When I return a bit after 10:00, there are seventy-five or a hundred people sitting or standing around the little stage, now cov- ered with deep purple, velvety cloth that has "Queen of Venice" in sparkly letters across its front. There is an air of quiet, good- humored excitement in the crowd, which I gradually realize is made up almost entirely of local people whose faces I know, though not many names. A somewhat speedy version of "Pomp and Cir- cumstance" is playing on a cassette recorder at the back of the stage.

Before too long, Sean emerges from behind the lavender tapestry, carrying a golden cardboard crown. He is shirtless beneath an old tuxedo coat with a red feather boa for a tie, the same bright red as his tight, short shorts. The video cameramen move up and zero in on him as he takes a bow, and the audience applauds and whistles as if on cue.

"As you must know," Sean says, holding the crown with both hands in front of him, "we have *come out* this morning to honor Babsy Babcock, *solid* Venice citizen and leader of *spirit* in this community. Why should Babs be crowned the Queen of Venice? Well . . . any of you who *know* her—and I'm sure many, many, many of you *do*—would never ask that question. Babsy just *is* the Queen of Venice, *that's* all. No contest. The girl's got royal Venice blood." The crowd applauds and whistles some more. "That's right," Sean says. "That's *right*. Let's hear it for Babsy Babcock, Queen of Venice!" We clap loud and long as Sean turns the music up and Babs emerges from the restroom door behind the lavender sheet.

"What were you doing in *there*, Babsy?" one of her friends calls out from just below the stage, and everyone laughs, including Babs herself. I must say she looks lovely in a sleazy sort of way as she steps to the stage in parody of stiff and regal grace. How *did* she learn to walk that well in those horribly sexy shoes? Her dress is slinky, full-length, flowing, a filmy, diaphanous lavender-blue. When she turns a certain way, the morning sun reveals the dark design of her panties and her bra.

"Oy vay," the elderly woman standing next to me says to her companion.

"Oy vay is right," the friend replies, but neither of them stops applauding.

The painter is up front on his knees, sketching away on a large white pad, and several people are snapping pictures as Sean attempts to quiet the crowd. Babs is standing perfectly poised, perfectly made up, perfectly smiling.

"On behalf of the citizenry of Venice of America, California," Sean intones as he rises on tiptoes with the crown, "I hereby proclaim you, Babsy Babcock, as our very own favorite queen, henceforth and forevermore."

"Let me through here mothafuckas, I got to piss," Glory shouts suddenly, pushing her way through the audience up in front of the TV cameramen, who stop filming instantly as the crowd bursts into a laugh. "Go to yo' *roooom*, faggots! Let me in there to piss." Mr. Fluffy very calmly threads his way to her, grabs her from behind forcing both arms to her sides, and carries her, cussing all the way, back to the outermost edge of the gathering. We applaud his valiant deed as Sean starts over for a second take.

"Well . . . as you all know, we're here this morning to honor a very, very, very special person. Babsy, on behalf of the citizenry of Venice of America, I hereby—"

"I'm gon' fuck you in yo' ass if you don't let me in there to piss," Glory shouts, brandishing a bottle of Ripple and shaking her fist as she heads once again for the stage.

"Oh for heaven *sakes*," Babs tells the entourage blocking the way to the restroom door. "Let her *in*, let her *in*." Glory rushes through the lavender sheet, and the crowd goes wild with applause and hoots. "The firtht royal pith," Babs says, almost as if she is mimicking Sean, and there is general pandemonium until Glory reappears and settles quietly once more at the edge of the group.

The cameras roll again, and Sean does his best to save the day for Babs. "As all of you gathered here must know, Babsy Babcock is a very, very, very special person, and that's why we have chosen her to represent Venice of America, California, as our very own special queen. I hereby proclaim you, our dear Babs, as the truest, utmost Queen of Venice, henceforth and forevermore." Everyone claps as Sean situates the cardboard crown, "Pomp and Circumstance" is turned up full volume, and a fourteen or fifteen-year-old effeminate looking boy rushes from the restroom with a dozen long-stemmed roses, which Babs clutches to her breast as she smiles, waves at the crowd, and parades back and forth on the short, velvet platform in true Miss America style. After a few minutes of this, Sean stops the music and announces that this also "just happens" to be Babsy's birthday, and don't we all want to sing? I get choked up at the sound of a hundred voices on "Happy Birthday, dear Babsy." I do hope she's having a Happy Birthday, and what a perversely loving thing for Sean to do. I wonder where her mother is and what my Aunt Lucinda would make of all this. I don't know who better than Babs could represent Venice with its sense of style, its capacity for abuse, and its bizarre, mysterious allure that so thinly masks brutality and ugliness.

As the crowd disperses, an aging hippie with a long black ponytail approaches me, crunching a granola bar. "Say, don't I know you from way back?" he asks, and I think he's feeding me a line, though he sounds sincere. "Weren't you in the movement down here around '66 or '67, along in there?"

"No," I say, not breaking stride.

"Oh man, there sure was a girl who looked like you. Used to organize meetings down here all the time."

"I only saw the '60s on TV back in Illinois," I say, and he laughs a sweet kind of laugh from a gentle kind of spirit.

"Well, how do you like it out here?" he asks, as if he really wants to know.

"I love it," I say, and he nods.

"Venice is great," he says. "There's room for everybody here. Venice gets into your blood. You want a bite?" He offers me the last of his granola bar, which I decline. "You sure you weren't here in '68?" he says as we move apart. "You do look like that girl, and she was something. Real good old Venice people, you know?"

Why do I feel so powerfully flattered?

When I get back to Westward, the painter is already there, studying his sketches and pacing back and forth in front of the gondolier. He sees me as I turn up the street. "I'm finishing today," he says. "Champagne at 4:00 for whoever's around."

"I'll be here," I tell him, "most definitely."

Each time I happen to look out my window, the prongs of the ladder are in a different place along the rooftop, disappearing altogether by three o'clock. Just after 4:00 I hear several corks pop almost simultaneously and look down to see the painter with his shopping cart full of champagne bottles that Mr. Fluffy and Luke are happily helping him open.

"You know he's a bro'," Mr. Fluffy keeps calling out as he struts around the pagoda serving all the regulars in paper cups. "Don't you know that dude's a bro'?"

By the time I go down, there is quite a little crowd clustered around the shopping cart. The painter stands off to himself a few yards, gazing at the mural with a bottle of his own. As I get my champagne, Luke raises a toast. "To a wonderful piece of work, young man, and all the pretty colors. May you win many and numerous prizes." Cups are lifted all around, and several people, most of whom were at the coronation, line up to congratulate the muralist, who is drinking fast and not smiling much.

As I lean against the Napoleon doorway, I see what he must have done today. With a coarsening of the mouth, a lengthening of hair and a few skillful strokes, the nude gondolier has turned into Babs. The breasts have been enlarged with one simple curved line each and the use of shadowing to suggest both cleavage and a masculine prominence of bone in the chest. The density of hair somehow adds to the power and weight that the figure is putting to the oar, which balances the pagoda scene in the opposite corner very well. The streak of red across the genitals carries much more significance now that this is Babs as Child of the Universe. The artist has drawn a black, rectangular frame around the entire edge of the mural, and in the lower right-hand corner, outside the frame, he has signed a first name only, "Joseph."

The champagne is dwindling and with it the crowd. "Congratulations," I tell the painter. "I admire the way you finished it up. Somehow I expected you to do another section."

"I probably would have," he says in a quiet voice. "But I got word yesterday the building's going down in six or eight weeks. Another apartment house on the rise."

"Oh my God," I say. "I was afraid that might happen. You must be heartsick—I'm heartsick myself."

"Yeah . . . well . . . that's the way it goes when you paint outside. At least I did it," he says, pouring us the last of his bottle.

"Yes, you did it," I say, "and here's to that. And nobody else could have done it but you." I head home with my own words echoing. Only Joseph could have painted that particular mural with its particular intent, particular richness, particular strengths and weaknesses. And nobody could write about Danny the way I might if only I had the courage to fail. Someone no doubt could write it all more perfectly, but no one can say what I have to say unless I say it myself. It's the doing that counts, and the painter did it, did it in spite of everything. I salute him for that and know I will have to follow his example.

When I get upstairs the phone is ringing. "Boy, am I glad you're home," Karen says excitedly. "That little house up the street I told you about has opened up for rent. The owner's there now and he said you could come, if you wanted to, and take a look."

"Oh, wow, I really don't know," I say. "How could I move, just like that?"

"You said yourself Venice is wearing you down. Quit being so goddamn stubborn," Karen says. "There's a little alcove in the bedroom for your desk and a good-sized living room. *And a kitchen that you can eat in, for a change.*"

"All right, all right," I say. "But are there any roaches? I don't know if I could stand a place without roaches anymore."

"If you don't get your tail over here this minute, I'll never speak to you again. The place is a steal at two-ninety-five."

"Okay, okay, I'm coming," I say, starting to feel her excitement myself. Her street in Santa Monica is only ten or twelve blocks from the beach. I could jog my way to the boardwalk every morning if I liked. I know I cannot stand it here if the new building next door blocks my view. Maybe I could write Venice stories better, anyway, without the constant influence that the muralist thrived on. Maybe I could cook more often, buy myself a double bed.

As I start down the fire escape, there's Mr. Fluffy, coming my way in his dingy fur coat. "There's my darlin'," he calls and stops below to wait for me. "Come on down here, darlin'," he says, stabbing a finger toward the pavement for emphasis. "Come on now. You get down here right now, darlin'."

There is nothing to do but do as he says. I feel like Audrey Lee's cat Fido, whom we used to order around that way after the fact, since he never obeyed our commands in the least.

"Come on down here now. You beautiful, darlin'," Mr. Fluffy repeats as I descend the last flight and pass him by. "Wait jus' a minute now, baby," he says, three steps behind as I head for my car.

On Westward the painter is sitting alone, watching his work in the softening light.

"Doggone, baby, I jus' wan' *tell* you somethin' now," Mr. Fluffy persists as I get in the car. "You beautiful, darlin', you beautiful now. Don't you ever forget that, you hear? An' someday darlin', some ol' day, a man gon' take control of you an' make you know it, an' then you will be *released*, darlin', an' then you will *be* released."

I pull out of the parking lot, turn back up the alley, and give Mr. Fluffy a goodbye wave.

About the Author

Ann Nietzke's novel, *Windowlight,* won a PEN/West Award for Best First Fiction. Her short stories have appeared in *Shenandoah, Other Voices* and *The Massachusetts Review.* In 1995, *Natalie on the Street,* her portrait of a Los Angeles "bag lady," was among six finalists for PEN/West's Nonfiction Award. Other nonfiction has appeared in *The Village Voice, Saturday Review, Cosmopolitan, Playgirl* and *CALYX Journal.*

Nietzke is a recipient of a Creative Writing Fellowship from the National Endowment for the Arts and a Residency in Writing at The MacDowell Colony. She has an Master of Arts in English and lives in Los Angeles. Her most recent work is *Solo Spinout.*